She crossed her arms, taking hold of the Basque shirt at either side. With an abrupt gesture she stripped it off over her head, rumpling the black hair; she dropped it, stood before him naked to the waist. Her breasts were boldly tilted. Reflected light touched her torso from the side, making soft highlights on the curves and swells of her body. She looked like the women of Egypt in ancient friezes, with their faces small and cold and cruel under the black hair; the women for whom special burial jewelry was made, the dancers who were buried with tiny pet antelopes.

"Remember?" she said.

"Yes."

They made their love on the coldly modern couch under the great window. She was sinewy, supple, taut with her eagerness. The only suggestions of softness were in lips, breasts, and hips. It seemed more combat than love, and upon his symbolic victory she gave a long cry of anguish as though he had thrust a dagger to her heart.

clemmie

JOHN D. MacDONALD

FAWCETT GOLD MEDAL • NEW YORK

CLEMMIE

All characters in this book are fictional and any
resemblance to persons living or dead
is purely coincidental.

Published by Fawcett Gold Medal Books, a unit of
CBS Publications, the Consumer Publishing
Division of CBS Inc.

ISBN: 0-449-14015-6

Printed in the United States of America

20 19 18 17 16 15 14 13 12

CHAPTER ONE

HE LIKED to drink sparingly after dinner, but now he realized he had let Chet Burney force three of his extra-potent highballs on him, and he guessed that they were the equivalent of six drinks at a bar. Chet believed firmly in the social prowess of alcohol, and when Chet and Alice gave a large cocktail party, there were many critical cases of remorse the next morning, and many earnest vows to be more careful at the next Burney affair.

Craig guessed that neither Chet nor Alice were aware that their parties were as much dreaded as anticipated. They seemed to feel that the noisier they were, the more successful. Also, such parties were breeders of the sort of anecdote Chet seemed to enjoy. "Remember the time Lew Carran decided Bunny's skirt was too long?"

To Craig it had an embarrassingly collegiate flavor, and he had long since learned to keep a cautious eye on his glass when Chet was circulating with the Martini shaker.

But this was not a party. This was family, Chet and Alice had insisted. "Just come over for some drinks and dinner, Craig. The kids eat on the first shift. Then, after they're out of the way, just the three of us."

Now he realized he was slightly drunk. It was nearly midnight. Tomorrow was a working day. He knew he would feel grim in the morning. Yet he knew he should not blame Chet. His restlessness since Maura had left had made it a little easier to take that next drink. When you were not having a very good time, you hoped one more drink would help. The evening had been a little awkward merely because the four of them had been together so often. The absence of Maura made a great gap and caused unexpected silences. Craig knew that during all the time Maura would be away, from this Wednesday, the tenth of July, until she arrived back in New York, six hundred miles away, on Friday, the sixth of September, the Burneys would have him over from time to time. Not too often, as this evening had not been entirely comfortable, yet not so seldom that his terminal report to Maura would indicate thoughtlessness.

He realized that Chet was telling a story that Craig had heard many times before. Alice was sitting on the floor in front of Chet's chair. She had held her cheek against the side of his knee and, as Chet talked and played with her cropped hair with his blunt fingers, she wore an expression that was at once smug and dreamy. She was a small lean woman with coarse dark-red hair, delicate pointed features, large gray eyes. She was not particularly intelligent, but she had a good sense of fun. She was a superb cook, and despite three children, she kept her house gleaming. Yet the clothes she selected for herself and the make-up she used were never quite right for her. This lack of style had absolutely no effect on the impression she made on most men, and the impression she so obviously made on her husband. This was a wife who, in spite of a boyish body, in spite of an absence of the mannerisms of the temptress, was obviously very capable and very eager. And with equivalent emphasis, those favors were available only to Chet Burney.

Chet was a big-chested blond man with a boyish face that made him look younger than thirty-nine, quite a bit younger. Craig, who knew that Chet and he were only three weeks apart in age, was sometimes faintly indignant about Chet's air of youthfulness. Yet, of late, the blond hair was thinning more rapidly, and the paunch was becoming more than a hint. In another ten years the situation would be reversed.

Chet Burney was a lawyer, a junior partner in the firm of Tolle, Rufus, Kell and Burney. The firm made a speciality of corporation law and, on local problems that were not of a serious nature, was quite often retained by the firm where Craig worked, the Quality Metal Products Division of the U.S. Automotive Corporation. Burney was a bluff and friendly man who liked to tell people that if it wasn't for lawyers, the law would be a very easy thing to understand.

Burney played good golf and had a weakness for important-looking automobiles. Craig suspected that when Chet and Alice had bought this house in the River Woods section, he had taken on more than he should have. But the odds were good that Chet's income would continue to improve. His political connections were good, and he was well-liked.

Chet was telling the story Craig had heard so many times. "Well, old Junior Thompson, the well-known wolf, had this little girl right here come to the house party on a football week end. We were playing Cornell that week end. This little Alice here was trying to look all grown up, but I found out she'd just turned seventeen and she was only a junior in high school, and she'd done some plain and fancy lying to get her people to let her come along. After I got a good look, I moved right in, and knowing how much of a chance she would have stood with a sharp operator like Thompson, I'll bet you I wasn't more than ten minutes too soon. Junior was sure sore. But I had me a date for that week end too. Big ole blonde girl from Smith. Name of Nancy. Nancy and Junior stayed sore for all of twelve minutes when we suggested we trade off, and you know ..."

Craig stopped listening. It had happened a long time ago. He had heard it before. Once he had asked Maura on the way home why in the world Chet, who wasn't usually boring, kept repeating that very ordinary yarn of how they met. Maura thought a moment and said, "He never tells it unless she's so close he can touch her. Then he seems to be talking to her more than to anyone else. I think it's a sort of love play with them. You can almost hear her purr."

Craig watched her. She had a sleepy, flushed, almost humid look. The heavy fingers toyed with her hair. She arched her back in an almost imperceptible way, and Craig felt a sharp sudden thrust of envy and desire. Not specific desire for Alice. Nor was it desire for Maura. It was not as specified. It was a desire for flesh, for togetherness, in which identity seemed of small importance.

When Chet was through and tried to give him another drink, Craig said he had to go. They told him he shouldn't run off so early, but their protestations were more glib than sincere. They walked out to his car with him. The July night was sticky. A passenger liner moved slowly overhead at about four thousand, running lights blinking, curving towards the big airfield on the other side of Still River.

"When Maura gets back, Craig, you two ought to consider moving out here. The new school will be going up next year. No through traffic. Playgrounds. No city taxes. It's great for dogs and cats and kids. And there's a damn fine bunch out here."

"It'll be even handier when the new shopping section is finished," Alice said.

"It's a little out of my reach, kids," Craig said.

"I think you ought to grab a good lot, though, before those go out of sight. Then you've got it, and when you get ready to change, you've got a place to build. You know, I can go from my garage to the Club in twelve minutes."

"And you ought to take twenty. You drive too fast," Alice said.

"We'll talk about it when Maura comes back," Craig said. "But, you know, she likes that old place. I guess because it's got all the inconveniences she's always been used to."

"If you want to make your limey bride feel really at home, you ought to have the central heating ripped out," Chet said, laughing.

"If I just leave it alone, it'll rust away. Look, thanks for a wonderful dinner and a good evening. I've enjoyed it."

"And we'll ask you again real soon," Alice promised. "I hate to think of you rattling around in that place. You should go to a hotel. It must be grim."

"It's pretty empty, but I'm beginning to adjust. She's been gone, let me see, two weeks and four days."

"Are you going to take a vacation?" Chet asked.

"Not much point in it while she's gone. I'm taking a late one. In October. That'll give her time to get settled

in, and we'll get somebody to stay with Penny and Puss
while we go away and get re-acquainted."

"Those parts you read us were charming, Craig. Do let
us know when you get another letter like that," Alice said.

They said good night, and he thanked them again and
drove off. He drove down the whispering smoothness of
asphalt, around the carefully engineered curves, past the
dark homes which made those severely architectured lines
against the night sky, lines that spoke of the wonders inside—the stainless steel, the immaculate plastics, the de-
odorized flesh. As he turned down another grade, moving
down toward the city, he saw out of the corner of his
eye, for just an instant, a child's tricycle on a high curve
of lawn, outlined against the night-pink halo of the city.
It stood contemplative under the sky, a small, lonely,
whimsical figure, half insect, half Martian. He felt a
quick touch at his heart and said to himself, you are
drunk, my friend, and damn close to bathos. Your mind
reaches out, seeking any possible excuse for a crying jag.

As he did not trust his reflexes, he drove quite slowly.
The car was a three-year-old Ford station wagon, maroon
with white trim. Lately there had been odd sounds in the
motor, and he kept forgetting to have the car checked.

As he drove toward home he wondered why the evening had seemed so flat. It was more than the fact that
Maura was missing. Tonight he had been unable to respond properly to the Burneys. He had felt a restless impatience with them, with conversation that seemed un-
necessarily trivial and predictable—gossip about mutual
friends, second-hand analyses of political trends. Such an
evening would have been satisfying in the past, but on this
night it had merely made him restless.

And when Chet had urged him to move to River Wood,
he had felt a sudden wariness, like an animal that senses
strangeness and thus avoids a trap. River Wood was a re-
stricted, carefully zoned community full of people whose
goals were the same as his. Yet he had the feeling that to
move there would make all of his future as predictable
as the conversation of this evening. He could look forward to making the final mortgage payment in 1968. By
then Penny and Puss would have long since been married, and there would be a grandchild or two. By then,
according to company policy at the time, he would be re-

tiring in either ten years or fifteen. And in another few years, he would die, and Maura, according to the actuaries, would live on several years longer. Craig Andrew Fitz, born the twenty-third of March, 1918, to die X years later in a little Florida retirement house.

He turned into the narrow driveway between his house and the house next door and put the car carefully in the garage that was too narrow for it, and not quite long enough. He walked slowly across the small fenced back yard, climbed the six steps to the back porch and stood there on the porch for a little time, listening to the night sounds of the city, reluctant to go in because he knew how empty the house would feel. The kitchen floor creaked as he walked across it. It was a narrow, ugly, two-and-a-half-story house in a decaying neighborhood, and it had been built in the early years of the century. The materials had been honest so the house was reasonably sound, but each room was small and square and unimaginative. They had improved it slightly by knocking out the wall between the living room and the dining room, but it was not a house you could be proud of.

He remembered 1946 when U. S. Automotive had re-employed him and sent him to the Quality Metal Products Division here in Stoddard. That was in January, and it had been a most bitter winter. Penny was born the following June, so Maura was four months' pregnant when they had lived in that furnished room while house-hunting.

Maura had been convinced that this was the land of plenty, but her education was abrupt. They spent a great deal of time looking at new houses. New little cracker-box houses, triumphs of monotony, concrete cracking before occupancy, sleazy plywood warping, tiny yards a wilderness of frozen mud—and they were priced to give a minimal profit of one-hundred per cent to the developer. They were selling because there was nothing else to be had in that price range. Future slums were being created with energy, venality and optimism.

He remembered Maura's shocked look after she did some mental computation. "Good Lord, Craig. Five thousand two hundred pounds for this—this absolute horror!"

The salesman had looked injured. "Lady, this is the best you'll find around here for this money."

Maura had drawn herself to full height. "I would far

prefer to live under a hedge like a rabbit. Let's go, Craig."

Even if a suitable apartment could be found, rents were exorbitant. The rent-control program in Stoddard had been administered with maximum advantage to the landlord. The fruitless searching finally reduced Maura to one of her rare periods of weeping. It made Craig feel apologetic about the whole country.

Finally they had found this house. It was a block and a half from a school, and not far from an area of stores. But the neighborhood was well advanced along the path of inevitable decay. Room to rent. Qualified Electropath Treatments. Music Lessons. There was an ancient and marginal textile mill four blocks away. There was a cellar barber shop on the corner. In warm weather old men sat in their underwear tops on the steps of shallow front porches, and tough teen-agers roamed in harsh packs. The school was aged, the playground paved with bricks and wire-fenced.

The price had been ninety-four-hundred dollars. The only pleasant thing about it had been a fairly deep front yard with one big elm tree. Craig had paid two thousand down and, after difficulties with the appraisal, had managed to get a G.I. loan on the balance. In 1949 the city had decided that Federal Street, all twenty-two blocks of it, should be widened to provide a cross-town highway to relieve traffic congestion in the cramped city. So the deep yard became shallow, and the tree was taken away, and Craig had received nine-hundred dollars which he applied to the mortgage principal. Maura had mourned the loss of the tree. Co-ordinated traffic lights had been installed. The widened road was smooth asphalt with vivid yellow traffic lanes. Day and night the traffic moved endlessly by, silent, orderly, with a sound like breathing.

Craig walked through the house to the front windows. Enough light came in so he could avoid dark shadows of the furniture. Down in the next street, an entire block of houses had been taken out. The skeletal steelwork of a new shopping section had already been erected. The block their house was in had recently been re-zoned to Commercial A. He'd heard that many of the people in the next block had gotten handsome prices for ancient, ugly houses such as this one.

And that, he thought, might be the answer. There was

less than two thousand left on the mortgage. Should the shopping center prosper—and the men behind it were hardly fools—the commercial value of this block might go up.

It would be good to get out of here. The kids in that school were rough. And sometimes you could have bad dreams about what might happen to a pretty, blonde, little girl caught out after dusk in such a neighborhood.

Yet the orderly ostentation of River Wood was not appealing. Not tonight at least. Not while he felt so restless. He turned on the light in the archaic kitchen and opened the refrigerator to get milk before he remembered there would be no milk. There were two cans of beer in the nearly empty refrigerator. He opened one and stood leaning against the sink and drank it. The refrigerator choked, stammered, and began to hum loudly. Turn the damn thing off when that next beer is gone.

And he went up the narrow stairs to the empty bed.

CHAPTER TWO

O N THE NIGHT he had too much to drink at the Burneys, he went to sleep very quickly. When the alarm went off he found he felt as bad as he had expected. Maybe a little bit worse. After he had breakfast in a diner, he left the car off at the garage and took a taxi out to the plant on the other side of the river.

It was a day when every possible thing went wrong. When he left at six-thirty, the other offices were empty, and he had forgotten he didn't have a car. The bus was nearly empty. He ate a tasteless dinner six blocks from home and walked back through the lingering summer twilight, back to the empty house.

It always seemed far emptier by daylight. There were dust motes in the last flat rays of the sun. With his fingertip he made an X in the dust on the top of the gateleg table. "X marks the spot," he said aloud, and his voice had an empty, eerie sound in the house. All hermits end up talking to themselves, he thought.

He wrote a letter to Maura. He had intended to make it a long letter, but at the end of the second page there didn't seem to be anything left to say. He told her about the Burneys and managed to make it sound like a pleasant evening. He tried a humorous account of the evil day at the plant, but when he reread it, the humor sounded forced and flat. He was tempted to destroy the letter and try again, but he suspected that the second attempt would be no better. He rolled the envelope into the battered portable he had owned ever since the Wharton School and typed her address:

> Mrs. Craig A. Fitz
> The Vinelands
> Long Melford, West Suffolk
> England

It was a damn long way away, and half an hour before midnight there—she and the kids would be asleep. He propped the letter where he would see it in the morning.

For a half hour he read a magazine that had come in the mail. Then he tried the five available television channels and found nothing that seemed worth looking at. Five minutes of nine seemed a strange time to go to bed, but there was no one to chide—or care. He made one stiff highball and realized that if he wanted to keep on having ice through the summer, he would have to keep the refrigerator on.

After he was in bed, he found himself thinking again of the Burneys. He imagined they had been glad when he had finally left. And, judging from Alice's heavy-headed look, the air of dragging languor that had come over her late in the evening, it had not taken them long to hurry to bed after he left. He thought of them and speculated on how she would be, quite idly at first, and suddenly, with both self-disgust and coarse amusement, he realized that he had all the physiological symptoms of strong and immediate physical need.

He turned on his side, trying to compose himself for sleep. He knew he did not want Alice Burney. She was not a type to appeal to him. Rather, he felt the need of anonymous flesh, of an unknown and uncaring warmth

beside him, of an episode where there would be no remorse, regret, guilt or responsibility.

This, he thought, is entirely too trite. My wife has gone
to the country, hooray. So I am nervous, restless, jumpy,
and perhaps itching for trouble. The Burneys try to be
nice, so I find them unspeakably dull.

As he thought of them there came another heavy surge
of the curiously uncontrollable desire. It exasperated him,
and he decided that the best way to short-circuit the nerve
impulse was to think of some dreary problem. Money was
easy to think about.

He could remember the bull sessions back in 1938, in
the fraternity house on Woodland Avenue. What was the
name of the little blond guy? Langer. Bucky Langer. "All
you Wharton hotshots aiming for the big buck give me
the cramps. Me, I'll settle for five-thousand bucks a year
forever. A nice clean hundred a week."

There had been many who had agreed with him. It
was a nice clean sum. You could see living on it and
having a family and getting alone all right. Fifteen thousand would have been gaudy riches. Genuine luxury.

And here I am, he thought. Fourteen-thousand, five-
hundred dollars a year. And there's nothing very gaudy
about it. Taxes bring it down to twelve five. Then take
out mortgage payments, food, car, insurance, clothes,
medical, and there is astonishingly little left. Look how
long it took us to save the money for Maura's trip with
the kids. We thought we could make it the summer before
last, and then we were positive we could do it last summer, and the only way we could handle it this summer
was by cutting corners wherever we could.

They had decided that Maura should visit her people
and take the kids. Since their marriage it had become increasingly obvious that her parents would not be able to
visit the states. Her father, George Thatcher, had to stop
work in 1948 after a heart attack. He had owned and
operated a repair garage and automobile agency in Long
Melford. The business had been sold. There was a small
government pension, plus the income from the proceeds
of the sale. Neither George Thatcher nor Maura's mother
felt that he should risk the strain of travel. They had a
comfortable home, a garden, a quiet and apparently satis-

fying life. Maura's two sisters were both married and both
living in London.

It seemed right that Penny and Puss should see England
while they were at the age when they would absorb im-
pressions and remember vividly. At first it had been
planned that Craig would fly over for his three-week vacation, but it had not been financially feasible. He would
wait out the long, hot summer and they would come back
to him, and she would write often.

In the very beginning it seemed to them a miracle that
they had found each other, because the very fact of their
meeting had depended on so many coincidences, so many
variables. Of course the meeting of any two persons who
fall in love could be described in the same way, but in
their case the coincidences seemed to have a curious
drama of their own. But in 1944, of course, drama was
not in short supply.

Craig had been a production chaser in the Camden Drop
Forge Division of U.S. Automotive on December 6th, 1941.
He enlisted on Monday, December 8th, thinking himself
both quixotic and noble, refusing to admit that one major
aspect in the decision was a boss with whom it seemed impossible for anybody to get along—a man of vile humor
and unpredictable rages.

After basic training, because he was rangy, rugged,
eager and reasonably well-educated, he had been selected
for infantry O.C.S. After graduation he was sent to the
Tank School, then assigned to an armored division that
was shipped west to train in the California desert.

During those days he sensed that the uniform suited
him well. He was baked brown and lean, and the tilt of
the cap went nicely with the slight heaviness of his features, the hollows in his cheeks. The deep tan made his
eyes bluer and more reckless. And there was the girl
named Kath, the nice, tailored, broad-shouldered girl of
good family, whom he had picked up in Los Angeles and,
after delicate maneuvering, managed to install in an airy
room in a small hotel in Riverside. Kath, of inky-black
hair, inexplicable tears, and frank and joyous hungers.

It was like a strange marriage, where they had over-
worked the word love, and agreed that marriage for real

would be unfair to both of them. He could remember
being beside her while her sleep was deep, and wondering
if he would ever see any of the war, and what would happen to him if he did. Her last name had been Mac-
Cullough or MacCullen. He could not remember which.

The division saw action in North Africa. Craig Fitz,
First Lieutenant, AUS, Ser. 0-776557, saw ten minutes
of the shooting war. He was in the lead tank and they
were unbuttoned because combat intelligence reports had
indicated they were five miles from trouble. But some
stuff had sneaked through in the night and it was in a
draw. When the first .88 hit between the bogie wheels,
the M3A1 medium tank bloomed into junk and Fitz was
blown up out of the unbuttoned hatch, scraping meat
from the top of his thighs. He landed with his legs afire
and he scrambled away from the furnace that had been
his vehicle, and put out the fire with sand. After the
action had moved away from him, he lay in the hole he
had scooped with his hands and wept from pain, humilia-
tion and shock. The broken tanks cooked and there was
a horrid meaty crackling in the heart of the flames. A
long time later they came and got him.

First was the field hospital, then the station hospital
and then the general hospital—a big ward where burns
were a specialty and pain was of a uniquely savage brand.
The legs were not too bad with the exception of the deep
burn behind the knee of the right leg and some tendon
damage.

He had time to think, and to wonder that he had been
able to think of this war in the juvenile terms of the
sports field, or the cheap movie. The good guys and the
bad guys. It wasn't like that. And he didn't want any
more of it. Not in this lifetime. The first shot his crew
had heard had fried them.

After weeks of the excruciating exercises designed to
stretch the pinched tendons to their normal length, he
was returned to limited duty and assigned to the casual
officers' pool in a replacement depot. In time he was re-
assigned to staff duty in London. He reported, thin and
tanned and tired, with a slight limp, three ribbons and a
small black and arrogantly bushy mustache.

He was given undemanding work in Theatre G-4, in the
Armored Vehicles Section of the Theatre Ordnance Officer.

He would work two or three hours a day for a week or two, and then have to work twenty hours straight on a priority report. He lived in a small, ancient and incredibly uncomfortable hotel, sharing a room with a fat, bald Lieutenant named Schiffler who kept odd hours and was very uncommunicative. Those first months in London were unreal. He felt gray and soured and out of touch with existence—half alive. He drank, but it made him feel more remote. He did not feel the need of friends or women.

Then, in November—the month the Russians retook Kiev and the Marines took Tarawa—Craig met Maura. One of the British intelligence groups sent over some classified material by courier. He had to sign for it. The courier was a blonde girl named Yeoman Thatcher, and she was wearing one of the most extraordinarily ugly uniforms he had ever seen. It was of coarse, lumpy gray wool with a dingy red piping, with a beret that was curiously shapeless and had a wilted red pompon on top. Her stockings were white and heavy, and her shoes were black and sensible.

But under the uniform was girl. Undeniable girl. She snapped into one of those prolonged, vibrating British salutes. Her round young face had clarity and loveliness, gray eyes wide-set, brows heavy and two shades darker than her blonde hair, color blooming in her cheeks, lips pink as a child's. She swung her arm down and clapped her hand smartly against her young thigh, and it seemed to him there was something extraordinarily touching about her, an awkward youngness. Under the ugliness of the wool her breasts were high and round, her waist narrow, her hips hearty, her long round legs balancing the pelvic basket neatly and delicately. She was, he guessed, about twenty, and she had the solemnity of a child playing an adult game. He wondered if the faint glint of mockery in her eyes was imagined.

She took the documents from the battered dispatch case she wore slung on a shoulder strap and handed them to him along with the receipt. After he had signed it, she stepped back and gave him that monstrous salute again. He wanted to keep her there for a time.

"Please sit down while I look these over. I may have a message to go back."

She hesitated, then sat on the edge of a chair, ankles

and knees together, back straight, hands resting in her lap. He was completely aware of her there as he read through the documents. He put them aside and said, "I'm afraid I don't know that uniform, Yeoman."

"I'm a fanny, sir," she said quite distinctly.

"I beg your pardon!"

"F. A. N. Y. First Aid Nursing Yeomanry, sir. But we haven't done any nursing since the Boer War. Now we work at—this sort of thing." Her voice had a precision, pitch, and clarity that he found most charming.

"Did you inherit the uniform from the Boer War?"

She smiled ruefully and touched her sleeve. "Horrid, I know. Makes me feel rather like a wash hamper."

"Been in it long?"

"Two years and a bit, sir. Is there a chit to go back? They'll wonder what kept me."

"No message, Yeoman. Is that what I call you?"

She stood up. "Right, sir. If I should be sent again and you find it odd to say Yeoman, you might call me Thatcher. That is correct, also."

Again came the great, sweeping, quivering, incredible salute, and she spun about and was gone. It was some time before he could get back to work.

It took him two weeks to arrange to see her again. He made contact through a Captain Hallowell who lived in the same hotel and had been seen with a girl in the same uniform, regularly. After he made friends with Hallowell, the man agreed to check on Yeoman Thatcher for him. He came back with a detailed report.

"Maura Thatcher, her name is. She's twenty. From Suffolk. Ella says she's very nice. Sound, middle-class background. She's been with the outfit for two years. She's unattached. She was in love with a Lancaster pilot who copped it in the Cologne do in May last year, and Ella says she's still broody about it. No dates. The other gals wish she would date somebody nice. But they're wary of us Americans. With reason. I gave you the big buildup. Ella is going to try to fix it up."

Hallowell reported later that Ella had talked to Maura and Maura had remembered him and agreed to go out. The date was set. They picked up the two girls at the FANY billet and took them to a small supper club. The girls were not in uniform. Ella was a flashing and decisive brunette in her middle twenties. Maura was lovely in pale blue. It seemed to require a conscious effort for him to stop looking at her. She seemed shy and subdued, answering when spoken to, but never initiating any comment. When he looked at her round arms, at the good lines of her shoulders, at the softness of her throat dropping away to the bodice of the blue gown, he felt flushed and breathless. Her conversation during the evening was so automatic, so uninspired, he would have thought her dull had he not caught, from time to time, a quickness of the gray eyes, sudden glances at him that were perceptive and alive.

The third time he danced with her he grew impatient with the triteness of their conversation and said, "I can't talk to you in front of them. Could we go?"

She pushed back and looked up at him rather gravely. "Wouldn't that be rude?"

"Yes, it would. Do you really care?"

They apologized to Hallowell and Ella and left. She came alive when they were out in the night. "That was horrid," she said. "I never felt such a fool. As if I were on display."

"Weren't you?"

"I suppose. Ella has been so anxious for me to go out. Could we walk for a bit?"

"Of course."

They took long strides. Her wrap blew in the wind. The sky was bright enough over the blacked-out city for him to see her shy and questioning glance when he took her hand. It was near the end of 1943 and the few air raids were nuisance raids, one or two bombers slipping in to drop a random death on the dark sprawl of the city.

When the sirens whooped they hurried to the nearest entrance to the underground. They stood close together, leaning against a dank wall, facing each other, and listening to the chugging of the guns. Faint light from a weak bulb touched her cheek and shadowed her eyes. He slid his hands inside her wrap, clasped the slim waist in his hands and pulled her close and kissed her. There was no response in her lips. She endured the kiss and pushed him away quite gently.

"Not like that," she said.

"Then like what?"

"Did they tell you about me?"

"About—the pilot?"

"Yes. I'm vulnerable, Craig. Craig. That is rather a nice name. I'm vulnerable. I don't want to get all emotionally involved. With anyone. Ella says I should have an affair. She's quite taken with you. She thinks you would be good for me. I can't be that cold-blooded. Do you see?"

"I think so."

"Poor Captain Fitz. Don't pout, darling. Please. It would be nice to have someone to walk with and talk with. But without any of—the other. Would you mind terribly?"

"I guess I wouldn't."

"Then could you get an auto on Sunday and could we go into the country and walk? I ache for a walk in the country."

And that was the way it started. When she began to trust him, she lost her reserve, and he found her delightful. They had good times together and he told himself it was enough for him. But, quite slyly, he managed to find a rather shabby little flat and get permission to move from the hotel to the flat. When he told her about it, she was angry that he had done it, and they quarreled.

It was weeks before he could entice her to come to his flat. Her reluctance had made him feel as though he should be twisting the ends of his mustache and leering. Finally he said, "Damn it, Maura, this is one hell of a cheerless town in the winter, and I'm damn sick of wandering around freezing. I liberated a tricky field stove from stores, and I've got fuel for it, and PX groceries. As near as I can tell, it's one of the few warm, comfortable places in London. I'm not about to bite you."

She agreed then, but she seemed strained and shy at the flat. She did not seem herself. He made no advances. By the fifth visit, she began to seem at home. After several ineffectual kisses, he had learned with the greatest difficulty to adjust himself to the fact of her physical coldness. It seemed grotesque that there was no physical warmth to match the provocative contours of her lovely body. There were ways she would stand, and ways she would turn, and the wanting of her, the pure physical need of her, would be like something closing around his throat.

On one Sunday he had to go back to headquarters, leaving her there. He had worked longer than he had anticipated, and it was dusk when he returned. He let himself in quietly. The stove was a red glow in the gray shadows of the room. He looked into the small bedroom. She was asleep on the bed, on her back, her head turned to the side, fine blonde hair spilled across the pillow. He went in on tiptoe and, with the greatest of care, sat down on the edge of the bed, shifting his weight a little at a time so as not to awaken her. Her leg touched the side of his hip, and he felt her warmth. She breathed slowly and deeply, placid as a child, and the gray light from the window was across her.

He sat for a very long time, until it was almost dark, just watching her sleep and getting pleasure from looking at loveliness and utter repose. She was dressed in a thing she had brought to the flat the last time she had come, something to give relief from the ugliness of the uniform. It was a one-piece outfit, not unlike coveralls or battle dress, with long sleeves and trouser legs. But it did not have the bagginess of coveralls. It was fitted to her, and it was of a soft gray-green, with knitted cuffs and anklets. She was sprawled there, looking leggy, almost boyish. Her breasts rose and fell with her soft breath.

On impulse he put his hand on her waist, and as she came awake, he bent over her and kissed her. She flung her arm up and tightened it around his neck, and her lips were electrically avid, her body, straining up for a moment to meet his. She made a sound like a sob and pushed him away, roughly and strongly, and moved around him with agility and fled to the other room. He followed her closely and, when she stopped, he took her shoulders and turned her around.

"No!" she said sharply.

He kissed her. Her mouth was lax and unresponsive. But he held her closely, caressing her as he kissed her. He felt the beginnings of response, and then she began to fight him with strength and violence. It was all he could manage to hold her, to keep his lips on hers. She stopped fighting suddenly, and her hips thrust strongly forward and her arms were strong around him, and her lips were alive. She sobbed again, and flung herself a bit to the side, sagging in his arms, head drooping, hair falling forward, breathing hoarsely. In time her breathing quieted and she straightened and said calmly, "Let me go now, Craig. Please."

He released her. She walked over and sat near the stove.

"I think I should explain something to you."

"I guess you should."

"It was a promise I made. After I found out. That in all the rest of my life there would never be anyone else. Rather like a shrine, I suppose. And rather foolish, I imagine. But there it was, and it was a sacred promise. I had promised God. Jeff and I had made love together, and it was all the love I ever wanted. But I'm so desperately weak. I've sensed that. When you kissed me, I tried to make my mind and my heart nothing but a great empty coldness."

"I think I understand."

"Thank you, Craig. Was it so childish?"

"I don't know."

"I'll never really love anyone else. Is that clear too?"

"Yes."

She turned toward him, and the only light was the red glow of the stove highlighting the curve of her cheek, glowing darkly in one eye.

"Do you know how weak I really am?" she asked.

"How weak?"

"I know you. I could ask you to help me. But I shan't. I—want you."

On that Sunday their life entered another dimension. Their physical need of each other was great, almost obsessive. They learned each other and became so perfectly attuned that each could be aroused by a word, a gesture, a glance. Her body was long and firm and rounded, and her skin texture almost unbelievably smooth. It was not long before the artifices and devices of physical modesty no longer existed between them. They took uncomplicated pleasure in the sight and touch of each other. And the compulsive frequency of their love-making seemed to renew rather than exhaust them. His capacity for work seemed to increase, and in her stride there was a new resiliency and energy.

There was a curious flavor to her love-making. She was not a creature of theatrical frenzies, of nails and teeth and whinings. She was earth-mother. She was like sunlit earth, like sea tides, like a slow wind in fields of wheat.

She was a deeply primal rhythm, clasping and enclosing, a rocking strength that underscored release with a long sighing breath, half-articulated, a sweet moist warmth against his face with that prolonged exhalation. In love play she delighted in tantalizing absurdities, in a child-like frankness of experimentation—yet always at one certain point she would revert to the primal woman, and it would be the same for them, always a renewal, a pledge, an unspoken statement of faith.

They never had a guest at the flat. It was their special and private world. As the weather improved, Craig managed to acquire two khaki and cumbersome G.I. bicycles. These could be stowed on a toy train and taken out to the country lanes when there was the rare coincidence of their days of freedom. But always, late in the afternoon, there would be a time when he would look into her eyes and both of them would be filled with a fevered impatience to return to the flat.

As June came closer, the tempo of staff work increased. They both knew D-Day was imminent. The symphony was building to a prolonged climactic coda. But the very intensity of the affair with Maura made the preparations unreal. They never talked of what could come afterward. He tried to tell himself this was just an exceptionally fortunate interlude and, after it was over, they could both forget it. But whenever he thought of never seeing her again, a coldness came into his mind.

On the fourteenth of June he received orders to go to France the next day. He was with Maura until three in the morning on the fifteenth. Their talk had a curious, electric emptiness about it. There were too many things unsaid. They agreed to say their final good-by the next day at eleven near her headquarters. He was to leave for the airport at noon.

As he walked toward their corner where they had met before, when she could leave her work for a few moments, he heard an odd thrumming, wobbling sound as though some fast-flying aircraft was passing overhead with something wrong with the motors. After the sound faded he heard a distant, deep-throated, smashing explosion.

He wondered if it was possible that the Germans could have rigged up some fantastic long-ranged gun to bombard London the way they had Paris in the first war. When he was a half block from the corner, he looked far ahead, trying to spot Maura. She was usually prompt, and he was several minutes late. There were quite a few pedestrians, not much vehicle traffic.

And again he heard the sputtering, thrumming noise, much louder than before. He looked up. A curious thing with short stubby wings moved into view. The sky was clear for a moment and it was outlined against the blue. It trailed puffs of white vapor. It seemed to be traveling slowly. The thrumming sound of propulsion died and at once it nosed over and came down like a stone. He saw that it was coming directly at him. He heard harsh shouts of alarm, heard women scream. There was a shop beside him, below sidewalk level, with three wide, stone steps leading down to the front door. He hurled himself down, banging his bad leg painfully against one of the steps, and huddled at the bottom, cheek against dirty concrete. Seconds later the crescendo of explosion seemed to lift him off the earth and drop him back. There were long seconds of dazed deafness during which he heard nothing. Then sounds came back. A prolonged tinkling of falling glass. A rumble of masonry. Something that cried hoarsely in a deep bubbling voice, endlessly, "Naaaa Naaaaa Naaaaa." Over and over, then it weakened and was silent. Cries and moanings mingled in atonal chorus, like an experimental choir.

When he got up, slowly and unsteadily, he found that there had been a short piece of wrought-iron railing lying across his back. He had not felt it fall. As he got up, the clerks came out of the shop. Their faces were gray.

"What was it?" a man demanded.

Craig walked up to the sidewalk. The thing, which had seemed to be aimed directly at him, had hit at the base of the building on the corner where they had usually met. The building and those near it had tumbled into the street. A bus stood half engulfed by the torrent of stone. The street was hazy with cement dust held in lazy suspension. Near the crest of the wave of stone by the bus protruded, horribly and ludicrously, a pair of naked, unmarked legs.

The dead lay smashed, and the wounded lay bleating. Now he could hear the other sounds of the city, the constant daytime roar. And he heard sirens, close by and coming closer. He saw flames begin in what was left standing of the big building.

He moved slowly and felt he was in a dream. This was the dramatic ending. This was inevitable, and it had been the result of his refusal to say last night what he should have said, and what she did not expect him to say. He knew the other portions of the script. It might be the ludicrous beret he would find.

There were so many dearnesses, now gone. From the small of her back to cleft of buttocks, the patch of palest down. A time of staring at a distance of inches at one gray eye until in semi-hypnosis, the whole world became one great gray eye, pupil like oiled and polished obsidian, and tiny flecks of tan and green pigmentation very near the pupil. Wide separation of breasts, so that in nakedness there was a heroic flavor to her stance, a reminiscence of the Greeks. Color of nipples—neither pink nor coral nor orange nor brown—but a special tawny shade of their own, without name. The one crooked tooth, this one here on the bottom, turned so that in one kiss too harsh it had made a cut on the underside of her lip. Tiny star-shaped scar on the knuckle of the little finger of her left hand, souvenir of a boy in Long Melford, a buck-toothed boy with what she had termed "a lewd and carroty smile."

He knew how she lifted her head when you reached to light her cigarette, how, after putting a shilling in the geyser for the privilege of sitting in the great stone tub in four inches of tepid water, she would come in and scrub with marvelous energies and sigh and say, "Oh, you have such a lovely, lovely back, my dearest."

"Leave some hide on it."

How she held a teacup in both hands, and rather than looking coy or consciously childlike, it had suited her. How she felt sternly disapproving of her own toes. "They're rather nasty, actually. Poor bent, pinched little things, always crouching in the ends of boots."

How once she had come up behind him and, catching him entirely by surprise, had locked her arms around him, around his middle and lifted him completely off the floor, all hundred and seventy pounds, holding him for poised moments after his whoop of surprise, then dropping him back on his feet. He turned and she, flushed with exertion, tapped herself on the chest and said, "Observe, you have a husky peasant wench, suited for heavy duty."

How she became grouchy and miserable with a cold, as

sorry for herself as a wet cat. How she had read aloud to him as he lay stretched on the floor, her voice rising and the words coming faster as she came to the exciting parts.

And she had known him as well as he had known her. All hopes, fears, desires, irritations, affectations. She had known him physically. He had felt ashamed of the burn scars, felt uncomfortable about the shiny redness and the puckered places. She had noticed his rather clumsy efforts to keep them out of sight. Finally she had made him tell her precisely how he had gotten them. He told her in all detail and tried to explain to her just how he had changed during the weeks in hospital. From the look of her eyes, tears had been close when she told him to stretch out on the bed, face down. The light was strong enough. She had run her finger-tips lightly, caressingly, over the tight hair-less reddened skin, and said, "And you thought this would put me off. This! Actually, Craig, you are sometimes such a fool."

Now he walked, looking for what might be left of her, and he walked with an almost imperceptible limp. The rescue people arrived, and one of them superintended the search through the fallen masonry. He went over to the helmeted man and said, "What did this?"

"A new bit of nastiness, Yank. A new great beast of a bomb with wings and a sputter. Bloody good thing the swine didn't have it two years ago."

He was standing looking dully at where the men worked when she came flying against him, nearly bowling him over, eyes adrift, mouth working, hands and arms unable to hold him tightly enough. They moved away from it, down a street, around a corner. And, in the boarded entrance to a building ruined long ago, they kissed.

When she could talk, she said, "I knew it killed you. And all I could think of was what I hadn't told you yet."

"What is that?"

"That nonsense about Jeff. My mealy mouth saying I'd never love again. I did not know what love was then. And I know now. I love you."

He had his hands on her shoulders. "We're going to marry."

"I know."

"I have to go now."

"Be dreadfully careful, darling."

"I'll find the deepest holes."

They kissed and he walked away and did not look back. The truck was waiting; the driver was cross. Late that afternoon he was in France.

During the next year he managed to wangle three trips to London and saw her each time and they managed, each time, to find a place where they could be together. He put in motion the red tape for permission to marry. At last it came through, but by then the war was over and staff details were so botched up he could not get orders to London. So he hitched a ride in a cargo plane, waited two days for Maura to get her release from duty, then went with her to Long Melford and met her people. They were pleasant and seemed neither terribly pleased nor particularly distressed that their third and youngest daughter should marry an American. It was a Church of England marriage and, after it was over, Craig and Maura went to Peterhead in the North of Scotland for a month. They walked the wild beaches and slept close and warm in a great bed as big as a lorry.

Back in London he did not run into the trouble he expected. Pre-dated orders were made out to cover his defection, and he was given new orders that provided for transportation by ship for Captain and Mrs. Fitz, and an honorable discharge at Fort Dix.

There was a life ahead, and Craig felt that this land was as strange to him as it was to Maura. That October, on the day Laval was executed, they learned that Maura was pregnant.

CHAPTER THREE

THERE, in the summer darkness of the small square bedroom of the ugly house on Federal Street, Craig turned restlessly, body weary, but his mind roving the backyards of memory, looking into corners, peering under things, searching for some unknown thing, thinking he would recognize it when once he saw it. His whole life seemed like a journey that could never be relaxing to him be-

cause there was constantly in the back of his mind the
certainty that he had left something undone. There was
some essential he had forgotten to bring, or there was
something he had neglected to turn off, or on, or something he had forgotten to lock.

He knew that this feeling had been with him for the
last few years, but it had been far back, barely on the
fringe of awareness. With Maura and the girls around,
life was sufficiently full, with little time for the loneliness
of subjective thought. He wished they were back. They
were his cushion, a padding to blunt the sharp edges of
this curious feeling of futility. He could close his eyes and
imagine them in the house, imagine it so vividly he could
almost hear her soft breathing in the neighboring bed,
scent the faint perfume of her, think that if he opened
his eyes, turned his head, he would see the mound of her
hip in the faint light.

The night was sticky and the sheet clung to his legs
when he tried to turn over. He kicked it free and lay
naked. This would be another Stoddard summer, long
and brutal. Maura was lucky to be out of it. The sun
would hammer the city all day, and the stone and asphalt
would absorb the sun. Then, in the airless night, the captive heat would radiate its misery.

Up at Riverwood there would be the illusion of coolness. Cooler air would move down the slope and across the
patios where ice tinkled in tall glasses and women in
shorts lazily batted the mosquitoes that landed on their
thighs and said, "Bet it's grim down in town tonight."

He went downstairs and made a tall, stiff drink of
bourbon and carried it into the living room and sat in the
dark room in the chair known in the household as 'his'
chair. The sodium vapor lights on Federal Street made a
yellow light in the room, enough for him to see the level
of his drink, the hairiness of his lean knees, the golden
glint of his wedding ring.

He remembered that eleven years ago he had sat this
way in a furnished room in this same city not more than
eight blocks away. A brittle Sunday afternoon in March,
sleet lashing at the west window. They had decided, solemnly, to get drunk, as an antidote to their feeling of de-
pression over never being able to find a suitable house.

She was seven months heavy with child then. They were gay for a time, and then she went, slurred and heavy and slow-moving, to bed. In those final months she slept on her back. He had gotten owlishly drunk, listening to the sleet, to the hiss of the gilt radiator and to her surprisingly loud snoring, looking at the mound of the belly —and thinking—what am I doing here?

And wanting to run and never come back.

The next day when he had remembered how strong the impulse had been, it had shamed him. He loved her. She was his wife. She was carrying his child in a strange country.

But tonight he could feel that way again. What am I doing here? What has happened to everything? What has happened to us?

Something had gone out of it the last few years. Something had gone out of the marriage. You weren't such a great fool you expected the magic to last forever, but you wanted a little more than was left. More than just the stylized responses. Though they had retained all of the habits and devices of ultimate intimacy, she had become something of a stranger to him. Once upon a time there had been a shy girl in a blue gown glancing at him across a restaurant table. Now there was, in her place, an American housewife, fifteen pounds heavier, waist thickened by childbirth—with a puffiness under her chin, a slight sagging of her cheeks, a tiny withering of the flesh under her gray eyes. The coronet braids were gone and her hair was cut short in current fashion, and it had lost its gloss.

Yet, where did the lean, brown lieutenant go? She is a mature and handsome woman, fastidious and warm. A good wife. Intelligent and ornamental—yet rather staid and conventional. And deeply passionate. And she's done a good job with the girls. They are solemn, thoughtful, blonde little girls. They have Maura's coloring, and they are neat and they do not whine, and they both adore me utterly. Penelope and Priscilla, almost as alike as twins despite the two years between them.

He was sure that Maura had sensed the way he felt about the trip. And he wondered if she felt the same way. Of late there had been a staleness. He did not want her to go, and yet he did want her to go away. It was not that they had quarreled. It was just . . . a certain indescribable staleness in their relationship, a weariness that he could not account for.

He sat in the darkness and drank a bit more than enough of the bourbon and went solemnly to bed at midnight, to a sleep that came moments after he had stretched out and pulled the sheet across him.

The Quality Metal Products Division was located in a heavy industry area on the other side of the river from the main part of the city of Stoddard. The original buildings, still in use, were quite old, and unsuited to modern methods of material handling and production flow. There had been many expansion programs, each adding new production areas of greater efficiency. The result was a great confusing sprawl of buildings, bewildering to new administrative personnel. Factory cost accounting indicated that an entirely new plant should be built, but the potential savings could not yet offset the losses that would be incurred by the interruption of production. In this jumble of buildings two thousand employees produced die castings, small forgings and stamped metal products for the automobile industry, for household appliances, for outboard motors, for chains of auto parts stores. The diversity of product lines was as much a headache as the awkwardness of the arrangement of the production areas. Inventory was in a chronic state of crisis.

Craig's office was in one of the older buildings, close to the clatter-bang of the stamping machines, the reek of the plating department, far from the air-conditioned orderliness of the accounting division and the design division. There were six assistant plant managers of which he was one. His office was small and high-ceilinged. The two windows faced the west. One door opened onto the corridor. The other opened into a large room where his immediate assistants worked at desks and drawing tables. There were two females, a secretary and a typist, and six males. On one wall was a huge board with multi-colored pegs to indicate production progress on the orders in the plant. Craig knew well that in spite of his impressive title, he was merely a glorified production chaser, with but one additional responsibility, that of feeding new or-

ders in on a schedule that would promote the most effective utilization of machines and man power. The job
required a man who could keep the maximum number of
details in his head, and make half a hundred minor decisions a day.

He had realized one day, while sitting at the counter in
a bean wagon, that his job was very similar to that of a
short-order cook. Remember the orders, feed them in with
the minimum of waste motion, send them out on schedule.

On Friday morning he took a cab to the garage, picked
up his car and drove to the plant. He was standing in
the large room studying the board as his people came in.
The board was the responsibility of Bucky Howell. It was
his control center, backed up by the production report
file. Bucky was young and alert and too inclined to fly
off the handle. He stood beside Craig and said, "122D
is stalled on account of a breakdown in stamping."

"Can't they put it on something else? No, there won't
be much over there that can handle those dimensions."

"Three units, and it wouldn't be worthwhile changing
the dies."

"How long?"

"I stopped by. Maintenance has been working most of
the night. Charlie says by noon they'll be rolling. So we
lose maybe twenty-five-hundred units. Is it worth having
another set of dies made?"

"No. But keep on top of it."

Bucky took off. He would go through the whole plant
picking up departmental production reports, then get the
consolidated report from shipping. Before noon the board
would be posted and current.

Betty James, his secretary, followed Craig into his office, closing the door behind her. She had been with him
a year and a half. She was close to thirty, a sandy woman
with a broad-shouldered, sturdy body, weak blue eyes, a
crisply positive manner. She was loyal and intelligent and
worked very hard. If she had a flaw it was that she had
a need to dominate. She often presumed to give him advice. But he had made clear to her the line beyond which
she could not go. They worked well together. He was not
attracted to her physically.

She placed the pile of inter-office and intra-office memoranda in front of him, sorted according to her guess as to priority, and sat with book in hand to record his instructions.

It took him an hour and a half to go through the memos and new orders, make phone calls, dictate new memos. When he was quite obviously through and ready to go out to the production areas, Betty still sat there.

"Well?" he asked, somewhat impatiently.

"A new latrine-o-gram, Mr. Fitz. Mr. Ober had Mr. McCabe in his office for over two hours yesterday. McCabe was in rough shape when he got back. Dorothy Bowman said he had the twitches. He went out for an hour and when he came back he was very jolly and slightly loaded. That has never happened before."

"Maybe he's been due."

"That's three so far. Mr. Ober seems to be working his way through the list. You ought to be about due."

"Not for a chewing, Betty. I do my ugly little job with neatness and a certain amount of dispatch."

"Maybe that's the way he operates."

"I hope he doesn't try it."

She looked concerned. "Please don't—blow up if he does. I mean—we both just work here."

The phone rang and she picked it up. "Mr. Fitz's office, Miss James speaking. Yes? Just a moment, please." She covered the mouthpiece. She looked slightly pale. Her freckles were more noticeable. "Can you see Mr. Ober at eleven-thirty?" He nodded. She said into the phone, "Mr. Fitz will be there at eleven-thirty. You're welcome." She hung up and said, "Speak of the devil."

"Why do you act scared of him, Betty?"

"Well, everybody knows his reputation."

"You aren't flattering me. Run along and type that stuff up. I'll be with Chernek and then I'll go right from there to Ober's office. Put what you've finished on my desk before you go to lunch."

"Yes sir," she said. And left, setting her heels down firmly.

As he walked to Purchasing to talk to Chernek, he thought of Paul Ober and what Ober might mean to him personally. U. S. Automotive was known throughout the industry for ruthlessness on the executive level. Competition between top men was savage. According to company policy, you did not stay in one place for long. You were promoted or weeded out. This lack of paternalism on the executive level seemed to keep the total operation, all twelve plants, more profitable. Though the name was still U. S. Automotive, horizontal expansion had taken the corporation into textiles, chemicals, plastics, and electronics. The Quality Metal Products Division was the only manufacturing facility which still had a substantial share of production taken by the automobile industry, but a lot of that output was flash merchandise for independents and retail chains—side mirrors, hood ornaments, hub caps, chrome stripping, dashboard accessories.

The previous plant manager, Harvey Haley, had reached retirement age in January. Paul Ober had arrived to take over. He had a reputation throughout the corporation and the industry as a tough and effective troubleshooter. His assignment to Quality Metal Products was an indication of the dissatisfaction of the Board with plant operations. It was rumored that he would spend a couple of years chopping out dead wood and tautening operations and then be assigned to the next problem plant.

Ober brought with him one tall, blonde, plain, chilly private secretary named Commerford—frighteningly efficient and apparently emotionless—and one small, fat, impassive man with thick glasses named L. T. Rowdy. Rowdy attended all executive conferences and never spoke. He could stand for two hours watching one manufacturing operation without seeming to move, or breathe. On rare occasions he would make a notation in a dime-store notebook with a slim, gold pencil.

Ober was not as ominous as his two assistants. He was a tall man in his early forties, without office softness or office pallor. He dressed casually, had roan, bushy hair worn too long, glasses with heavy black frames, a shaggy mustache, and a pipe. He was languid and gracious and soft-spoken. The hair, mustache, pipe and glasses made it difficult to remember just what he looked like. But you couldn't forget the eyes. They were large, brown, moist eyes, harmless as a puppy's. He had the absent-minded manner of a visiting professor. He seemed to know the personal history of every executive at Quality.

As the weeks went by they learned he was unmarried,

that he was living in one of the newest apartment buildings in Stoddard, that he drove a rented car. He kept casual working hours and took frequent trips. One by one he entertained the executives and their wives at his apartment. When Craig and Maura had been invited, it had been a disarming evening. Ober left no opening for shop talk. He was amusing in his own quiet way. The excellent dinner was served by a Negro named Howard.

On the way home, Maura had said, "I hope we passed inspection."

"Why do you say it that way?"

"He's a very intense man, darling. Intense and watchful and guarded. And cold as a snake. There is a word for him."

"Dedicated?"

"No. That seems to imply moral values. Committed is a better word. He is one-hundred per cent committed to his function, and it leaves no room for anything else. No room for softness or friendship or love. He would be frightfully impatient with anyone who isn't also committed."

Craig knew that Ober made him uneasy. He had been too long in his present job. Though it was not his fault, the job was a dead end job. There seemed to be no place to go. He knew he did the demanding work well, but the record would show that he was static. There was really no reason to be uneasy.

He went over the new materials list in Bill Chernek's office, and they changed the scheduling on two orders to give a less dangerous safety margin.

Craig sighed and stood up, glancing at his watch, and said, "I'm off to see the wizard."

Bill grinned. "Take away the hair, mustache, pipe and glasses, and what have you got?"

"You haven't got Shirley Temple."

"Stop dating yourself, Fitz."

"Okay. You haven't got Julie Harris."

Bill crossed his fingers and said, "Don't lead with the right."

Ober's private office adjoined the main conference room. It was the first time Craig had been in the office since Haley had retired. He had half expected to see it unchanged, but the redecoration was extensive. It was no longer an office. It seemed like a small private lounge, with leather chairs, draperies, decorator colors, a large photomural of the industrial complex on the east side of the river, showing Quality Metals and the neighboring plants. Miss Commerford showed him in and closed the door behind him without a sound.

Ober was alone, sitting on a couch, studying papers fastened to a clip-board. Craig felt relieved that Rowdy wasn't present. Ober put the board aside, stood up and shook hands, and had Craig sit near him on a chair turned toward the couch.

"Maura and the kids enjoying England?"

"Very much, from her letters."

"Good, good." Ober packed his pipe carefully. "I've been thinking about you, Craig. About your work. Your record is good."

"Thanks."

Ober got the pipe lighted. "What you are doing seems to be essential. But I can't imagine you being satisfied with the work."

Craig said warily, "Why not?"

Ober shrugged. "It's pretty mechanical. It has no scope. Got any idea how we could eliminate your job?"

"There's several ways, all of them impossible."

"What are they?"

"Put nothing through the plant but large runs of standardized orders. Eliminate design changes. That's one way. Or tear this down and build a new plant, modern and flexible. That will have to happen some day, when this old crock finally won't give any return on the investment. We're operating on the basis of patch and pray."

Ober nodded mildly. "You're called an assistant plant manager. You're a glorified production chaser, Craig."

"Call it co-ordinator. It sounds better."

Ober slouched and closed his eyes. Craig sat uncomfortably for several long minutes. Without opening his eyes Ober said, "Here we have a pretty problem. Fifty-five per cent of production proposes no special problems. But we can't show a profit operating at that per cent of capacity. So we scramble for orders, and shave prices to build capacity up to the point where we get a return on the investment. The plant and at least half the equipment is obsolete. We get a lot of nuisance orders through the shop. Small quantities. The index of your efficiency, Fitz, is the Percentage of Utilization Report. You fight with the order takers, with engineering, with purchasing, with production. And design. You're caught in a closed circuit."

"I guess that's right."

Ober straightened up, leaned forward and tapped Craig on the knee. "So let's come up with the Fitz plan. A plan to get this plant—and you—out of this closed circuit problem. Bring me an idea a week from today, Craig."

"But—"

Ober stood up and Craig stood up. "It's an old gambit, Craig. I'm asking you to think yourself out of a job. Fly high. Look down on the jungle. Don't try to cut a trail through it."

He eased Craig into the outer office and said, "Commerford, set Mr. Fitz up for the same time next Friday."

"Yes, sir," she said in an outer-space voice.

"And bring me the Chernek file. See you Friday, Craig."

As he went back to his own office he felt a sullen resentment. So Quality Metal Products was tottering along. That was obvious. But there were a hell of a lot of smart people trying to figure out an answer. Why expect one Craig Fitz to come up with a miraculous solution? You couldn't pick and choose the kind of orders you wanted to fill. You couldn't suddenly come up with a miracle item and make it and market it yourself.

He was correcting and signing memos when Betty came back from lunch.

"How did it go?" she asked quickly.

"I don't know how it went. I don't know what he's thinking. I don't know what he's trying to do."

"Did he criticize?"

"I don't know that either."

"But what did he want?"

He looked up at her impatiently. "Nothing at all. He just wants me to come up with a genius-type idea that will eliminate my job."

"Dear God!"

The rest of the day was peaceful, relatively speaking. A vacation snarl caused an intricate rescheduling. An anticipated re-order didn't come in. A breakdown turned out, for once, to be noncritical, as stand-by equipment was immediately available. Stores made an inventory error which could be corrected by an air-express shipment. John Terrill came in to grouse about the jigs and fixtures required for one of the new orders. Even though the troubles were minor, it seemed to Craig that he could very easily react to them too emotionally. He wanted to yell and wave his arms—or break into tears. It seemed like a monstrously long afternoon. He would have to come in Saturday to catch up on some paper work, and then endure the rest of the long, empty week end.

Bill Chernek left at the same time he did and, as they walked to the lot, Bill said, "Ruthie left me. For a week. She took the kids and went up to her mother's place at Lake Ruskin. So how about we howl a little, brother bachelor? Take off some of the Ober-bearing pressure."

"Not if you make puns like that."

"Come on, boy. I join Ruthie a week from tonight when my overdue vacation starts. You've looked and acted sour for weeks. You're stale, my friend. We'll get tight and act loose. So say yes and start to cheer up."

Craig cheered up immediately. "Where do we start?" He liked Bill Chernek. Bill was about four years younger than Craig. He was the purchasing agent for Quality Metals, buying all those items not centrally purchased out of New York. He was a big, cheery, blond man, rapidly taking on too much weight. He had been a college football player, a Marine, and later a salesman. He liked to explain how he'd had so many purchasing agents say no that he thought the only defense was to get on the other side of the desk. He was bright and shrewd and likable.

"I want to clean up first," Bill said. "I like to drink clean. Tell you what, you go home and leave your car and take a cab down to Nick's Bar on Mallory. I'll do the same. Then we don't have to sweat out anybody's driving. After a little of Nick's liquid inspiration, we'll cook up something."

Part of the enthusiasm faded while Craig was on his way home, bucking the heavy traffic on the bridge. Bill had a reputation for getting thoroughly loaded and becoming a problem. But it was certainly better than an evening alone, no matter what happened.

There was a letter from Maura. He threw it on the bed. When he was ready for his shower, he opened it.

CHAPTER FOUR

CRAIG, DEAREST,

It is one of the loveliest days, so clear and bright. It is like a day sent back out of my childhood. Yesterday was almost as good. We made a picnic and I took the girls in the Hillman to Lowestoft, to the beach there. We walked on the rocky beach. The sea was running very heavy. Puss just sat and stared at it, while Penny became quite a mad thing, running, waving her arms, and shouting at it.

I must tell you that I have been dealt with firmly by the girls. They consent to return to their normal identities when we come back, but while here they will be Priscilla and Penelope from now on. It seems to them more suitable. Long Melford is positively acrawl with children, and a great many of them seem to be children of my childhood friends. Penelope and Priscilla are quickly taking on protective coloration, dressing as the other children do and aping their speech. They indulge in long intricate games in the back garden, and become very sticky indeed if tea should be late. Poor dears, they seem to be caught between two worlds.

And now I must tell you about myself. I was half afraid to come back here. I had the idea I might slip back into this world I came from so completely that suddenly all the years with you would take on the quality of a dream. But I cannot get back into this world. I am a visiting American. I hardly know or remember the child who grew up here. I have talked endlessly with old friends, and they seem to recall perfectly so many things I had quite forgotten. They tell me of horrid things that have happened to people I cannot remember. It seems as though I am impersonating Maura Thatcher and I have not been properly briefed.

I made another poor estimate of the situation. I had imagined they would all be avid to hear about how we live. But they do not wish to hear about the States. They make me feel a liar when I say anything which goes contrary to what they have learned from the flicks. They live behind what I shall call the tea curtain, and do not care to have anyone attempt to dislodge their odd notions about the States.

Yesterday, darling, I met a man from my past. I believe I must have been all of twelve years old when I had a crush on him. He was very important then, because he had the only motorbike in the village, and it was a gaudy red. I had but to come upon him unexpectedly, and my knees would go all cottony, and the world would swim, and I would bumble about on the verge of a swoon.

He is a greengrocer now, and he must weigh close to twenty stone, a great gross man with an incredible number of chins, smelling of suet and spices. His wife is wispy and defeated. I knew her as a rather mild girl, some years younger than myself. After his wife went to the back of the shop, Harry seemed to think it required of him to puncuate our conversation with little pats and nudges. Believe me, it was a very short talk we had.

My mother, of course, is anxious to know all the details of how we live. But she has gone quite deaf and refuses to admit it. She nods and smiles and then says things that show clearly she hasn't heard me. In some curious fashion her deafness does not keep her from hearing my father's voice. She is somehow adjusted to it. They both quite obviously adore the girls. Tomorrow Elizabeth arrives from London with her two little boys. How we shall all fit in this house, I cannot say. It seems much smaller than it did before. Penny and Puss are all electric about meeting their cousins, and ask odd questions.

America has spoiled me. I had not remembered the inconveniences, the awkward things. The shops are very grim. Their stocks are so limited. Television is the current rage. Everyone talks about it, and spends endless time peering at tiny little screens which receive so badly that part of the time it is difficult to make out just what is being shown. I have had to be very firm with the girls.

They have a tendency to expound on how much better
things are in Stoddard.

My darling, it is very late and everyone else in the
house is fast asleep. I think of you a great deal, and I am
drearily lonely for you. The summer stretches ahead of
me and it is endless. I am a displaced person, and I do
not believe I shall come back here again. I think of how
your lips and your hands might feel, and I grow as giddy
as that little girl who watched Harry on his motorbike.

I hope your summer is not too desolate. Do not rattle
about in that empty house like a lost soul. Go out where
people are, my dear, and it will do you good. I did not
like the sound of your last letter. The gaiety seemed so
dreadfully forced, like a person laughing nervously while
someone else stands upon his foot. Do not work too hard,
and eat properly. The girls, of course, send their love.
They whine for you at least once day. And so do I. In the
next letter I shall send the pictures. I love you so very
much.

                                                    Maura

He put the letter on his pillow, knowing that he would
want to reread it when he went to bed.

Bill was on a bar stool when he walked into Nick's.
Nick's was a Stoddard institution. Female trade was permitted in the glossy cocktail lounge adjoining the bar,
but was firmly discouraged in the bar itself. The men's
bar was shabby, poorly lighted, with big brass spittoons,
sawdust on the floor, dusty trophy heads on the wall. But
the bartenders were deft, the drinks both generous and
expensive, the bar stools comfortable. At five-thirty on
any weekday evening, Nick's was crowded with men from
nearby office buildings, the courthouse around the corner, the city hall two blocks away. Lawyers, newspaper-
men, realtors, judges, politicians crowded the bar and sat
in the dark oak booths that lined the wall opposite the
long bar. It was a place to give and receive information,
patch up feuds and make new ones.

Now, at six-fifteen, the quick-one-on-the-way-home
crowd was thinning out. Craig looked at Bill's Martini
and decided it looked good. He sipped the first half of
his drink standing half behind Bill, with Bill twisting

around to talk to him. Then the stool on Bill's right was vacated and Craig was able to sit at the bar. By the time they ordered the second round, half the bar stools were empty.

They talked in low tones about Paul Ober. "My opinion is very easy to state," Bill said ponderously. "It is a little gem of simplicity. It requires little elucidation. I think he is a spherical son of a bitch."

"Spherical?"

"Sure. That means no matter how you look at him, he's a son of a bitch. From any direction. So God-damn sweet and gentle. He's a sadist. He'll cut your throat or mine just for the exquisite pleasure of watching our expression. He's a specialist in keeping you off balance. He wants everybody sweating to keep their job. L. T. Rowdy is a prop. A menace, like a bit part in a Hitchcock picture."

"I think you've got him wrong, Bill. Do you want him to get us all together for a big fat pep talk? Fight team fight. You know damn well old Q.M. is the lame duck division of the whole works. He's here to do a job."

"On you and me. Let's stop talking about the sweat shop, for Christ sake. Let's get this ball rolling. Joe, hit us again." The drinks were potent.

"How many of these are we going to have?" Craig asked.

"Too many. Nobody's driving. Hell with it. A big red steak will knock the edge off later and then we can start again. A big drunky bachelor evening, kiddo."

Craig lost track of the drinks. He felt that he was talking persuasively and importantly. It had become necessary to him to explain exactly how he had felt the last few days. It was a highly personal thing that without drinks he would never have thought of trying to explain to Chernek. He could hear his own owlish voice, but he could not turn it off. "I don't feel like me any more. It's like losing hold of something. You know what I mean? I'm not wearing my own skin. Hell, it's like there was a great big gap in time. I'm twenty-four and all of a damn second I'm right next to forty and where the hell have I been? What have I been doing? Like amnesia. I'm looking around and right now—get this—right now I got less time to go than I already had. That's important. Less

time to go. I've used up more than half. Doing what?
Eating, sleeping, working. A wooden man. A wooden man
with wheels running along a track down a hill, and when
the track ends you fall off the edge of the world."

Chernek nodded heavily and thoughtfully. "It's tough
all right."

"Now you got to get this too. It's important. People
gotta think about this. Okay, you look at some old bastard."

"I look at some old bastard."

"That's right, and you think he's old all the way
through. Old inside his head. But you gotta realize he
isn't. Inside his head he's maybe a kid. And this age thing
has happened to him. Like—like a disease. You get it.
Suppose this old bastard, he's sitting in a bus station and
he's wearing busted shoes and he's got a bad heart and he
can sit there and listen to his bad heart and look at his
busted shoes and wonder how all this time happened to
him. Where it all went, and what he was doing with it."
He felt the sting of tears in his eyes. He tapped Bill on the
shoulder. "It's happening to you." He hit himself on the
chest. "It's happening to me. Every minute. It's leaking
way from you."

"Leaking," Bill said, his eyes half closed.

"So whatta you going to do about it. That's what I
want to know. In a few lousy little years I can be a grandfather. Me! Craig Fitz, a grandfather, and right inside
here I'll still be twenty-four and nobody will know it but
me. You get it? It's a great tragedy—tragedy."

Joe, the bartender, drifted over and said, "It's nearly
nine o'clock, gentlemen. Don't you think you should get
some dinner?"

Bill stared at the small polite man. "When I want some
eating advice, I'll go to a dietician, buster. In Spain the
right people don't eat until eleven. But what the hell
would you know about Spain?"

"Take it easy," Craig said.

"Easy, hell! Scurry off, you little jerk, and whip up some
more of these delicious Martinis. We'll go for doubles this
time."

Joe had turned dark red. He turned white. "I'm afraid
the bar is closed to you, Mr. Chernek. I can't serve you
another drink."

Bill studied the paper money and change on the bar. He picked it all up very deliberately, hesitated, put down a dime. "This is for you, Joe. For superb service. And might I add that this is the last time I shall ever be seen in this over-rated saloon. Good-by forever, old buddy. Screw you, and the same to Nick."

Craig lingered behind as Bill lumbered toward the door. He made an apologetic gesture, and left two dollars of his change on the bar. Joe nodded curtly and picked up the money. Craig hurried after Bill. Bill could be a very troublesome drunk. But he was the only man in the world who could understand how Craig had felt and what he was trying to say.

Bill stood, swaying slightly. "Never come here again. Craig, by God, I think you're the best friend I've got in the whole world. You're a deep thinker. You're sort of a quiet-type guy, but by God I like you. I like you a hell of a lot."

"I like you too."

"We'll have us a ball, old buddy. I'm going to do you a favor, and you're never going to forget it. Come on. Let's get a cab."

"Are we going to eat?"

"Sure we're going to eat. Come on."

They found a taxi in a hotel stand. They got in and Bill said, "We want to be dropped off at the corner of River Street and State Street, kiddo."

The driver turned around in the seat and looked at them. "You gents sure you want to go down there?"

"Why, all of a sudden, is every little son of a bitch in the world trying to give me advice?" Bill complained.

"Suit yourself, chief." He pulled the flag down and started up.

"Where are we going?" Craig asked.

"Leave everything to old Uncle Bill."

The driver snorted.

"Skip the editorial comments, buster," Bill said.

It was a fifteen-minute ride. Bill hummed tunelessly and refused to answer questions. When Craig saw the section he knew what the driver meant. It was the oldest part of the city, down near the sour smell of the polluted river, an area of old warehouses, missions, fleabag hotels, derelict bars. One portion of that area had been razed two years before and a Negro housing development built to help relieve some of the pressure of the rapidly growing Negro population. The July night seemed stickier down there in the narrow streets.

"Where now?" Craig asked.

"You nervous? I haven't been down here in two years, but I know a good thing and I remember it. We're going to see an old friend of mine. Name of Connie. We got to walk a block and a half. I couldn't remember the name of the other street, so I had to tell him here."

"A friend of yours lives here?"

"Sort of. She's got a nice place. Best damn people in town come down here. Hell, we'll probably run into the Mayor. She's in the big leagues. She's in the big circuit. She gets the best merchandise you ever saw. They're no tramps. Every damn one of them looks like a model. They can carry on a conversation too. It's fifty bucks for all night."

Craig stopped. "Are you talking about a whore house?"

"What else? And you never been treated better. This is on me, Craigie old buddy."

"Damn it, I want some food."

"Food you'll get. This is a set up, kiddo. It has atmosphere. She's got a freezer full of steaks and a little old nigger who really knows how to cook 'em. And we'll have us a bottle of champagne. And you get yourself first choice of those nice leggy gals. Come on. Don't just stand there."

They walked. They passed corners where men leaned against darkened store fronts and fell silent when they passed. A man slept on newspapers in a doorway. They turned onto a darker, narrower street. The buildings were all old, all joined together. The street was littered with paper, and the alley mouths smelled sharply of urine.

Craig walked woodenly beside Bill. He was conscious of how conspicuous they were. He felt nervous about the black mouths of the alleys. Stoddard, with its undermanned police force, its industrial expansion, its venal city government, had a high ratio of crimes of violence. Muggings were commonplace.

Now that he had adjusted to Bill's program, he felt recurrent quivers of excitement.

"Right in here someplace," Bill said. "Right along in here."

He stopped and looked at the stone houses. They were two and three stories high. Each had stone steps from the sidewalk up to the front door, and many of them had a second flight going down at an angle to the basement. There were not many lighted windows on the street. At some of the houses people sat on the front steps. As Bill studied the buildings, Craig could hear a faint discordancy of music, of mingled reception from many sources.

A dark sedan drew up to the curb two houses away. The horn blasted the night twice. A girl came quickly out of the door, hurried down the steps and into the car. It was moving before she could pull the door shut.

"You wait here," Bill said. He climbed the steps and thumped on a door. When the door opened he said, "This Connie's place?" The door slammed in his face. He came down the steps. "Bad guess."

He tried the next house and the next, without luck. He was getting angry. He was kicking the doors instead of knocking. He said, "You know, I'll bet you the damn place is across the street. You wait here, pal." Craig waited and watched him. Craig felt the whole street was watching them, watching the pair of noisy drunks.

Finally, Bill lifted his head and filled the night with a brass roar. "Connie! Oh, Connie! Where the hell do you live?"

It was at that moment the prowl car came around a corner, moving swiftly and almost silently. A white spotlight swung onto Bill Chernek and the car stopped close to him. Craig saw Bill glare into the light and heard him yell, "Get that damn light off me!"

Craig had been leaning against the side of a building in the shadows. As he pushed himself away from the wall to cross the street he felt a twist of dizziness. He staggered sideways and tumbled down an unseen flight of stone steps, landing on his hip and shoulder. The fall jolted him and sickened him and he lay there for a moment. He came up the steps, swallowing hard, and when his eye was above sidewalk level he saw the two cops tumbling the unconscious body of Bill Chernek into the back of the prowl. The people on the shallow porches had moved quietly indoors. Craig could hear the cops' voices clearly.

"Big bastard, isn't he?"

"Two bits says he's from that furniture convention. We'll get the I.D. when we get him in."

"Figure he was alone?"

"Looks that way." The sedan doors chunked shut. The car moved off.

Craig stood in the shadows, down in the blackness. The small sounds of living began to be audible again on the street. He told himself it would have done no good to cross the street after Bill had already been knocked out. The damage was already done by the time he had started back up the stairs. They would have taken him in too. He suspected he would have been unable to conceal his intoxication. The fall had sobered him, but only slightly. He felt dulled and witless standing there in the stale night air. The buildings were out of perspective, leaning toward him. A drop of chilled sweat ran down his ribs and he wondered if he was going to be sick. He took several deep breaths, squared his shoulders, marched up the stairs and down the street. He tried to look sober, purposeful, a man with a place to go.

He had enough idea of direction, enough knowledge of the texture of the city to know that he should walk away from the river. There was no chance of stopping a cab down in this area. He walked through the fringe of a Negro district, past jukes turned to maximum volume, past a white-haired white woman who vomited in the gutter, past a child who wept, past a woman who spoke to him insinuatingly. He walked the narrow blocks away from the river and found a small grocery store that was open and put a dime in a pay phone fastened to a sidewall and phoned Al Jardine.

"Al, this is Craig Fitz. I think I've got a little problem."

"*You're* not in some kind of trouble!"

"No. Not steady old reliable Craig. Not me. Bill Chernek. I was with him. We were drunk. The cops knocked him out and took him in."

"And let you go? You sound funny."

"They didn't spot me. It happened about two blocks from the corner of River Street and State Street. He was looking for a place called Connie's."

"Sane people don't go down there, and Connie moved away over a year ago, I hear. She runs a call business. Is it just a D and D?"

"I don't know. I guess he fought. They knocked him out."

He could hear Jardine sigh. "Good old Bill. I'll see what I can do. Want to meet me at the station?"

"I don't think I should. I don't think I'm an asset."

"If he's got one of those streaks on, I'm going to let him stay right there. I'd never be able to get him home alone. It won't get in the papers. If it has to, I'll make sure they typo the hell out of his name and address."

"Thanks a lot, Al."

"You take care of yourself, now. Say, how about coming around for dinner some night. Irene and I were talking about you the other day."

"I'd like to, Al. Have Irene give me a ring at the plant."

He debated calling a cab, decided against it. He was out of the worst of the area now. In a block or two he could cut over to Turner Street, and then it was only about five more blocks to the fringe of the theater district where he could get something to eat—if he could force it down.

When he came to an area of small frame houses with small lawns, where people sat on the front porches and kids ran whooping from lawn to lawn, he turned left and cut over to Turner. Two blocks up Turner he came to a lunchroom that looked sparkling clean. There was a low counter to sit at, and waitresses in yellow uniforms. He ordered black coffee. After that was down, and stayed down, hunger began to stir. He ordered a bowl of chili. It was hot and good. When it was gone he had a glass of milk and then another cup of coffee. He felt a great deal better. It was twenty after ten. It seemed to him that it should be much later. He realized there was nothing left to do but go home. It gave him a let-down feeling. After violence, the evening had dwindled off into nothing. He wondered about late movies and decided he had no urge to sit in the dark with strangers.

He paid and left. He walked slowly. As he passed a neighborhood bar near the corner, he paused and looked through the screen door. There was a good crowd in there, and they were watching a fight on television.

". . . a left hook to the head and another right and a left to the body . . ."

He turned the corner, heading toward Federal Street.

There was a small parking lot beside the bar, with over a dozen cars in it. He glanced idly into the lot. He heard a girl's voice, shrill and indignant. "That's enough, God damn it! Stop! That's enough!"

He paused, staring into the lot. He wondered if she was in one of the cars. He walked a few steps into the lot, listening. He could hear grunts and thuds and, in remorseless rhythm, the meaty splat of fists on flesh. He moved gingerly toward the sound. Just then a car swung around the corner and as the headlights swept by, he saw movement beyond the hood of a car thirty feet away, a car parked almost against the side of the bar.

"You're *killing* him, damn you!" the girl yelled. Craig moved more quickly and when he went around the car, he could see the tableau. Enough life came from a high window. A short, wide man had wedged a taller man into the angle formed by a fence and the side of the bar. The taller man's arms flopped and dangled. His face was a darkened smear. The short man worked on him with the rhythmic tenacity of someone chopping wood. A slim girl was hurling herself at the wide man's back, yelling at him, kicking at him, striking at the back of his neck with her fists. She was having no effect on him at all. Craig hurried toward them. The blows were heavy, sickening, murderous. Just as he got there the man cuffed backhand at the girl without looking at her. He hit her across the face and she stumbled and sat down hard on the cinders.

Craig locked his arms through the man's elbows. The man was shockingly powerful. Craig was whipped around, his feet frequently leaving the ground, but he managed to hold on. The beaten man, no longer supported by the tempo of the blows, had sagged into the corner.

Suddenly the stocky man stopped struggling. He seemed to exhale at great length. "Okay," he said quietly. "Let go me."

Craig let go and stepped back quickly and warily. The short man spat and turned around. He had the blunt face of an ex-fighter, cropped gray hair. He seemed to be about fifty, and solid as the stub of a tree. He was not breathing hard.

"You could have killed him," Craig said. The girl was standing six feet away, hand to her cheek.

"Maybe I did, hey. Let me know. Pepper Henry is the

name. I'll be right there in that there bar." He worked his hands, flexing the knuckles. He spat again and walked away with a shoulder-rolling strut.

Craig and the girl went to the unconscious man. "Dewey is such a tiresome slob," the girl said. "Is he breathing?"

Craig found the man's pulse. It was steady and regular. "He's not dead. His face is an awful mess, though. He'll have to go to a hospital."

"*I'm* not going to take him there. They can come and get him. Let's not phone from the bar."

"There's a pay phone in the lunchroom."

"Wait a minute. Can you sort of roll him over? Just get him stretched out flat."

He moved the man gently. The man moaned but made no other sign of returning consciousness. She worked his wallet out of his hip pocket, opened it, took out the bills and put them in her pocket.

"Is it right to do that?"

"Don't be a moralistic ass, my friend. It's my money. Anyway, the first character who cuts through here will take it away from him. Get his watch too. I'll make sure he gets it back."

Craig unstrapped the man's watch. She took it and put it in her pocket. He could not figure her out. He could not see her distinctly. Her voice had a finishing-school flatness to it, that husky polish rubbed there by money.

They went down to the lunchroom and she went back to the booth. It was the first time he had seen her in bright light, as she walked away from him. She had a trim little figure. Her hair was shiny black, and red-ribboned into a high pony tail. She wore a basque shirt with narrow, horizontal red and white stripes, lusterless black pants that came midway between knee and ankle and were slit at the sides, flat sandals with red straps. She walked with utter confidence; pony tail bobbing, small buttocks flexing under the tight pants, arms swinging, sandal heels clacking on the tile floor.

Just as his coffee was brought she sat on the low stool beside him and said, "Same for me, please."

He turned toward her and they studied each other with frank curiosity. She looked to be about twenty. Her features were small and pointed and quite delicate. Her face was heart-shaped. Black, shiny bangs came almost to thick, unplucked eyebrows. Her eyes were a very pale blue.

"Clemmie Bennet," she said, and smiled widely and held out her hand. Her teeth were small and even and very white. They looked like the milk teeth of a child. He took her hand. She winced and pulled it away. She had gouged the heel of her hand on the cinders. "Damn," she said. She dipped a paper napkin in his water glass and scrubbed at the hurt. Her hands were small and broad, with short fingers, thick pads at the base of the fingers.

"Craig Fitz," he said.

She looked at him and tilted her head a little to one side. "You're older than I thought. You know, you've got a hell of a reliable look. They could send you out with brandy around your neck."

Craig was suddenly and uncomfortably aware that she had nothing on under the tight basque shirt. Her breasts were small and sharply conical. "I'm the reliable type," he said.

"Maybe some day you'll meet Dewey and he should thank you. He was being a slob and he had to stop for another drink so he could keep fighting with me. But he was yammering at me so loud they couldn't hear the television fight and they couldn't shut him up so that wide little man took him outside. Pathetic. Dewey couldn't sucker-punch a stud butterfly. You should see him stripped. He looks like he was made out of pipe cleaners. There they come."

He heard the siren come through the night, growl to a stop fifty yards away. Clemmie sipped her coffee and wore an expression of mild interest. Soon the siren went away. She said, "Later we'll phone Stoddard General and see how he is." She looked and frowned. "Fitz, this is a hell of a bright place. It must be the brightest place in town. Let's move along. Are you always so quiet?"

"I haven't had much—"

"Don't start now. Let me guess." She took his hand, turned it over. "Nice hand. No manual labor. An office type. College man. Conservative. And reliable. Pay the girl, Fitzie, and let's get out of this operating room."

They went out into the night. When she walked beside him she seemed quite small. He had felt conspicuous with her in the bright lights. He felt more at ease in darkness.

The dulled feeling had left him. He looked down at her and felt a tingle of excitement. "Where to?"

"Ah, some dim café, my love. With muted music. And people without faces. Where we can continue this mad affair between the innocent child and the conservative elderly type."

"Flattery will get you nowhere."

"I will use all my elfin charms to lead you on and destroy you. Former friends will avoid you. They'll say poor old Fitz. The dangerous forties, you know. Fell in with a bit of fluff and they drummed him out of the club. Tore off his Rotary pin and broke his six iron. Pitiful thing for his wife. Poor Laura. Splendid girl. Salt of the earth."

"Maura, not Laura."

"Honestly? Brother, I'm hot tonight. All ESP."

"What happens to me after this mad affair?"

"Isn't it obvious? A broken man, slouching down shabby streets, begging on corners. Everything gone but the memory of me and how once we burned with a hard gemlike flame. Remember the night, darling, when you gave Fritz five thousand marks and the orchestra played for us until dawn?"

"Hans, dearest, not Fritz."

She spun and walked backward in front of him, beaming at him appreciatively. "Hey, I think you could play my game too. Dewey always slobbed it up. No talent. Come on. Play some more."

He hesitated and said, "Do you remember how long I stood outside that hotel in Madrid in the rain, darling?"

"And do you know, I can't even remember that bullfighter's name. His embroidery was all scratchy. I do remember that."

"How about this place?"

She looked in. "Ideal. Time out on the game. It'll be your lead next."

They found a dark corner, a padded bench with a low table in front of it. They drank. He was able to play her game. It flattered him that he could play it well enough to please her, to make her laugh, to make her eyes gleam with her pleasure.

"That time in Spain," he said, "it was a good and true

thing for us, because all brave things are good and true."

"But don't you see, dearest? That was the beginning of the end. When you went with the countess to Málaga, expecting me to follow you."

"But you did follow me, remember?"

"Certainly, you fool. But you were killing my love, little by little." She sniffled. She was hamming it, but she was uncannily convincing. She sighed. "We had so much, my darling. So very much, such riches. But we squandered them madly. We threw it all away." She threw her head back and looked at him through tiny thickets of black lashes. "But . . . still . . . perhaps . . . a tiny ember is left in the ashes of my heart. And it can be fanned back to life."

"I am too old," he said, "to go through all that again. Too old and too weary. I have the missions, the soup kitchens, my broken shoes and my memories. I can't walk back into your life."

"Do you ever hear from Maura, dearest?"

"No. She married a wealthy industrialist named Paul Ober."

"I wanted only joy, excitement. I did not mean to ruin your life."

"You enriched it, Clemmie dear."

"And Paris was the best, wasn't it?"

"The very peak."

"But by the time we reached Italy it had begun . . ."

". . to wither."

"Exactly, Craig. I cabled Daddy. He sent me money. I came back alone. For months I couldn't smile. Tears would come without warning. I'm rich now, my darling. You need a year in a rest home. Good food, treatment, kindness. I shall write you a check."

Over his protests she wrote an imaginary check. He took it, folded it, put it carefully in his pocket. There were more drinks. He did not seem to feel them. They played other games, took other parts. He played with an increasing facility that pleased her. It was a game, but in another sense it was love play. It made him intently aware of her, of the quickness of her body and the mobility of her face. When she would turn toward him as he lifted his glass, so that the back of his hand brushed the warmth and tautness of her young breast, he could not tell if it was accident or design.

And quite suddenly she ended the game, looking at him almost without expression, her pale blue eyes wide, her mouth still and level.

"Now walk me home, Fitz," she murmured.

When they were out in front he asked her if she wanted a cab. She said it was only a few blocks, and turned toward the river.

"Down this way?"

She hugged his arm against her. "Down this way, yes. Don't sound like Daddy. Don't go all moral and stuffy. You've been lovely so far. Don't get stuffy, please, darling."

She hummed as they walked and then began to sing in French in a voice that was husky, sweet and true.

"Pretty," he said when she was through.

She giggled. "Then you don't know French. A girl from Paris taught it to me. In a boarding school near Lucerne. A long time ago. Daddy was on wife number three then. The Canadian one. So they popped me off to school. The song is filthy, actually."

"Is he still married to her?"

"Oh, no. She died. And that was the damnedest thing ever happened to Daddy. He thought you divorced them. It seemed indecent to have one die. He's alone now, and he keeps making animal sounds about how I should give up my mad, mad life and go out and make like the lady of the house in that redwood stadium of his. I keep telling him to go live at one of his clubs, but he couldn't bear to part with the three incomparable and loyal servants who give him a screwing on the household bills every month. I'm the only chick he has, but he can't force me because two years ago, when I turned twenty-one, a lovely little income started coming in. Thank God my grandmother had some sense about money. If old Georgie didn't want to spend his senility alone, he should have thought twice before sending a lonely kid off to schools on other continents."

"If it's a nice income, why this neighborhood?"

"So I won't have stuffy neighbors. Wait until you see the layout. Here we are. Down this alley."

"Isn't this a warehouse?"

"So it is! Imagine that. And all the time I was thinking it was an apartment house."

"What are you getting so sore about?"

"Every time you open your mouth you lose five yards. This is a warehouse. That is a shed. Inside the shed is my car. This is a door. That is a loading ramp and— Oh, for God's sake!"

"What's the matter?"

"Wait right here. Don't join the group. Be right back."

She went over toward the loading ramp. A tall figure came out of the shadows. They spoke to each other in tones so low he couldn't make out a word. The man had a deep rumbling voice. His words had a plaintive begging sound. Her voice had a sharpness, an impatience. Finally he turned and went off into the darkness. She came back to him.

"Who was that?"

"A creep. He depresses me. He hangs around like some kind of kicked dog. He has a big thing about me. He gets so stinking tragic about everything. He's a writer. Now he says he can't write anything and he can't sleep and—the hell with it. Now where is that key?"

She found the key in the left hand pocket of her pants. The metal door was big. It creaked when it swung open. She went inside and turned on a light. There was a staircase with steel treads just to the left of the door. He could make out a freight elevator, and he had the feeling that the blackness around them was vast and empty.

"Three flights, honey," she said. "If those arthritic old legs can make it."

"You young people run on ahead."

The metal made an echoing sound as they climbed. The still air had a smell of dust and oil. "How did you find a place like this?"

"I met the man who owns it. He told me to fix up what I wanted. He got the strange impression that I was fixing up a home away from home. For him. I must act too friendly or something. Here we are."

There was a huge room. She went around turning on low lamps. The shades were opaque, so that all the light shone down and was absorbed by a black tile floor. There was one huge window of fixed glass, with big awning windows on either side of it. There were no buildings to obstruct the view. He could see the heart of the city, the turn of the river, the traffic on the bridges, the floodlighted spires of self-important buildings.

"This is really something," he said.

"I wanted to put a window in the roof, but that was out. So I had this one made high enough. I get good light in here. If I haven't mentioned it before, I paint. I paint lousy. But I work at it. Nobody will buy them. I make them too damn big."

She went over to another switch. "I'm nuts for lights," she said. "High drama, courtesy of T. Edison." The floodlight struck a painting hung on a vast expanse of wall. For the first time he could see how high the ceiling was. It was at least twenty-five feet above the floor level. The painting was truly enormous. He could only guess at the dimensions. Perhaps eight feet by twelve feet. The colors were vivid. At first it looked to him like a fire, with tall red, yellow and blue flames. And then he saw that the flames were people. Not precisely people. He could make out a thigh, a breast, a suggestion of a tilted face, a curve of back, buttocks. It seemed to be people all writhing together in flame, dance, orgy or panic.

"Don't try any sage opinions, Fitz. It's the most recent one. I had a lot of trouble with the son of a gun. I had to rig a scaffold even when it was standing on the floor. The framer had to come up here with his tools to frame it. It made him pretty jumpy, I think."

"What do you call it?"

"I stink in the title department. I have to lean on my friends."

"How about, uh . . . Weenie Roast on the Banks of the River Styx."

She gasped, ran to him, strained up against him and kissed him heartily. "Fitz, you weather well. I can't call it that, but by God you've come awful close to what I had in mind when I was doing it. Even Dewey couldn't top— Oh gosh! Dewey."

There was a phone on a low table. She trotted over and began to look up the number. He stared at the overpowering picture. There was violence in it. Blood and sex

and fury. It seemed curious that all of that could have
come from this small erratic person. She did not seem to
be the sort of person who could exercise self-discipline
and control her energies long enough.

The tall, slow drinks he had taken had an entirely
different effect than the numbing impact of the Martinis. Then he had felt dulled, confused. Now it was very
late and he knew he should be weary, but instead he felt
vivid and alive. He felt as though he could see all physical
objects very clearly, as though in form and color they
were making a deeper imprint on memory. The great window came to within two feet of the floor. Directly under
it was a long couch, an upholstered slab of foam rubber
on an austere base, narrow legs. In a far and shadowy
corner was a long trestle table littered with the tools and
tubes and stenches of the painter. There were two Eames
chairs, looking very alone in their individual islands of
space.

He turned and looked at the girl. She was at the phone
table, standing grotesque as a teen-ager, standing hipshot,
bending abruptly forward, elbow on the low table, free
forearm resting with double-jointed ease across the small
of her back. It was awkward, yet so seemingly suitable
for her that it was a strange kind of grace.

Her voice became suddenly, startling imperious. ". . . I
am afraid I am not satisfied with that sort of answer.
You cannot? Then connect me with your emergency people, the people who saw him when he came in. I beg
your pardon? Young lady, I certainly do not wish to have
to disturb Mr. Entwistle at this hour of the morning. He's
the chairman of your hospital board, is he not? Even
though he's a close personal friend, I think he would be
displeased. All right. I'll hold the line. Thank you for
your co-operation." She turned and made a face at Craig
and murmured, "Ghastly little bureaucrat. Hello? Doctor
who? Lenetti. Sorry to bother you, Doctor, but I must
really have some idea of how seriously injured one of your
patients is. He was brought in earlier this evening. Mr.
Dewey Maloney. What? Oh, no. I have no idea. Was it
an auto accident? Someone phoned me. A mutual
friend. No! That isn't like him. What? Doctor, I'm afraid
I'm terribly dull about anatomy. Can you tell me in lay-

man's language? Yes. I see. Yes. Thank you *so* much. Good night, Doctor."

She hung up. "Concussion. Broken jaw. Broken cheek-bone. Mouth lacerations. Cracked ribs. Possible internal injuries. The police are interested."

"Do you always get your way like that?"

She looked surprised. "Don't you?"

"I'm the milk toast type. They give me the song and dance. I hang up."

"The system is easy, Fitz. You just keep insisting, and sooner or later something gives."

"Do you really know this Mr. Entwistle?"

"Daddy knows him. He's always sneaking up obliquely when they have fund drives. Come and see the rest of the nest." He had wondered what lay behind the three dark red doors so evenly spaced against the off-white wall.

She swung one open, clicked a switch. "Kitchen." It was a bare room about ten by ten. The height of the ceiling made it grotesque. There was a bank of the most modern equipment. It looked implausible there, as though in storage.

"Bath," she said, opening the next door. Again the new and expensive equipment had the look of not even being hooked up. The shower stall was very large, with sliding opaque glass doors.

"Cell," she said, opening the last door. There was a cot, much bright clothing hanging on an exposed pipe that stretched from wall to wall. Under the clothing was a battalion formation of shoes and sandals. One low bureau. One stool. A barred window.

"Why the bars?"

"They were there. One of the original windows. They give me sort of a special feeling. You know. Guilt. Retribution."

They went out into the huge room. She stood in front of him. There was an intentness about her that made him uneasy.

"And now back to Maura," she said, "with careful story of how after the lodge meeting, the boys decided to play some cards and you didn't want to phone because you thought she'd be asleep."

CHAPTER FIVE

H E LOOKED at the questing girl and knew that out of
some curious honesty, or perhaps a desire of experimentation, she had handed the decision over to him. It was
unsettling. For a long time he had watched all the young
girls. He had seen them on the summer streets, arms
locked, giggling, calves ripe as pears, walking close with
sweet billow of breast and hip, full of their own promise
and their secret lunacy.

There had been the imaginings that stirred him. Such a
one, gentle as peaches, a gasp in his arms, turning toward
his strength and experience, turning away from her pim-
pled gallants. These were all the tireless rovings and
imaginings of the mature male.

But this was not one of those. This one was odd. In
this there could be trouble. In this very way a man
might contemplate murder, not only weighing the chances
of secrecy, but trying to guess at the eventual effects of
his own feeling of guilt.

During all the years of marriage Maura had been
enough. Not enough to quell the imaginings, yet enough
to make any overt act of infidelity worth less than the
risk. And so, during all the marriage, he had not strayed.
But he did not pride himself on that. He knew, objectively,
that there had been but very limited opportunity.

She faced him boldly in the light, arms crossed under
her breasts, putting it squarely up to him. He felt
that he had taken no initiative this night. He felt that had
she wished it, she could have maneuvered him into her
bed without it ever reaching a point of decision. It would
just happen, as the conversation had just happened.
Maura was a doll figure in a dim room in the back of
his mind, her back turned to him. But Clemmie stood
waiting and watching, facing him, her face a speculative
mask.

He hesitated a moment, licking his lips. "I thought I
told you about Maura, darling. They tell me she's happy
now."

And the face of Clemmie came alive, piquant. "There *is* a last ember left, my dearest. We can find each other again. All is not dead between us." She drifted into his arms, and it was the first time he had held her. He had expected to feel a slender fragility. She was lithe enough and slender enough, but hard warm muscles slid under his hands as he held them to her back, as she raised her arms to hold him more tightly.

She backed away from him suddenly, moved quickly around the room and turned off every light except the high spot that brought the huge painting alive and made a reflected glow in the room. The night outside was more vivid, with the moving distant lights of traffic, and the neon-misted stars of July. She stood apart from him, tugged the ribbon from her hair and it fell straight and glossy, the heavy bangs giving her the look of a carving on an Egyptian tomb.

"Remember?" she said softly.

"The way you used to wear it," he said, knowing his voice was thickened and husky.

She crossed her arms, taking hold of the Basque shirt at either side. With an abrupt gesture she stripped it off over her head, rumpling the black hair; she dropped it, stood before him naked to the waist. Her breasts were boldly tilted. Reflected light touched her torso from the side, making soft highlights on the curves and the swells of her body. She looked like the women of Egypt in the ancient friezes, with their faces small and cold and cruel under the black hair, the women for whom special burial jewelry was made, the dancers who were buried with tiny pet antelopes.

"Remember?" she said.

"Yes."

They made their love on the coldly modern couch under the great window. She was sinewy, supple, taut with her eagerness. The only suggestions of softness were in lips, breasts, and hips. It seemed more combat than love, and upon his symbolic victory she gave a long cry of anguish as though he had thrust a dagger to her heart.

There was a time when he looked up through the window at the stars. They seemed directly overhead. He sensed that she slept beside him, that all of this made no difference to the stars.

And another time he knew she was up. She brought a pillow for him, spread a sheet over him.

He awoke again before sunup. She was not beside him. When he turned he could see the top of her dark head. He rolled to that side of the couch and saw that she sat naked, cross-legged, on the floor, carefully taking the cards and identifications out of his wallet. He watched her, puzzled, too sleepy to be angry. He imagined that she did not know he was awake, yet when she came to the picture of Maura, the one taken on the beach in Scotland, she said, without looking up, in a conversational tone, "She *is* pretty, Craig. Is she this young?"

"That picture is—twelve years old. We were on our honeymoon."

"Has she gotten a lot heavier?"

"A little. Not very much."

"She looks the type who might." She looked up at him. "Do you two get along?"

"Yes. It's a good marriage."

"Then where do you and I fit, darling?"

He felt a quick alarm that destroyed the last dullness of sleep. "Do we have to fit somewhere?" he asked, hoping he sounded casual.

She laughed at him, then said, "Poor Craig. I wanted to see you flinch, dear. And you did, nicely," She sobered. "I don't fit anywhere. I never will. I used to think I might, but I got over that. Everything is so neat and orderly for dear Maura, it makes me hate her. She found herself such a nice dependable man. I found mine early, you know. Sometime maybe I'll tell you. I found him eight years ago." Her face hardened in a suprising way. "Oh, the tender mystery of a first love. The love of a young girl for a brave and gallant man. My little heart went pitty-pat, pitty-pat. He liked to be amused, you know. And after he's exhausted every method he could think of of amusing himself with the little love-struck fifteen-year-old girl, he got his kicks by getting her blind on brandy and loaning her out to his friends. And he had a lot of friends. And they had friends. But somebody had the sense to pry me loose and pop me into a rest home. I recovered. Completely."

He reached for her, wanting to touch her, to comfort her, but she scrambled back out of his reach and stood

up, indifferent to her nakedness. "Take that sloppy look
off your face, Fitz. I don't want pity or understanding or
a lot of wet philosophy. I can't imagine why I told you
that. I'm sorry I did."

He sat up and bent over and picked up his scattered
cards and put them back in his wallet. She came quickly
and sat beside him and put her arm around his waist.
"You are such a stable citizen, dearest. A joiner. Daddy
would be enchanted. He adores earnest men. He keeps
hurling them at me as if we were an Indian club act. Or
is that a Freudian simile? Oh, dear. I hope not."

"In case you missed anything, I make fourteen thousand
five. I almost own my own home."

"On Federal Street. Horrible neighborhood."

"I have a loose filling that needs fixing. Penicillin
gives me hives. I need reading glasses, but I've been stalling. Vanity, I guess. These scars are burn scars from the
war. I was blown out of a tank. This is my appendix
operation scar."

She hugged him. "You sound so stuffy and indignant.
I think I love you, somewhat. You have almost all your
hair, and your voice makes me feel tingly, and I like the
way you look fierce when you're annoyed, like right
now. You could be in better condition, but your shoulders are just wonderful. You've got a funny unexpected
kind of shyness and nice flat cheeks, and you're gentle
and fierce and luscious in bed, and I am going through
this inventory because maybe I am not going to let you
get away."

He twisted and pushed her down on the bed and held
her pinned there, his hands on her shoulders. She lay in
the gray, soft, pre-dawn light. "Are you nuts?" he demanded.

"I love the way you look so scared when you think I'm
going to make trouble for you.

"I will make a little trouble for you. Like this. And
like this. And, also, like this."

The sun awakened him. It streamed across the couch,
blazing on the white sheet. He knew at once where he
was. He sat up and looked for her. She was on the far
side of the room, at a bar set waist high, an exercise bar
he had not seen before. She wore a black leotard, soiled

white ballet slippers. Her face was shiny with sweat, intent with effort. She smiled at him and said, breathlessly, "Halfway through, lamb."

He sat on the edge of the couch, the sun hot on his back, and watched her. She worked with fury, twisting and contorting her body. If this was a daily routine, he now knew what caused her firmness, the muscled hardness of her body, the tension of thighs like spring steel encased in warm rubber. She left the bar and moved to the center of the room and whirled and leaped. Her slippers scuffed and thumped, and he could heard the hard tempo of her breathing. When she finally stopped she looked wilted. "Phoof," she said, and smoothed sweaty hair back from her forehead with her forearm.

"Once I saw ballet," he said. "They seemed to float. Are you just learning?"

"If somebody who knew ballet said that, he'd get a hit in the eye. I started too late, Craig." Her breathing was beginning to slow down. "I was twelve. That's six years too late. But I've got the right sort of body for it, all but my hands. I do this because it makes me feel firm and good. Maybe I'm too fond of my body. But I'm willing to work to keep it. You saw, there at the end, a linked *ballonné simple derrière, pas de chat* and a *ballotté,* with a little *glissade* stuck in just for the hell of it. And all reasonably well done. Now I am not coming near you because I smell like a horse. Firsties on the shower. You make coffee while you wait, please."

"You did get pretty high off the floor," he said.

She paused in the bathroom doorway, looked back over her shoulder at him, waggled her hips saucily at him and said, with hauteur, "My *ballon* was always considered excellent."

He folded the sheet and knotted it around his middle. He found what he needed in the kitchen, made coffee, poured a steaming cup and carried it out into the studio. Her strenuous exertions had made a faint scent of gymnasium in the air, a slightly acid taint of her perspiration. It was not unpleasant to him. He could hear the soft thunder of her shower. He stood, sipping the coffee, looking out at Saturday morning. He felt very good. He suppressed the dim stirrings of conscience, the fear of consequence. He did not want to feel remorse. Not yet.

It was enough to taste hot coffee, feel the hot sun on your chest and belly, look at the bright morning and try to remember each specific micro-second of their tousled union.

She came out of the bath, black hair damp, leotard and towel in hand, as casually naked as a child. "Next," she said, and smiled at him and walked into her bedroom. The shower was good. He spent a long time under the water. He found a razor and blades, and used bar soap for shaving. He brushed his teeth with the corner of a towel, and used her brush on his hair.

When he went out she had pulled the draperies across the whole expanse of window. They were an odd shade, more green than blue. They were heavy, but enough light came in to give the studio an underwater look, still and deep and green. She lay naked on the couch, a sheet under her, her eyes closed. When he sat on the couch beside her she said, without opening her eyes, said in a small far-away voice, "Be very slow and very sweet, darling. Make it happen like we're dreaming it happening."

Later on when the sun was so high they could open the draperies, they became very brisk and practical. She was crisp in pale blue linen shorts and a tailored white shirt, her hair pulled back into a shiny black bun, emphasizing the delicate modeling of her face. They worked together and prepared brunch and served it with the utmost ceremony. There seemed to be a shyness between them. Sixteen years apart, and it was a generation. He realized there was less difference between Penny's age and hers than between hers and his. They spoke politely, almost formally, and he watched her eat, and there was a small flavor of greediness about the way she ate, small white teeth neatly incising the toast, red membrane of lips closing quickly over the fork of omelette. Over coffee she changed the mood with characteristic abruptness. "What's happening to us, Craig?"

"Is something happening?"

"Don't *try* to be dense, please."

He smiled and shrugged. "What do I say? Thanks loads. Thanks for all the hospitality."

She banged her small fist on the table. "Crap! Just say what you think."

He looked at her and looked away and said, "I don't

think I want to say what I think." When he looked back at her she was smiling broadly and contentedly. "Now what?" he asked.

"I like what you said."

"My God, you want to jump at things."

"I always have. This time Paris will be good, but Spain will be even better."

"This makes me nervous."

"I know it does, darling." She reached across the table and patted his cheek. "I love to make you nervous. You're such a pillar of the community, darling."

He could not understand which way this was drifting, or what his response should be. She could have a compulsion to rationalize a one-night stand by making it sound like love. Or it could be another of her games, an attempt to scare hell out of him, which, if she succeeded, would be followed by her husky, ribald laughter. The third possibility, and the least likely, was that she had fallen in love with him. The pleasure they had taken in each other had been intense. In any event he knew he had to make his position very clear.

"So I'm stuffy and dull, Clemmie. But listen. I have a good life. I don't want to change anything. I don't want to complicate anything. I don't want any emotional responsibility, not any more than I already have."

She leaned back and studied him somberly. "What do you want, Craig?"

"What I wanted I've had, and I'm grateful to you."

"And never climb those stairs again?"

"I don't think it would be very smart to climb those stairs again, Clemmie."

"All right. I'll be honest with you. I think you're good for me. I think I'm good for you. So while your Maura is in England, I offer you a summer affair. I'll play it your way. No tricks or sly gimmicks. I shall be available Clemmie, your summer love, and when it's time for it to be over, we'll shake hands, shed one tear and part forever. Will that suit your lordship?"

"It's—a damn flattering offer. I'm tempted. But I'm also a coward. I don't think it would be good for either of us."

She shook her head sorrowfully. "Fitz, you are a highly

moral type. Will you settle for this, then? It is now one-twenty on Saturday afternoon. It is thirty-six hours until one-twenty Monday morning. Let's see just how sick of each other we can possibly get."

After a long moment he grinned and nodded. "A deal."

"Thank you, sir. Thank you so much, kind sir."

"But I can't face it without fresh clothes."

She opened the drawer of the telephone table and threw him a keyring. He caught it in the air. "That's the key to the shed and the key to the bug. Porsche Speedster." She explained the shift to him. When he was ready to go she hugged him by the door and leaned back and looked up into his face and said, "Bon voyage, lover. And don't be shy. Bring spares. Bring a toothbrush. Sort of move in on Clementina. The girl doesn't mind. She loves it."

It was a little white convertible with a black top. After he fathomed the shifting, he found it responsive, a pleasure to drive.

He went into his own home like a thief. He did not want to give himself time to think. Thought would bring guilt. Maura was too much with him in this house. Her hands had touched too many things too many times. He changed quickly to a lightweight suit, fresh shirt. He yanked a small suitcase down from the closet shelf, threw in underwear, sports clothes, toilet articles. As an afterthought, he went to the kitchen cupboard, found the last two bottles of bourbon and put them in with his spare shorts, socks and shirts.

When he reached the door again, he stopped hurrying. He put the suitcase down and lighted a cigarette and made himself look around quite calmly. No great decision had been made. He could unpack and phone her. And then drink the bourbon and go to bed alone. She was dangerous. She was a girl who lived too close to the unpredictable edge of hysteria. She hunted trouble. The breasts, too evident under the basque shirt last night, had been an invitation to trouble. She walked the night streets with chippy stride. She was an exhibitionist, body-worshipper, sensualist—without discipline, morals, scruples, ethics, a child in search of the father she had never had.

But, after all, it was only one weekend. He stubbed his

cigarette out in a pottery ashtray Puss had made in the second grade, a Father's Day gift with a melted image that was indubitably a duck. And he left.

CHAPTER SIX

ON MONDAY, the fifteenth of July, Craig was a half-hour late to work. Everything looked quite different to him, as though he had exchanged eyes and color sense with someone else. Everything was intensely familiar, and totally strange. As he went through the main room to his private office, he tried to make his morning greeting cheerful but not boisterous. It sounded too loud, and he saw Betty James start and look at him strangely.

"Watch it, son," he said to himself. "You are just the slightest loveliest bit tight, and you feel absolutely wonderful, and when it all wears off you are going to be lucky to be able to hold your head up. So step carefully."

Betty followed him into the office as usual and shut the door. "You didn't look at the board."

He leaned back in the chair. "A terrible oversight. And I'm a half-hour late."

"I waited Saturday, but you didn't come in."

"Did I ask you to come in?"

"No, Mr. Fitz. But I knew you were coming in. I didn't have anything else to do. I thought I could help."

"I changed my mind."

"Sooner or later they're going to start hollering for those back reports, you know."

The jubilant mood soured in an instant. "Miss James, if you want to sit here and let me sit there, I'll see if I can clear it with Personnel."

She flushed and abrupt tears stood on the sandy lashes. "I just thought I'd—"

"Sometimes you think too much."

She got up very quickly and quietly and started for the door. He moved more quickly and caught her right at the door, put a hand on her shoulder and turned her around gently.

"Sorry, Betty. Wrong side of the bed."

She stood with head bent and then looked up slowly, the tears still there. "Is anything wrong, Craig? Is there any way I can help? You've been so—odd."

He concealed his annoyance with her. She was too adept at gamesmanship. Make a bad slip and when you comfort her, she moves a step closer and starts calling you Craig.

"I'm fine, Betty. Nothing wrong. Let's get to work."

His mind felt clear enough. He went through the morning stack of memos, reports and orders quickly, so quickly that twice she had to ask him to repeat. He studied the board, made a few phone calls, then went out into the production areas. When he got back to his office Betty said Mr. Chernek had phoned.

"Get him for me, please."

When Bill got on the line he said, "What the hell, Craig?"

"What do you mean, what the hell?"

"Where can I talk to you?"

"Come over here. I've got a breathing space."

He told Betty that while Mr. Chernek was in his office, he did not want to be disturbed.

Bill came in and sat down wearily. "Does it show much?"

"It shows some." The left side of Bill's mouth was puffed. His left eye was discolored. There was a large flesh-colored Band-Aid on his left temple.

"Those God-damn cops beat the crap out of me. They had no reason to do that. Thanks for alerting Al."

"Did he get you out?"

"Right away. There was no more fight in me, brother. I was sick. He says I shouldn't try to sue those cops."

"He's right."

"How would you know?"

"You swung first, Bill. Before I could have gotten across the street to help you argue, I fell. Then it was too late."

"Nice guy. Great friend."

"Don't be a fool. If I hadn't, we'd both have spent the night in there."

"I guess you're right. Thank God Ruthie wasn't there to see me when I got home. Christ!"

"Did Al tell you Connie's isn't there any more?"

"Yeah. Great big deal. Steak. Champagne. You know, I never expected to see you in the office."

"Why the hell not?"

"Al said you sounded funny over the phone. I told him about the overload of Martinis. I phoned your house when I got home. No answer. I got worried about you. I called you again Saturday at least a dozen times. Then I went over there late Saturday afternoon. Your car was there, but you weren't. I waited around. I phoned in the evening. I phoned all day yesterday and I stopped around again. What the hell, Craig?"

"I was all right."

"I thought maybe you'd phone me, to find out how things came out. You haven't even asked."

"Okay. I'm asking."

"I'm out on a thousand-dollar bail. Al is getting it set back until after my vacation. He thinks he can soften it up a little, get it cut to D. and D. without that resisting-arrest rap. Then it should be just twenty or forty bucks and costs."

"He's got connections."

Chernek stared at him. "Just where the hell were you?"

"Staying with a friend."

"What kind of a friend? You got a nice color on you. Like putty. Shack job?"

"Why don't you just drop it, Bill?"

Chernek stood up. "The hell with you, Fitz. You make a dandy buddy on a binge."

"What are you sore about?"

"If you can't figure it out, skip it."

Craig stared at him for a moment, shrugged, and said, "As long as you're here, what luck are you having on that aluminum alloy on 770 F?"

"Write me a memo and I'll look it up, you stuffy son of a bitch." Bill left and slammed the door heartily behind him.

Betty came in immediately. "What's the matter with Mr. Chernek?"

"I don't think I know, and I don't think I care. Will it foul up any of your plans if I go to lunch first?"

"Why, no!"

He drove far enough to find a restaurant where no

plant people would be. He drove east, away from the
river, and picked a roadhouse at random. He had two
Bloody Marys at the bar, and then a sirloin-steak sandwich at the bar. He looked in the back bar mirror. He decided he didn't look at all gray. Bill had been fishing.

But there seemed to be plenty of reasons why he should
look gray. On the way back to her place he had found a
delicatessen and had loaded up, carried a great heavy bag
up her steel-tread steps.

There was no coherency about the thirty-six hours.
They had started drinking and had drunk too heavily.
There were curious distorted images in his mind. A play-
ful, boisterous sharing of the huge shower stall. A time
when she had him doing fiendish exercises of her own
devising. He had strained and groaned and the sweat had
poured from him, while she stood like a drill major, count-
ing sharply, tolerating no deviation. He was still sore
around the middle, and in his thighs and his biceps. He
remembered that they had talked about going off in the
car, going out into the country for a long, long walk. But
when that was nearly arranged, the big thunderstorms
had hit, in sequence, flashing and banging, and it suddenly became essential to her to make love at the very peak
of the storm, there under the vast window. Sleeping, eating, showering, love-making, they were all jumbled and
mixed in his mind, like a film from which entire sequences
had been cut. She was tirelessly inventive, incorrigibly experimental, and when he remembered bits and pieces of
the week end, he had that same hot-cheeked feeling of
incredulity that the party guest feels when he awakens the
following morning and remembers that, with drinks and
persuasion, he was trapped into playing games that destroyed every last device of personal dignity. The very
last straw would have been a venal boy friend behind a
peephole with a splendid camera.

That thought made him choke over the last bite of his
sandwich and look with wide-eyed consternation at his
own reflection in the mirror. No. That wouldn't be her
style. The week end was over. He had had it. When he
thought of her there was not the faintest suscitation of
desire. It had been a damn fool thing to do, and now it
was over and it would not happen again. The problem was
to get his clothes back. She had driven him to his house

and let him off in front at eight that morning. Clemmie wouldn't miss him. She led a busy life. He remembered the hooting and hammering on the big metal door. She had said it was the kids, and giggled against his chest. And one time the phone had rung twenty-seven times before the caller gave up.

He would return her to the kids, gratefully. He felt a thousand years old. When the endless day finally ended, he drove home. He was too tired to eat. He showered, tumbled into an unmade bed and fell endlessly down black velvet cellar stairs.

He awakened at seven, after thirteen hours' sleep. The muscles which had been sore from the ballet exercises she had made him do had stiffened. He got out of bed like an elderly man. He remembered the exercises she had told him would limber him up. He grunted his way through them and then took a very long and hot shower. They seemed to help. He went to a better place than usual and ate a monstrous breakfast. The previous day's work was like a dream remembered.

On Tuesday he worked with a drive and intensity he had not been able to manage for weeks. Though numerous problems required his attention, he was able to handle those and also dig deeply into the back work that had piled up. He drove all of his people and drove Betty James particularly hard. Though she claimed to thrive on pressure, she was looking particularly harassed at the end of the day. At five-fifteen, when the others had gone and the only shop noise was on the double shift over in C Building, Betty leaned limply against the door frame and said, "Is that all, I hope? Uncle."

"That's all, Betty. And thanks."

"If you aren't a madman tomorrow too, Craig, I ought to be able to finish the typing by late afternoon, if both of us work on it."

"No latrine-o-grams today?"

"Gosh, no!"

"When does your vacation come up? I've forgotten."

"The last two weeks in August."

"Where are you going?"

"Staying in town, I guess. We've got a nice backyard. It's easier to take care of kids at home than on a trip. And Mother doesn't like to travel. Well, good night now. Don't you stay too long."

" 'Night, Betty."

He sat at his desk for another fifteen minutes, with blank paper in front of him, and he devoted those fifteen minutes to Ober's curious request to "Think wild. Think big." He made aimless doodles. He crumpled the paper in disgust. The chair creaked as he leaned back. All through the long demanding day he had held image and memory of Clemmie Bennet back in a neatly sealed compartment of his mind. Now, with caution, he let her out. She stepped out of the compartment, smiling, vivid and nimble. He felt a hollowness in his stomach, a sudden heavy pressure in his loins, a weightiness. And he breathed lightly and quickly, using the shallow tops of his lungs. His heart raced. He could not have responded more quickly or violently had she suddenly slipped onto his lap. It frightened him. It was actual fright. The thrust of desire was as tangible as her hard, smooth legs.

He went out to Betty's typewriter, rolled paper into it, and typed a letter to Maura. He made it quite a long letter. He knew he was saying very little, but at least it was long. He felt as though he were writing to a stranger. When he slipped it into an envelope, he knew the whole letter was a lie. But he sealed it, and when he left, he took it with him to mail.

As he was on a party line at his house, he phoned Clemmie from a drugstore booth.

"Yes?"

"Clemmie?"

"Oh, darling! You didn't call yesterday."

"I just barely got through the day."

"Poor dear. Poor old beast."

"What have you been doing?"

"I don't know. I've gone all helter-skelter. I tried to paint, but you got completely in the way. Then I drove. I went out to the pike and I had the top down and I went just as fast as the bug would go."

"Hey!"

"I'm a wonderful driver. I sang at the wind, and then I cried a little and had to go slower because it blurred the road. I cried a little while ago, too. First time in years. I'm so terribly happy."

"Now wait a minute."

"Can't I be happy without permission? You have a nice voice on the phone, darling. What will we do tonight?"

"That wasn't the agreement, was it?"

"Did we have an agreement? I forgot to take minutes of the meeting."

"Clemmie, listen. I just want to get my stuff and—"

"Poor baffled beast. I know what you mean of course, darling. But I have an idea. Nothing like last time. There's no harm in it. Nothing bawdy and decadent. Just boy and girl. I saw a fair. A county fair, forty miles away, with midway and cotton candy and rides, harness racing and square dancing. There's no harm in that, is there? Is there?"

"But—"

"I hope you have a ratty work shirt and a corny hat. Because I have a beautifully faded cotton dress, dearest, and we can go sort of in costume and play my game, Fitz-lovely. Please don't disappoint me. I'll pick you up at the corner of Federal and Butternut in one half of an hour." She hung up. He could hear her voice, like a distant echo ... "There's no harm in it. There's no harm in it."

She swung the little car up to the curb and clambered over into the other bucket seat so that he could get behind the wheel. The black top was down. He felt extraordinarily conspicuous. He knew it would not be wise to be seen too often with this girl. Though Stoddard had a half-million inhabitants, if he was careless he would be seen by someone who knew Maura was away for the summer, someone who would make the correct inference and delight in passing the information along. He hesitated, but felt it would be awkward to try to put the top up. He grinned at her. She had a look of clean glowing youth, of virginal eagerness. She looked so young it touched his heart.

Her thin cotton dress was a blue and white print, quite faded, with a small edge of lace around the bodice. She had made a kerchief of a blue and white bandanna and it was knotted under her chin. He felt relieved to see that she had confined the sharp impudence of her breasts in a bra that rounded them.

"You don't shift very well yet. Miss me?"

"Like being hit on the head with a hammer."

"Get on the pike. The hat is perfect, ole Fitz. Look, I bought this because it suits."

He glanced at the purse she held up. It was a confection

of a purse, a shiny blue embellished thing, in the worst possible taste.

"Now drive fast, Craigman. Pour it to her. Goose this bucket."

The wind sound was too loud to make conversation easy. It was not long before he found the driving rhythm of the little car. The steering was quick, and it sat deep and stable on the road.

He remembered a movie he had seen long ago. A horror movie, full of trick camera work. The villain had stood, and an alter ego had sort of slid out and away from him, stepped away and become another person, a younger person, smiling and plausible. Craig had the sensation that he had remained back in the house, with the news magazines, the television programs, the dusty silence of the house, the gargle and hum of the refrigerator. This other person had left him back there, this younger man. This was being twenty-four, with a scented date, money in hand, a place to go.

That other Craig Fitz, alone in the house on Federal Street, would never put on a work shirt with patched elbows and a billed khaki cap that smelled faintly of fish and take a young girl to a county fair. But this Craig Fitz could, and would.

Suddenly he felt very good, very strong and young and alive, and he laughed aloud. Anything that could make you feel this good and this alive could not be harmful.

"What's funny?" she shouted against the wind roar.

"A man I used to know."

"What about him?"

"Nothing about him. He's just a silly bastard. Very self-important."

He drove into the dusty, lumpy lot, and when he turned the motor off they could hear the sad nostalgia of the merry-go-round. They put the top up and locked the car. She took his arm and they walked toward the main gates. She took small steps, prim and shy, and he sensed she was fitting herself into a character.

"Pa wants you to find out if he deeds us that forty acres on the mill road, your father will give you the rest of the piece down to Thompson's line."

"Said he would, honey. Now hush and let's have us some fun here."

"Where do you figure on putting the house?"

"On the little rise near the southwest corner. Best place," he said firmly.

"Maybe it's better by the crick," she said dubiously.

He paid their way at the main gate. The midway was crowded. He could hear the talkers, the music, the mumbling of the crowd, the ratchety slam of the rides and yelp of the women. They played her game as they toured the fair grounds. They built new identities, staying within the rules. He took her around the corner of a tent and kissed her, and somehow she made her lips dainty and fresh and shy for him.

The summer dusk came and the lights went on. They saw the exhibits, rode on the crack-the-whip and the caterpillar, and banged into each other enthusiastically on the dodge-em cars. There was a group of young and husky boys, sleeves rolled high and tight over bulging bronze biceps. They dominated the dodge-em car rink, ganging up on the prettiest girls. Clemmie had almost no competition. They drove into her grimly, riding her off into corners, swinging around and coming back to thump her again just as she was getting clear of the boards. Clemmie squealed in a manner that Craig guessed, sourly, was most satisfactory to them. Craig could not duplicate their dexterity with the little electric cars. When he tried to get near Clemmie, he was thumped away expertly. He was glad when that ride was over. As they left, one of the boys who had been most diligent about whacking into Clemmie strolled along a little behind them, thumbs tucked in the belt of his jeans, arm muscles tensed for display, hair and brows burned to the color and texture of straw. He knew Clemmie was aware of her new admirer. Her voice became more clear and high, she giggled more frequently, and twitched her hips as she walked. It annoyed him. He maintained the pretense of the game, but his responses were glum and uninspired. He thought she was acting like a damn filly with a frail fence between her and the stallion.

She wanted a ride on the merry-go-round. She sat primly sidesaddle on her wooden horse, one on the outside. Craig took the one next to hers. They went up and down in opposite rhythm, suspended from the shiny brass poles. Craig realized he had made a tactical error. The husky boy took the horse directly in front of Clemmie's. Sweat stuck his khaki shirt to his thick back muscles. Both the boy and Clemmie reached daringly for the rings. Clemmie whooped each time she snared an iron ring, and the boy grinned back at her. Near the end of the ride he reached and Craig saw that it was a gold ring. The boy almost took it and pulled his hand back. Clemmie hooked it and yelped and waved it at Craig, her face alight. "Free ride! I got a free ride!"

The boy spun around, laced his hands behind his neck, leaned against the brass pole, crossed his legs, resting them along the rump of the wooden horse, and grinned at Clemmie as he went up and down in perfect balance. Craig felt depressed, asinine in his work shirt and billed cap. He felt as though he should be riding in one of the unmoving swan chairs with the aunts and grandmothers. He paid for another ticket and endured Clemmie's free ride. The boy ahead of her showed off until the attendant made him stop his acrobatics. Clemmie squealed with delight at each new trick, and Craig found himself mildly despising her.

When they got off, the boy, bolder now, sauntered along beside Clemmie and said, "It'll get a lot better later on. You going to the dance?"

Clemmie turned to him a little too sweetly and said, "We are, aren't we, dear?"

"I don't know."

"Me and my brother got some damn good corn stashed in the car if you folks want a drink. It goes down smooth."

Craig stopped walking, holding Clemmie's arm. The boy came to a stop, his eyes on Clemmie.

"No thank you," Craig said.

The boy looked at him. He shifted his feet uneasily. He half shrugged and said, "See you around." He moved away slowly, holding his shoulders very square.

"Honey! It would have been real corn. I've *never* had any."

"Too bad."

"What's making you so *grim?*"

"Maybe I'm the sensitive type. Maybe it offends me to watch you waggling your butt at a plow jockey."

Her eyes narrowed and she thrust her chin forward. "We came here to have a *good* time. You've spoiled the game. You're acting like a—" She stopped suddenly and eyes went wide and her mouth widened in a pleased smile and

she took hold of his wrist hard and gave it a little shake.
"Oh, you great lamb! You're jealous! Over that big baby
with his cute muscles."

"That big baby is going to get full of corn, and when he
does, he's going to be as easy to stop as a runaway truck."

"But we have to go to the dance."

"No thanks."

"Please. If there's any kind of trouble, we can leave
right away. Now I want root beer. A big mug with that
creamy foam on top, and then I want to go on that ferris
wheel and hold hands and be kissed when we're right at
the very top. Then after that I want to go see those awful
things in the bottles. Come on."

He kissed her when their chair was at the very top of
the wheel. It was full dark. They could see all the lights
of the fairgrounds, see traffic on the pike. He felt good
again, and felt ashamed of the way he had acted.

The dance was held in an open pavilion. Electric bulbs
in paper Japanese lanterns were strung criss-cross under
the eaves. It cost fifty cents a head to get into the pavilion.
The man at the small gate stamped the back of your hand.
There was a low wall around the four sides, and folding
chairs aligned against the wall, facing inward. The band
was on a raised platform in one corner. They would play
one set of round dances, sodden, thumpy, uninspired fox
trots and waltzes, then a set of square dances. The band
came alive for the square dances, fiddles squalling, caller
yelling incomprehensible directions through the metallic
blur of the P.A. system, spectator heels thumping the
wooden floor, the dancing groups stamping in unison.

He danced a round set with her and was surprised to
find she was not easy to dance with. She had a tendency
to lead, and she was more resistant than pliant in his arms.
They sat out the square set, and she watched avidly,
leaning forward on her chair, heel tapping, lips parted.

When the next square set came she said, "Let's try!"

"Not for me. I don't know what he's saying or what to
do next."

"They all know. We can do it."

"Let's just watch. God, it's fascinating."

The groups were forming. He looked away from her for
a moment. When he looked back she was gone. The husky

boy was leading her onto the floor. She looked back at him with expression and gesture to show that she was helpless.

He half stood up to go after her when the music started. He sat down again. He watched her. She was in a set with the huskies from the dodge-em rink, four of them, and three slim young girls. Of all the groups, they were the wildest, the most muscular. The girls were swung completely off the floor, hurled from man to man with a roughness almost brutal. Clemmie handled herself without confusion, controlled and graceful. When the other girls flapped like rag dolls, Clemmie could not strike a pose without grace. He looked at all the flushed faces. He looked out into the night. On the dark side of the pavilion three men passed a bottle around, each wiping the neck on the palm of his hand, keeping it tilted for long seconds. After the second circuit they tossed the bottle away. It gleamed in the light.

After the set the boy came back with Clemmie, flushed, proud and swaggering, just slightly unsteady on his feet.

"Craig, this is Mickey." Craig was not set for the childishness of matching grips. His knuckles ground together and he barely kept from wincing visibly.

"Clemmie can really fling that thing," Mickey said. "She's got it. By God one time there she got aholt of me and if I wasn't set right I'da got flang out into the weeds." He squeezed Clemmie's arm. "Clemmie, you got a muscle on you there. Where'd you get all that?"

"Pa says a girl's got to be strong. He had me chinning myself when I was so high."

Mickey lowered his voice. "Come on out, folks. I know where my brother is."

Craig was very dubious about it, but he fell in with it. They went around to the dark side of the pavilion. Mickey spoke to a group of half-seen figures under the trees. "Ralph? Get on over here, boy. Bring the juice."

Ralph came over. He was an older, shorter, wider version of Mickey. "This here is Clemmie and this is her friend Craig. I want they should sample some of that smooth corn."

"You got a cup for the girl?"

"I can drink out of the bottle."

She took the pale, unlabeled bottle. She wiped the neck professionally, tilted it high. Craig could see her pale throat work, and he counted five swallows. She lowered it and said, "Haaah."

Ralph said, "Mickey, you got you a drinkin' woman here. Here you go, Mr. Craig." He took the bottle from Clemmie and gave it to Craig. He tilted it up. It was lukewarm, and it burned like battery acid. Three swallows was all he could manage before he felt his gag reflex threaten to work. Mickey took the bottle, carefully braced his feet, tilted it and finished it.

"Well damn you," Ralph said. "You're a damn hog, Mickey."

"Go get another jug. You saving it all for yourself?"

Ralph disappeared into the shadows. The band was plodding its way through *Paper Moon*. Ralph came back with another bottle thumped the bottom of it with the heel of his hand and pulled the cork with his teeth. "My turn," he said, and drank sparingly.

He held it out toward Clemmie.

"Well, just to be sociable," she said. And again she drank five full swallows.

"Damn me!" Ralph said, awed.

Clemmie giggled. "Smoooth," she said. "Smooth as a hay rake. Here you go, Craig."

He held his tongue over the mouth of the bottle and pretended to drink, working his throat. He handed it to Mickey, but Ralph snatched it away. "No more for him for a time. This Mickey here, he's got to show off. You go sweat out some of that last jolt and then you can have some more."

"Gimme that," Mickey said thickly.

"Boy, you make a grab and you get it. Right across the head."

The band came to the wooden end of *September Song*. The fiddles began to make anticipatory sounds. Mickey grabbed Clemmie's hand and said, "They're going to play *our* song, baby," and hurried her away.

Ralph said sagely, "It might take another ten minutes before that little lady falls flat on her can. Then again it might only be five. This batch runs about a hundred twenty-proof. Friend of yours?"

"Yes."

"I don't want to cut my own brother out of any business, but if he and them Hernons and Dill Quinn get her off in a dark place for her to pass out, they'll sure enough line up on her. Girl slugs herself like that, she's taking her own chances. And she won't get much chance off in the brush. None of my business, but I figured I'd tell you. Another knock?"

"No thanks."

He pushed his way through to the group between square dances. Clemmie looked glazed and unsteady. He took her by the arm and said, "Sorry to break it up. We got to take off." And he hurried her off the floor, paying no attention to the shouts of annoyance behind him. Clemmie came along woodenly, without protest, stumbling frequently so that her weight came against him. She whined about going so fast.

He got through the main gate and headed toward the far end of the parking lot. He looked back and he saw two of them running after him. He took Clemmie's wrist and managed to get her into a fumbling run. But she soon tripped and fell heavily. When he had picked her up, they had come up to him, and they slowed, advanced warily.

Mickey was in the lead, thumbs in his belt, shoulders rolling. One of the other huskies from the dodge-em rink was a step behind him.

"What are you busting up the set for?" Mickey asked.

"We have to go."

"Clemmie don't want to go. She's having a ball. Right, Dill?"

"She sure is."

"Clemmie, you come on. We're going on back. You want to go home, pops, you go right on. We'll see she gets home."

Clemmie, at the moment, was beyond response. She sagged against the side of an old Hudson. Mickey moved around Craig, moving closer to the girl. Dill circled the other way. They were hard young animals, sensing the helplessness of the bitch in heat. Dill slid in quickly and grabbed Clemmie and pulled her off to one side. Craig spun toward them and Dill said, "Take him, Mickey. I'll get her on back."

He turned as Mickey rushed him. Mickey swung ponderously, with a strange slowness, and Craig realized he was both drunk and muscle bound. He caught two road-house blows on his arms, but the third hit the point of his left shoulder. It was like being hit with a rock. His arm sagged. There had been a course, long ago, in unarmed combat, at Benning. He had not realized that he could remember any of it. He hit Mickey in the throat as hard as he could. Mickey gagged and floundered. He kicked at the kneecap with the side of his shoe. Mickey gasped and went down onto one knee. Craig laced his fingers, slapped them down on the back of Mickey's neck, pulled his head sharply down into the upflung piston of a knee.

He turned and ran headlong after Dill and the girl. Dill was pulling her along. They were in silhouette against the main gate lights. Another couple had just left the fair. They were each carrying a small child and two other children trailed them. Dill tried to go faster, then turned, letting go of Clemmie. He turned and swung in one quick fluid motion. Craig ran into the punch. It hit him flush on the forehead. His neck was wrenched; his feet left the ground. He landed flat on his back. He lay still for several seconds, until a white light in his head faded away and he could see the stars overhead. He got up with an effort. Dill was walking around and around in a small circle, shoulders hunched forward, hugging his fist against his stomach. Clemmie stood slack-faced and swaying. Craig moved toward Dill. Dill turned and walked toward the main gate, still hugging his hand, not looking back. The couple with the kids were hurrying toward a far line of cars and looking back toward them.

Clemmie came along with him. He found the car and got her into it. She was going to need all the air she could get. He put the top down. He was weak and trembling from the exertion of running and fighting. His forehead throbbed. His left arm felt deadened. It ached in a dull way when he moved it. By the time he got out on the highway, Clemmie had slid down in the seat and gone to sleep. She did not awaken all the way back.

CHAPTER SEVEN

On Wednesday morning at the plant Craig felt disgusted with himself and ashamed of himself. It required a serious effort to respond properly to the anticipated comments about his bruised forehead.

"Dropped the soap on the floor and went after it too fast and hit my head on the edge of the sink." It seemed to be a slight improvement on the tired story of running into a door.

It was a day when it was hard for him to concentrate. His attention span seemed as short as a child's. At one point during the morning he was talking with John Terrill about the feasibility of a gravity conveyor between the first and second floor of A Building, and whether or not Maintenance might be able to knock something together that would serve the purpose.

Terrill was in his early forties, a small man who, unlike most small men, moved slowly, talked softly, and got a great deal done. He had broad production experience. Craig sat on the corner of John Terrill's desk. He suddenly realized that John had asked him a question, and that he had been nodding and looking attentive for several minutes without hearing a word.

"How's that again?"

"What's the matter with you? Did that thump on the head put you to sleep?"

"It's one of those days, John. I'm sorry."

"Here it is again. I said the conveyor will be better than loading racks and taking them down in the elevator, but unless we can get enough room for the racks, and room to load them, it isn't going to help. Here. Take a look. We can knock out this wall, move this stuff back. This is light stuff. It doesn't need special footing. Just unbolt it and move it, set new bolts and tie it down."

"Looks okay. Why don't you make a joint recommendation and I'll sign it too?"

"No more questions? No bitching about the patch and pray policy? Not like you."

"I repeat. One of those days."

"Better not have too many. The new broom is starting to make sweeping motions."

"I know. John, can you think of any real radical idea that'll fix us up so we won't go constantly nuts over all these subcontracts?"

"Sure. A nice fire. A nice hot one. If it started in paint storage, that ought to do it."

"Thanks. Thanks a lot, pal."

When he got back to his own office, he shut the door, shoved his chair back so he could put his feet on the corner of his desk, laced his hands across his stomach and tried to do some logical thinking. Style changes were the big headache. Short runs were another. Think big, the man said.

He sighed and shifted his position. He couldn't stop thinking about last night. He was too damn old to get mixed up in Clemmie's nonsense. It was all fine for some kid, playing that asinine game of hers and rescuing the fair drunken maiden from the biceps set. He'd been lucky with those two, luckier than he deserved to be.

I broke his hand by hitting him on the fist with my head. This Clemmie affair is too ripe, and too unpredictable. I'd better stop being an eager old goat and pull out of that. There's an unhealthy flavor to it. And I am not going to be permitted to retain any dignity. Once the ring is firmly locked on my nose, all she has to do is tug the rope. A fine picture I made. Riding those dodge-em cars. Sulking on the merry-go-round. Drinking corn with kids.

He didn't want to think about the rest of it, but his mind kept turning back to it, the way a child will persist at picking at a scabbed knee.

When he got her home she had been a rag doll, barely able to climb the stairs with his help before collapsing again. He couldn't awaken her. So he had carried her to her bedroom, undressed her, hung up her clothing, and then, without premeditation, had taken his quick and angry use of her, punishing her for the humiliations of the evening and, on some primitive level, seizing the spoils he had won in battle, taking a bitter satisfaction in his knowledge that, though she moved in feeble response, there was not enough consciousness left for her to know who he was, or care. He used her the way they would have used her had they won, with a savage selfishness. Then he slept beside her.

When he awakened at five the sky was light. Her breath was stale, her long black hair across his throat, her arm across his chest, their bodies sweaty-moist where they touched. He eased away from her without awakening her, dressed, drank four glasses of water and walked the full seventeen blocks to his home. He made the bed with fresh linen, set the alarm for eight. He slept so deeply that when the alarm awakened him the incidents of the previous evening had become remote, like things that he had imagined in delirium, so that he was not responsible for them.

It was easy, perhaps too easy, to make a most plausible analysis of what had happened to him. He knew that over the past years his emotional scale had narrowed. He had felt anger, joy, disgust, fear, contentment—but all in a minor key, blurred, softened, diluted by the very predictability of his stabilized and well organized life. He saw that in one way he had been like a sailing vessel that had been anchored in a safe harbor, after short years in the wild seas outside. He had ridden out those seas and found harbor and protection. The waves were still high outside, but by the time they reached him, rocking him in his refuge, they were muted, no longer dangerous.

Now he had foolishly left the harbor mouth, and he was shocked by the strength of the waves, by the unpredictable furies of emotions he had felt capable of surviving. The quiet years had made the vessel less seaworthy. The hull was bearded and barnacled, the rigging half-rotted, the compass unadjusted. These were the same choppy seas he had ridden out long ago, but now the safety margin was less, and he had lost confidence in his own seamanship.

Now it was time to run for the harbor.

He told himself that he was a sane and decent man, and this was an ugly affair, and now he would get out of it.

He was aware of another factor within himself. He had always been wary of strong emotions. There had been too much of that in his childhood. Too many scenes, too much violence.

His own mother had died when he was four. He had lived with an aunt for two years until his father married again, married a young and rather coarse and very erratic redheaded woman named Katherine. When Craig was eleven his father died of a heart ailment, leaving Katherine with Craig and the two younger children of that marriage. Fourteen months later, when the insurance money was nearly gone, Katherine married a man named Gochak, the resident manager of one of the middle-sized mines in the Scranton area, and began to have babies by him.

The frame house was too small for the size of the family. It was a tumultous marriage, full of violence and outrage and quarrelings. Katherine throve on continual emotional crisis. Finally Craig achieved an immunity to the environment. He could no longer respond. He knew there was only one escape for him, one escape with honor. Rather than run away he stayed and achieved the second highest grades ever given at the high school, and, given a choice of scholarships, took one at the Wharton School of Finance at the University of Pennsylvania. Katherine and Gochak gave him a watch.

Katherine died while Craig was in college, died at fifty-one in the backyard when her heart, damaged from too much work, gave out while she was beating a rug in spring frenzy.

Craig got along well in college. He was desperately anxious to conform. And he was so anxious to forget his origins that he made for himself a fictional autobiography that came to be more real to him than the actuality. He went home for the last time when Katherine died, and sorted what he had left there, and took a few small things with him when he left. Pictures of his own parents, a few documents.

When he graduated in June of 1939 with a good record, he was offered several jobs in industry. He accepted the U. S. Automotive offer, went through their training program and then was placed on a permanent status at three hundred dollars a month at the Newark Drop Forge Division, as a production chaser. He had escaped.

He did not talk of his origins to anyone. The fictional autobiography was a better substitute. He even told Maura the false history first, but later, one night in the flat, she lay in darkness in the curve of his arm, and he talked to her for a long time and told her just how it was, and how it felt to be in a place where you did not belong, just because there was no other place to go.

And now, after all the years, he had come much too close to being seriously involved with a woman whose emotions were so raw and so quick and so flamboyant that she inevitably reminded him of Katherine. Clemmie lived with the same carelessness and hunger. And, like Katherine, she could goad and madden anybody who became emotionally involved with her.

Now he wanted to get back to quietness and stability, back to a placid place. In a sense she had cured his old restlessness, but left him with shame and guilt. He felt as though she had marked him in a way that Maura would discern with her first look at him.

He would break away before any more damage was done. He had known of men ruined by an inexplicable infatuation. He had wondered how it could happen. Now he could sense how it could happen. But it would not happen to him.

CHAPTER EIGHT

CLEMMIE PHONED HIM at the office at twenty minutes to five. Betty James was checking over a report with him when the call came in, and she scooped up the phone.

"Mr. Fitz's office, Miss James speaking. Yes? Just a moment, please." She covered the mouthpiece. "A Miss Bennet, Mr. Fitz." Betty seemed to be looking at him oddly.

"I'll take it. Hello?" He held the receiver close to his ear to let no sound escape.

"Craig? Oh, honey, I'm so abject and miserable and sorry and everything."

"Don't worry about it."

"You sound frighteningly gruff, dearest. I *must* see you."

"I'm afraid that's impossible, Clemmie. I'm all tied up."

"I suspect the presence of pointed secretarial ears, darling. And I understand. I shouldn't have called you there. Give me a ring as soon as you get out of that salt mine. I'll be waiting right here." She hung up.

Craig handed the phone to Betty and she put it back on the cradle. "Clementina Bennet?" she asked.

It startled him. "Why? Do you know her?"

"Gosh, no. But I know *of* her. Don't you read the society pages?"

"Maura does. Is she in there often?"

"Not lately." She changed her voice to a haughty tone, little finger crooked. "Miss Clementina Bennet, socialite daughter of George LaBarr Bennet, is hostess at Hunt Club Breakfast. Miss Bennet is shown modeling a Paris original at the Pelton Club Charity Bazaar. Miss Clemmie Bennet returns from Nassau where she was a guest of Miss Cynthia Whosis, daughter of Lord and Lady Bluntwhistle. How did you get into the top levels, Craig?"

"I didn't know I was. I—I met her at a friend's house. The name didn't mean anything. I guess she wants to do a public service by entertaining the lonely bachelor. Some kind of a dinner party."

"You *ought* to go. I'd die to hear about it. Her father has a perfectly enormous place out in the Robinson Woods section. He's very, very rich. It was inherited, I think. His mother was one of those financial wizards who always knew what to buy and when to buy it. Clemmie came into quite a bit of money of her own when she was twenty-one."

"You certainly keep track."

She sighed. "I guess so. Those people are sort of dream people. They don't seem like us. I don't see how they could possibly think the way we think. I mean—so much of our every day is taken up just—by the ways and means committee. You know?"

"Yes."

"Where were we? Stock level, 718 D. Material on hand —complete. Percentage of order complete—86. Percentage shipped—78. Units in process—80,000 of a total of 110,-000. Estimated date of final shipment—August 10th. Does that check?"

"Check."

"Mr. Fitz?"

He looked up. "Yes, Betty?" He had never seen her look so wistful.

"Maybe I'm going to be out of line. You tell me. I mean you're just as alone as I am right now. I thought maybe a Sunday picnic, with the kids. Mother likes a breather on Sundays. I can forget it ever happened, if you think it would be okay. And if you think I'm out of line, kindly forget I got brassy enough to ask."

Had it not been for the phone call from Clemmie, he would have managed to say no in a way that would have saved her pride and retained her loyalty. "I think it would be fun, Betty. I'd like to do it."

She stared at him. "I was positive you'd say no."

"Want to retract?"

"Oh, no. Look, Mother is a little odd. She's full of dire suspicions. She'll want to see who I'm going out with. She knows your name and I've described you, but she's never seen you. Could you, when you pick us up, let me call you something else? I mean she knows you're married. You will? Good. The kids are really good kids. It won't be a painful picnic. But if you want anything to drink, you better bring it. That's another of Mother's peculiarities."

He was already regretting the impulse that had made him say yes. Betty was difficult enough to control as it was. After the picnic she would be harder than ever to restrain. She had a curious talent for continually enlarging her areas of decision and command.

"Let's finish this up," he said.

Bucky came in at five and made a final report. McCabe came in with a design for a welding jig. He and Betty finally finished the report at quarter of six and she said she would get the typist on it the first thing in the morning. He heard the clack-tock, clack-tock of her heels as she left the empty office. There would be a jolly Sunday picnic, and it would be interminable. But, in a sense, it would be refuge. There could be no duplication of the previous Sunday. Curious, he thought, how much and how little Betty had known about Clemmie Bennet. And he could imagine the awed horror, the disgusted fascination on Betty James' face had she been able to see into Clemmie's studio apartment the previous Sunday.

He wanted to stay and work on the idea he was supposed to present to Paul Ober on Friday morning. But it would perhaps be better to phone Clemmie and be firm with her, let her know it was finished. He left the office, walked a half block to a small cigar and candy store, a place of loungers and punch boards. The last person in the booth had left behind the stale aroma of cheap cigar.

"This is Craig, Clemmie. I was tied up. I don't like you phoning me at the office."

"So stern, Craig, So severe. I don't blame you. I was a mess. No more corn. Ever. Gaaa. I don't remember coming home or going to bed or anything. I vaguely remember a fight which you seemed to be winning. I can't apologize over the phone. You come on the dead run, darling, so I can do a better job here."

"Sorry. I accepted a dinner invitation."

"Then leave as soon as you dare, dearest. I'll be waiting for you. What a day, dearest! I've been pummeled by a masseuse, and I called on the sick, and I bought a very sexy dress all for you. It's kind of a schizo dress, all prim in front, and in the back it is open all the way down to imminent disaster. And I am teetering on new red shoes. Please come as soon as you can."

"I'm sorry, Clemmie. I don't really think I'll be able . . ."

"I'll tell you what. If you think it will be too late, this will be an easier way. I've got a spare key and I'll leave it on the right side of that little ridge over the shed door. On the right corner as you face the shed. And, my Fitz-darling, spend all of your stuffy evening thinking up the most interesting way of waking me up that you can de-vise."

He started to object again, but realized he was talking to a dead line. He took out another dime, then changed his mind. She had no intention of listening to him, or permitting herself to believe that he wouldn't stop by. She could wake up in the morning and be astounded.

He drove home. The phone was ringing when he walked in. He hurried to it.

"Craig? Craig this is Irene Jardine. Can you hear sounds of revelry in the background? I don't see how you could miss them. One of Al's grateful clients came through today with a huge package of the most monstrous steaks you ever saw. There's absolutely *no* room in the freezer, so this is turning into a pickup party. I do hope you can come."

"I'd like to, Irene, very much."

"You better hurry, or you'll be too many drinks behind. I'm dying to see you. We're out in the yard mostly, and it's mighty informal around here."

He showered and dressed hastily in sports shirt and slacks. The Jardines were among the early settlers in the five-year-old River Wood section, and had appropriated one of the best sites, a hilltop site. He and Maura had been entertained there often, with a kind of hospitality that could not be returned on Federal Street. There was an acre of backyard with a wading pool for the kids, a wide concrete terrace, an outdoor grill. When he realized no one would hear the front-door chime, he went in and through

the house. There was the usual confidential group in the
kitchen, Joe and Jeanie Tribbler, Chet Burney and a young
couple he did not know. They were introduced as Dave
and Floss Westerling, house guests of Steve and Lollie
Chews, who lived next door. Chet Burney built him a dark
hairy drink from the kitchen supply, and Craig wandered
out to find his host and hostess.

He found that the Westerlings were the only strangers.
He knew all the others. They were all part of the same
social group as he and Maura, all but Bill Chernek who,
he guessed, had been invited because Ruthie was out of
town. He stiffened when he saw Bill, but Bill saluted him
with his glass, friendly enough. He spoke to Steve and
Lollie Chews, to Vince and Bobby Hellgren, to Anita Osborne and Ralph Bench. They asked him about Maura,
about the latest word. There was the expected banter about
the discolored bruise on his forehead. He sensed that the
party was at the three-drink level, just a shade overly
gay, but not yet frantic.

It was, as Irene had explained, informal. The sun was
still high enough to slant into the yard. Petite Jeanie Tribbler and gross Lollie Chews both wore sunsuits. Jeanie
looked as charming as Lollie looked grotesque. The house
guest, Floss Westerling, wore a sort of cabana costume of
cape and swimsuit. The only overdressed one was, as might
have been expected, Anita Osborne. She wore a cocktail
dress and had seen her hairdresser that same day. When
Craig spoke to her he noted that she was slightly ahead of
the others in the number of drinks consumed, and he
made a mental note to give her a wide berth.

Everyone had thought that Tom and Anita Osborne,
despite their childlessness, had a good marriage. They
seemed warmly happy with each other. It had shocked the
group when, nearly two years ago, Anita had gone to Reno
for her divorce and got it on the grounds of mental cruelty.
Tom married a girl of twenty-five, fifteen years younger
than he was, the day after the decree became final. And
shortly thereafter, he had wangled a transfer to another
city, leaving Anita with the house and moderate alimony.
Anita had not properly gauged the change in her social
status, not at first. She had been a slender, graceful
woman of thirty-six with prematurely white hair, a golf-

club tan, a knack of dressing well. She had apparently believed that her social life would go on as before and, sooner or later, she would find another man and remarry.

But ever since the divorce, there had been a gradual disintegration of Anita. The invitations were far less frequent. Friends made efforts to introduce her to eligible men, but the men were always less than suitable.

She began to become slightly frantic. She had the white hair dyed blonde. Though she had paid a great deal for the change, and though it had been carefully done, it served only to harden the lines of her face and made her look suddenly and shockingly older. She began to drink too heavily. When she drank her conversations became larded with sexual innuendoes. She greeted friends with such extreme cries of surprise and affection that she became almost hysterical. She began to buy clothes more suitable for a junior miss. The poised and gracious wife of Tom Osborne no longer existed. This woman was a menace, a lonely and frantic human being who, though she was trying dreadfully hard, seemed to expend all her efforts in the wrong directions. Everyone knew she was moving constantly closer to a breakdown, and no one seemed to know what to do about it. Craig had an uncomfortable memory of a party in May when she had clung to him and wept. He wanted no recurrence this evening. Al and Irene were two of the old friends still loyal enough to invite her. Yet Al and Irene did not ask her when there were other guests who might not understand.

Lately well-meaning friends had been asking her and Ralph Bench to the same parties. He was a newcomer in Stoddard, an insurance company executive. He was a widower with grown children. Though he looked distinguished and alert, his conversation was composed entirely of the dullest sort of platitudes, and of personal experiences he told over and over. He seemed to like Anita, however, and chuckled fondly at her overdrinking and her hysterical posturings.

Al Jardine drew Craig over to one side. "No grief for you the night our Bill got it?"

"None. I was drunk, but I stayed out of trouble. Bill's got a rough touch with a Martini. How will he come out?"

"Okay. The fix is in."

"How do you mean?"

"I hesitate to explain it to you, my idealistic friend. We've had too many arguments about this sort of thing, with you on the side of truth and beauty. But I'll explain. Both cops have to come up with the same story. One of them is named Cooper. He's a real hardnose cop. The other is a kid, still on probation. His name is Fenelli. And he got on the cops because his uncle is a ward worker down in the ninth ward and his uncle went to Manny Brancci whose name you have heard and who delivers the vote from the eighth, ninth and tenth wards, and asked Manny to back the kid for an appointment—which Manny did, because the way you hold wards together is by doing favors. So when I had my facts, I went to Hal Reiter, the people's choice, who gave Manny the word, who gave the uncle the word, who gave the kid cop the word. Now when it comes up, this kid, who was absolutely positive, will be very dubious about who swung first. Reasonable doubt. No reprimand for anybody. But a quiet little disturbing the peace fine for our Bill. Such are the procedures of justice in fair Stoddard. Like it?"

"Do I have to?"

"You want the book thrown at Bill. Public disgrace, and a can tied on him by Quality Metals because he's a lousy purchasing agent."

"No. I don't want that."

"You have told me the same laws should apply to all. So some River Street bum takes a swing at a cop. He gets six long months. I think you're a little mixed up. The law applies differently to each social strata, Craig. That's the way it works here, and that's the way it works in any city in the land. Except maybe more so here. Here I bet that if George LaBarr Bennet ran down an old lady pushing a baby carriage at high noon at the corner of DeWitt Boulevard and Long Bridge Avenue, sodden drunk and with a pocket full of reefers, give me some grease for the right bearing surfaces and I could get him off with a parking ticket."

"Why mention him?"

"What are you startled about? I just pulled his name out of a hat. He's one of the untouchables. We've got several of them in the area. You don't stomp on a man who bought immunity by putting a half million into the hospital fund. Understand, Craig. I'm not proud. I was going

to hold juries in the palm of my hand. I was going to have
one hell of a courtroom manner. But I'm just a very capable and very well paid Mr. Fixit. And they all know, from
judge to pimp, from senator to whore, that when I give
my word it's as good as any legal contract that can be
drawn up. But it's still a dirty business, and I rant at you
like this because sometimes I get a little fed with it and I
have to go around defending myself to the bleeding hearts.
Let's drop it. You need a drink. You're behind in the bar
batting average."

He had a drink and he talked with Irene and Jeanie
Tribbler for a while, and then had another drink and was
talking to pretty little Jeanie and Floss Westerling, the
statuesque young bathing-suited one, when Bill Chernek
moved into the group.

"Ole Fitz," he said. "Cuts himself out the two best looking dolls at the clambake. This guy is cozy. You want to
watch him."

"Is that a sort of warning, Mr. Chernek?" young Mrs.
Westerling said.

"Sort of! I'm giving you the straight facts."

"Lay off, Bill," Craig said.

"No, I mean it. You lovelies don't know what a chance
you're taking. This ole Fitz is surely on the prowl these
days. Wife away for the whole dang summer."

Jeanie smiled up at Craig and said, "You're a lamb.
Bill is trying to give you a dangerous reputation. Bill, I've
known Craig long enough to know that it'll take more
than press agenting."

Bill leaned closer, put a thick finger to his lips and said,
"Shush, honey. Now I make with the facts."

Craig realized Bill was drunk in a way not normal to
him, a sly drunkenness. When Bill glanced at Craig his
smile was broad, but his eyes had a small pinched look.

"Here's the facts, you lovelies. You underestimate ole
Craig. You won't ever find ole Craig home. He's got a
shack job all lined up. This boy is real sneaky. Look at
him. Manly and honest and stuff. But I got five bucks
says he goes right from here to her."

"That's not particularly funny, Bill," Jeanie said.

"Isn't meant to be, sugar. I'm just ready with the facts.
You gals watch out."

He turned and lumbered away, heavy elbow nudging

Craig painfully in the ribs. Jeanie said to Floss Westerling, "Forgive the local types, Floss."

"We've got 'em where I come from. Think nothing. Are you really a lady-cruncher, Craig?" she asked looking at him guilelessly.

"I read a book."

"Oh, of course. One of those do-it-yourself texts."

After her husband came and got Floss, Jeanie said, "Craig, Bill acted pretty nasty. Is he sore at you?"

"I guess so. It's a long dull story, though. Come on and I'll buy you a drink and promise not to inflict the story on you."

As they walked across to the outdoor bar, Jeanie said, "You know, Craig, you've never made any hint of a pass at me."

"I've managed to restrain myself, Jeanie."

"Thank God. Kitchen kissings and hallway goosings and little trips out to the car or into the brush sicken me. Hey, not so heavy on the Scotch, Craig. Maura and I have talked about this pass business. We both feel the same way. And we both congratulate each other on having husbands who aren't—sleazy." She patted his arm and smiled at him. "Now I'm going off and be constructive and tell Al to start to think about the steaks."

He watched her walk away. The last of the slow dusk was gone and Al had turned on all his spots and floods. Al was fond of lighting. There was a theatrical number of them. Al, with no encouragement at all, would tell you his theories about the relationship between good lighting and human emotions.

Craig stood with stiff drink in hand, in a patch of shadow, and looked at all the people he knew so well, all of them predictable. Bench had the Hellgrens blocked in a hedge corner. Bill, Joe and Chet stood in a tight group, making giant shadows against distant trees as they told jokes. Al was poking his bed of coals, and it made a pink light on his face, intent under the high chef's hat. Steve Chews was trying to help him, with customary ineptness. Lollie Chews, talking to Irene Jardine, bent over to slap a mosquito on her ankle and Craig saw the spotlight on her gargantuan buttocks that strained at the lime sunsuit she wore, staggering monuments to self-indulgence. Jeanie Tribbler was sitting on a redwood table, swinging her little legs that were so perfect that somehow they were impersonal, beyond desire. Alice Burney leaned against the table, talking to Jeanie, a spotlight touching the amber in her glass. Beyond them he could see lightning on the western horizon, silent car lights crossing the bridges, and a yellow-orange neon glow over the city.

This was the mixture as before. Craig stood and rubbed the coolness of his glass against the side of his face, and felt he looked at them with an equal coolness, with a speculation. He remembered all the other times and all the other places. The group changed, but it remained the same. There was economic attrition, and marital attrition, and bad hearts and malignancies, but new ones filled the vacant places. Only the names were changed, but the parts were played in the same old way.

He stood there as though he were an uninvited neighbor watching them from beyond a hedge. The Westerlings, though they were strangers, fit into a very familiar pattern. She had a look of restlessness and boldness and discontent, and her young husband had all the uncomplicated eagerness of a setter pup. Like the Carrans, who weren't here tonight.

Craig shook off his feeling of detachment and, both physically and emotionally, rejoined the group. He had another husky drink and twenty minutes of idle and interrupted conversation before the steaks were served and they ate. Bill Chernek had to be wheedled into eating. There was steak and hot rolls and a huge bowl of chilled salad and strong coffee.

Craig sat on the edge of the raised terrace to eat. Floss Westerling sat with him, at his right. He finished before she did and he sat there smoking a cigarette, aware that she was glancing at him from time to time.

"You work up a pretty heavy silence there, my friend," she said at last.

"Sorry, Mrs. Westerling. Floss, isn't it? How do you like it here?"

He had taken his finger out of the dike. Her talk washed over him. She had a sprightly way of expressing herself, but it only partially masked the whine of her discontent. They had a month vacation, and it was half gone. They had three small children—six months, nineteen

months, and not quite three. She had put her foot down
when Dave had wanted to bring them along. What kind
of a vacation would that be? Dave's mother took the kids,
but they had to pay for a full-time practical nurse to help
her, and a good one, so it had taken the money for the
nurse instead of the vacation they had planned.

She complained about how the kids had her so tied down
she'd lost her golf game. She complained about how dull
the vacation was. She had wanted to go to Las Vegas. She
complained about how she would be forty before she could
pack the youngest off to boarding school, and what was
there left after that? She spoke in an amusing way, in a
young and husky and defiant way, but it was a paean of
woe.

Finally she asked about his wife and he explained, and
she asked what he did for a living and he explained that
too, and said Bill Chernek worked there too, and she leaned
closer and told him that Chernek was drunk and was looking for a playmate. Then she wanted him to get her a bourbon on the rocks with a dash of soda.

He went and fixed her drink and decided he would
make himself a tall Scotch. He poured a reasonable amount
in a tall glass with the ice, started to fill it to the top
with water and then, on an impulse he did not understand, he put the pitcher down, took the bottle again and
slugged the drink so heavily there was little room left for
water. He wondered why it should seem such a necessary
thing to do, why he should feel such a strong desire for the
amnesiastic refuge of a dive into the bottle.

When he went back and sat beside her, he looked at her
for the first time directly and intently. She sensed it and
turned so the light struck her face more directly. She had
changed from her cape and swimsuit to dark slacks and a
short-sleeved white cotton knit sweater, an off-the-shoul-
der sort of sweater. She had brown short hair, a broad
brow, high, heavy cheekbones, eyes wide-spaced, a rather
rudimentary nose. Her mouth was broad, with lipstick
applied in an almost rectangular pattern. She was a big
girl with good shoulders, large breasts, and a waist made
more trim than it was by the clever tailoring of the slacks.
It was a face patterned to current standards of beauty, as
glib and mannered as the face on every billboard.

They stared at each other in an utter silence. Her eyes glittered in reflected light. She ran her tongue along her lips and said softly, "Well, now!"

"A sudden awareness," he said. "Like in the books." And felt a slow inner turn and coil and stretch of need for her.

"I'm a sucker for the gloomy ones," she said. "You're unhappy, aren't you?"

A tired gambit, he thought. Shallow and silly and pointless. Very like one of Clemmie's games, but not as honest. This would be full of stock phrases, and perhaps if all cautions and precautions were observed, and if she was certain he would not talk or become a problem to her, she would award him her special favors and expect breathless gratitude. She would insist on a lot of emotional posturing, phony tears, posings and worn romantic devices to surround, obscure, glorify, saccharin-coat, justify and make more memorable some twelve spasmed seconds of revenge against her environment and compensation for her inability to feel love.

"Unhappy. Up to a point. So are you, Floss."

"I know, I know," she said, and sighed, and looked away. "In two weeks the long-expected vacation will be over, and ole Floss will be back in a welter of diapers and pablum and Spock, and what has happened, I ask you? Absolutely nothing."

"What would you like to have happen?"

She looked at him again. "That's it. I don't know." She turned just enough so that her knee rested warm and round against his thigh. He looked at his glass and saw to his surprise that it was empty.

He filled it, as heavily as before, and brought her another. And coldly, purposefully, half amused at himself and half disgusted, he steered the conversation toward marital fidelity. This heavy-breasted discontented wife might be turned into a fine antidote to Clemmie. A double negative. Two infidelities would cancel each other out.

"I think I know what kind of man you are, Craig. Most husbands would get into the most horrid kind of trouble if they were left alone all summer. I shudder to think of how Dave would react. He needs a tight rein. He's got dandy taste. Greasy little car hops and elevator girls and girls behind counters at the five and dime. It's depressing. When I was in the hospital having Margot— she's the middle one—it got very messy. He's like a puppy that has to roll in something dirty. That hurts, you know. I told him that if he could do that to me, I could do the same to him. But I haven't. But he doesn't know that."

"Does it have to be dirty?" he asked, seeing his cue as clearly as though she had handed him a script.

"I don't think so. Not really. It depends on the people involved. I mean if they're sensitive and so forth."

"I'm the steady type," he said.

"Well, really! I'm not exactly round-heeled. Did you think I was?"

"No, Floss. I'd never think that." And the pressure of her knee became more insistent and she smiled and squinched her eyes a little and arched her back to make the breasts more prominent against the white of the orlon sweater.

"My father was the steady type too," she said. "It's funny what happened. You take Dave. With him it's like a little kid stealing cookies. But my father wanted to be a good man and he was. He was a thousand per cent loyal to my mother. And when it ended, it was horrible for both of them. I was eighteen. Mother and I went through hell and so did he. He took it so seriously. He divorced my mother and married her, and she's made his life hell ever since. He's pathetic now, honestly. He's trying so hard to be a Princeton boy. I see him when he comes to visit our kids. He bounds around, very springy, wearing hairy sports jackets and suede shoes. He has a Jag and a Cad convertible and a heart murmur and a bitch-cat wife three years older than I am."

"So you think that will happen to me?"

"My God, don't get mad."

"I'm not mad. It was an interesting analysis, Floss." He checked on his degree of intoxication. His mouth felt numb, but his mind felt cool and still and competent.

"Like we said," she whispered, leaning toward him, "it depends on the people involved. And—what they want. I wouldn't want anything cheap. Without any meaning. Would you?"

"Never," he said gravely.

"We're not cheap, are we, darling?" she whispered. "But there won't be any chance, will there?"

"Remember the saying. Where there's a will." The knee had been away and it swung back, blunt and warm and confident, and it went with the arched back, and with the four-color reproduction of the same smile that sells orange juice, motor parts, retirement policies and Tampax. "Don't go 'way," she said and got up easily and smiled down at him and touched his cheek with the back of her hand and went away then, long round legs swinging in the dark slacks.

Irene Jardine came over and sat on her heels beside him and said, "People were beginning to talk, Craig dear."

"Let them talk. This is bigger than both of us."

"You are a little bit tight, my boy." She smiled at him. "Be careful of these out-of-town gals."

"Very careful," he agreed solemnly. Irene went away. I am merely setting up an antidote, he thought. Get bitten by a snake and they give you a shot made from snake venom. They grind up polio germs to make a polio shot. So I take her like medicine. Cures Clemmie-itis.

He got up and he felt adrift in a world where the lights made the leaves too green. Old Goodman band music came over Al's outdoor speakers. He saw Floss taking Dave a drink. Dave was wobbly. The drink looked very dark. He felt smug and very sophisticated and very wise about being able to prescribe for himself, and pleased that he was able to line up a suburban roll in the hay with all the ease of a man who made a habit of it.

At eleven o'clock Anita Osborne, who had been drinking with an almost hysterical compulsion, fell down in one of the bathrooms and hit her face on the edge of the sink, cutting her mouth badly and knocking out her two front teeth. Craig met her inside the house before anyone else had seen her, and the look of her sobered him slightly. Ralph Bench took her away to see a doctor. He led her to his car. She leaned on him, sobbing into the bloody towel she held to her mouth.

The party continued.

He had a very deep and very confusing talk with Irene Jardine about ethics and civilization. The party shrunk abruptly to thirteen when Bill Chernek stretched out on the chaise longue under the partial roof of the terrace and passed out peacefully, moving not a muscle when Alice Burney and Jeanie Tribbler filled his every accessible pocket with potato chips. Craig was glad to see Bill fold. He had been growing uglier by the moment.

Craig had eased off on his drinking, trying to maintain a certain level of intoxication. Vince and Bobby Hellgren organized a drunken and disorderly session of The Game. Craig played, though usually he was more than content to pass it up. He found himself on the same team as Floss Westerling. Dave Westerling was on the other team. When Craig's team held their strategy conference over in the shadows, Floss took every furtive opportunity to rub against him.

When it was Floss's turn to act out something for her team to guess, they never found out what it was she was trying to do. She laced her fingers behind her neck and began to do a slow series of bumps and grinds, after indicating that it was a book title.

David, her husband, came charging across the grass and grabbed at her so awkwardly and roughly that he knocked her down. He was very drunk. He swayed over her, looking down at her and said, in the sudden silence, "Don't wantya doin' that stuff, ya hear?"

"Dave, for God's sake," she said, starting to pick herself up.

"Showoff bitch," he mumbled, and kicked her heartily in the ham and sent her sprawling. The scene held everyone avid and motionless.

Floss scrambled up quickly, her face contorted and her voice shrill. "You don't know just what that cost you, you silly clown! You don't know what that cost you!"

Dave ignored her and turned with stately dignity toward the others. "Teller this. Teller her husb'n went home and she can damn well come home when she's ready or damn well never come home. Teller."

He stalked across the yard, stumbled over a small bush and walked into the darkness, headed for the home of Steve and Lolly Chews. Steve Chews said, in the silence, "Looks like cuz has had it."

The scene broke up the game. When Craig went in the house a little later, he found Irene Jardine crying, sitting alone. He tried to find out what the trouble was and at last he understood that she was weeping because she had wanted it to be a nice party and it was turning into the worst party she had ever had. It was turning out as messy as one of Chet and Alice Burney's parties. Unfortunately Alice Burney came in just in time to hear the comment. The Burneys left, Alice rigid with indignation, Chet bewildered and apologetic.

Party down to ten. He suspected he was losing the splendid edge he had acquired, and he made himself a tall strong drink. Floss Westerling came up beside him as he was fixing it, and made a rueful face at him and held out her empty glass.

"Indignant type husband," he said.

She rubbed her bruised hip. "He's a clod. He's going to pay and pay and pay."

"Are you going to follow him home?"

"Not bloody likely. Walk me to the end of the garden, darling, but let's not be too conspicuous about it, hey?"

They walked to the end of Al's yard. He looked back. They did not seem to be missed. There was a small tool shed, dimly lit by the reflected glow of the spots and floods. She took his glass out of his hand and put it down on the grass beside hers. She looked at him demurely and said, "Now I would be kissed."

The kiss started in a demure manner. Almost a shy manner. And after that concession to convention and to her ideas of herself, she kissed him with enthusiastic and muscular abandon; she became a panting wilderness of rocking, thrusting hips, press of breasts, avid mouth agape, arms tugging, nails biting. It was like being eaten in the shadows by hungry animals. They lost balance and swayed and thumped against the side of the tool house. She giggled and said, "Where can we go, darling? Where can we go? Your house?"

"No. Not there."

"Where then, darling?"

"Motel?"

"That's so . . . grubby. And isn't it too late? Well, I suppose we can try. Look, my honey, let's go back. Here's your drink, dear. And I'll say good-by and go home. Give me fifteen minutes and then you leave and drive down to the bend at the end of the street where the playground is. Will you do that?"

"Will do. Roger."

"Don't be too drunk, baby."

He finished the drink and had another and then he

left. The world was a crazy tilting place. Awareness came in short grotesque flashes, with meaningless blackness in between. He was in his Ford wagon, but she was driving, and it was hard to remember her name. Then there was red neon that said "vacancy" and he walked, very carefully erect, across gravel and pushed a door open and gave a fat woman with pouched eyes and stringy gray hair a ten dollar bill and signed, in a cheap ruled notebook, Mr. and Mrs. Jonathan Johnson, and was given a key fastened to a piece of soiled shiny wood six inches long.

Then there was the rancid cabin that smelled of linoleum and a harsh disinfectant, and the small lamp was on the floor beside the bed with a towel over it, and she was gasping and slippery with her efforts, and very cross and abusive because he couldn't. Then he was able to be better, and for an eternity endured the rubbery bucking and tossing until he heard, with relief, her contrived and theatrical cry of completion and felt her body clench totally, like a doughy fist, and he was glad because then he could stop trying and slide away into welcome blackness.

CHAPTER NINE

HE AWOKE to a great thirst and a blinding, battering pain that hammered at the backs of his eyes and the inside of his forehead. He was on his back and he opened his eyes cautiously and looked up at no ceiling he had ever seen before. It was a peaked wooden ceiling with two-by-fours as cross beams, all painted a pale, poisonous green. Nausea rolled up toward his throat and receded. He closed his eyes. The room was bright. The light source was on his left. The room was hot. His body was sweaty.

He became aware of something soft and warm and heavy that rested across his left leg, just below the knee. A faint alarm stirred within him. He turned his head slowly and painfully to the left. It moved irregularly, in tempo with the hard thudding of his heart, moved like a rusty ratchet. He opened his eyes.

The woman slept with her back to him, on her left

side. Her left leg was across his left leg. They both lay naked on top of a wrinkled, grayish sheet. She had brown hair, worn short. A sheen of perspiration made highlights on her shoulders and on the massive mound of her hip. There was a purple pimple on her right shoulder, and a cluster of three moles at the small of her back.

He did not have the faintest idea who she could be. Or where he was. Or what day it was. He closed his eyes. He groped through memory for a starting place. And suddenly remembered the Jardine party. Just then the woman stirred and sighed and rolled over, taking the weight of her leg off his. She still slept. Her face was toward him, and, looking at it, he remembered the name. Floss Westerling. Her breath was sour. Lipstick was smeared around her mouth. Her hair was tangled and matted. He could see the coarse pores in the skin across her cheekbones. He could see where the plucked eyebrows stopped and the eyebrow pencil began. And see the gunmetal gleam of a filling between the parted lips. Her left breast was uptilted by her left forearm. It stared at him with a blind brown nipple. There was a blue vein in the white skin of the underside of the heavy breast.

He knew the sun was high. He lifted his left arm until he could look at his wrist watch.

Ten after ten.

Dear Jesus.

"Floss!" he said. His voice was thick and rusty. "Floss!" She sighed and dug her head into the pillow. He took her shoulder and shook her. It hurt his head.

Her eyes opened. They were utterly blank. She looked at him without recognition or comprehension, and then her eyes went wider and she looked startled and alarmed. She sat up abruptly, looked around for something to cover herself with, and then held her arm across her breasts.

"My God, what time is it?"

"After ten."

She looked terrified. "I wasn't going to go to sleep. I knew I shouldn't go to sleep! What are we going to do?"

"Where are we?"

"I don't know. Outside of town someplace. Fifteen miles, maybe. I drove until I saw the vacancy. We're in trouble, Craig. Bad trouble. My God! This is awful. We've got to get dressed."

She swung out of bed and trotted into the bathroom,

fatty hips bouncing. She shut the door. It took him a very long time to get to a sitting position. He sat on the edge of the bed, elbows on his knees, face in his hands. Water ran in the sink and a toilet flushed noisily. He heard her come out into the tiny bedroom.

"No peeking now," she said with a sort of frantic coyness. He did not move. He fought waves of nausea.

"Please get dressed, Craig! Now."

He lurched to his feet and stumbled to the bathroom, dropped onto his knees in front of the toilet and was agonizingly, monstrously sick. Each paroxysm felt as though it would burst his forehead open. When it was over he washed his face, drank a glass of tepid water and threw that up. He washed again and drank more water. It stayed down. He drank five glasses of water. It had a metallic taste.

He went back out. His clothes were piled on a chair. Floss sat on the bed in bra and panties, smoking a cigarette. As he started to fumble with his clothes, Floss said, "Wait a minute, dear."

He straightened up and stared at her. "What now?"

She looked at him archly. "Such long hairy legs, grandma. Darling, the damage is all done. It can't get any worse. And while you were in there, I remembered that little love kick he gave me. So he can sweat a while longer. Later on you can drive me into the city and I'll register at a hotel, and when I get around to phoning him, he'll think I've been at the hotel all along. He'll come down on his hands and knees. Now come here, Craig dear. It wasn't very good for you last night, was it? You were too drunkie, baby. This will be lots better."

He shook his head helplessly. "I'm too damn sick, honest."

Her face grew cool. She shrugged. "Suit yourself. Then we might as well dress."

When she was dressed he realized that she had changed from the slacks and sweater to a dress, and she had picked up a small suitcase he did not remember. On the way back to the city they were distant with each other. She said she could get breakfast after she registered. He let her off in front of a good hotel. She walked in without looking back. She looked tall, cool, fresh and pretty—and above reproach.

As soon as he was in the house he went to the phone

and called his office. It was eleven thirty. Betty James
sounded concerned. He told her he had been sick in the
night and had taken a sleeping pill. He said he would be
in later in the afternoon. She explained how she had
taken care of his appointments, and he thanked her. He
had missed an appointment with John Terrill.

He drank more water and went slowly up to the bedroom. The day was getting hotter. The sun was brass.
Insects shrilled in the baked leaves. He could see a slice
of Federal Street. The cars moved through a shimmer of
heat waves. The sun on chrome was like needles in his
eyes.

He undressed and lay on the bed.

Be proud of me, Maura. I was ghastly drunk and if my
heart keeps going like this it is going to scare hell out of
me. Be delighted with me. I am a big man. I kept myself
from going to Clemmie. I substituted a lesser vice, a
drunken and cynical romp with a big and breasty young
housewife and mother, and I didn't enjoy a minute of it.
I played the standard subourbon game.

And I can't stop thinking about Clemmie.

But the first giant step has been taken. And the worst
of it is over. I'll work like a horse, and I'll get myself back
in good physical shape, and read some of the books I've
been planning to read, and maybe when you come back
I'll be able to look you right in the eye and smile at you
and you will know that everything is all right between us.

He picked up the bedside phone on the second ring.

"Hello?"

"Fitz darling, are you terribly ill?"

"How did you . . . Did you call the office, Clemmie?"

"But of course, darling. I was worried."

"I told you not to call there."

"But I get along just beautifully with your little secretary. She's most cordial."

"Don't phone me there. Ever."

"Do I make you nervous? Are you always so ugly when
you're sick, darling? I couldn't understand why you didn't
come by last night."

"The party broke up late."

"But I told you I didn't care how late it was. Remember?"

"I know that. I know that. How plainly do I have to
say it? I didn't *want* to stop by."

"Oh." Her voice was small and hurt.

"I think we ought to knock it off right . . ."

"I know I was a mess the other night, but actually do you think I deserve this kind of punishment? I was willing to apologize."

"That isn't it."

"Then what in the world could it be? I know I was a problem to you. But you couldn't have been too upset. You did stay here."

"This is a party line."

"Do you think I care about that?"

"I do, damn it."

"Craig, I'll come right over. I must talk to you. Can I bring you something? Medicine or soup or something?"

"I'm leaving for the office in twenty minutes."

"You don't feel well. Let me drive you down and then I can pick you up after work. I've got some off-beat types stopping in for a drink about sixish. They might amuse you, dearest."

"I've lost a half day. I'll be working too late tonight. We better skip it."

"What have I done?" she wailed.

"You haven't done anything, damn it. I feel lousy. I got stinking drunk last night. I don't want to see *anybody.*"

"Poor honey."

"Clemmie, will you please . . ."

"I know exactly what the trouble is now, dearest. I was so stupid I didn't understand before. And it's one of the things about you that makes me love you so."

"What thing?"

"That great, bloated, ridiculous conscience of yours. You're just all crawling with guilt, aren't you? Clemmie will fix."

He heard her hang up. He had no idea what she might do. There was something terrifying about her intensity and determination. He dressed as quickly as he could, and was out of the house within ten minutes. As he drove away he looked in the rear view mirror, half expecting to see her car pull up in front of his house.

All afternoon he drove himself. He was curt with Betty, and when he found a mistake on the control board, he was savage with Bucky. Yet he could not get so far into his work that he failed to hear the ominous reiteration of her final words, "Clemmie will fix." Each time his extension rang he felt a wary tension until he knew who it was.

Before Betty left he had her bring him a sandwich and milk shake. When the office was entirely empty, he began once again to work on Ober's assignment. For a long time he could think of no starting place. His mind felt numbed. Finally he decided to make a summary of available data. He took all of the production orders that had been completed during the past three years, those orders that were taken on to fill the forty-five per cent slack left after standard orders were scheduled. He divided the orders into three groups, the desirable, the average, the undesirable—all from a production rather than a cost or profit basis. From that he was able to work up a statement describing what constituted a favorable sub-contract. He typed his statement on Betty's machine. The recommendation was the most difficult part. It took a half pack of cigarettes and an hour of walking before he got any glimmer of light. Then he typed three drafts, and made numerous pencil corrections on the last one.

He read it over, trying to look at it as Ober would look at it. "Statement of Problem: To find some way of achieving optimum utilization of existing equipment at Quality Metal Products Division of U.S. Automotive Corporation. An estimated fifty-five per cent of capacity is utilized by standard product lines. The remaining forty-five per cent is taken up by sub-contracts from prime manufacturers in the home appliance, automotive and marine fields. A limited number of sub-contracts are placed by retail chains. These sub-contracts are expected to pay their fair share of overhead and . . ."

He put it aside. He had thought he had been working with the greatest of efficiency, but actually all he had done was restate the problem and suggest that they go after orders which would be easy to handle efficiently. Make brochures. Set up a regular campaign.

He knew it was trite and he knew it wasn't what Ober was looking for. But, hell, something had to be submitted. This could be dressed up. He put it on Betty's desk with instructions to type it carefully, make four copies, put them in the new spring-back binders, and have them ready for his eleven thirty conference with Ober.

It was after ten when he left. The gate man said good night to him, and Craig asked, "Am I the last one out, Jeff?"

"Next to last, Mr. Fitz. Mr. Ober's still at it." Craig turned and saw the wide-lighted windows of Ober's office over in the new building. As he watched he saw the tall, narrow figure of Miss Commerford pass the window, papers in her hand.

"He work like that often?"

"Comes in a lot around eight, eight-thirty, and lots of times he's still here when I go off shift at twelve."

Craig walked thoughtfully to his car. Another clue to the man. His daytime hours were elaborately casual, some days, when he was in town, an hour in the morning, then another hour or two after a long lunch. It was not exactly disarming or heartening to learn of this particular habit. He stopped by his car, hand on the door handle. He stood there and thought of his recommendation. It was not what you would call thinking wild or thinking big. There seemed a fair chance it would work. Even ten per cent effectiveness would improve the operations. Ober would be able to see that.

He wondered why he should be so wary of the man. Just another man, a little more complicated than most, a little more devious. But probably a fair man. Basically fair. Suddenly he remembered Clemmie again, and forgot Ober immediately. He looked up and down the street for some sign of the pale car parked in the shadows.

What could she fix, anyway? What could she do? Just gad-fly around until she had the word. It had been an upsetting episode and that was all. Clemmie and her damn fool games. Her complete lack of either self-consciousness or restraint. There was all the rest of the summer, and during that time he could push her firmly into the past and be whole again by the time Maura came home.

On the way home he stopped at a small Italian restaurant named Marino's where the food was excellent. He had an antipasto, a small filet mignon and coffee espresso while he read the late edition of the *Stoddard News and Ledger*. In spite of his cigarette tongue, the food tasted superb. Somehow, during the day, he had thrown off the lingering effects of hangover, and now he felt wonderfully tired. He knew that part of his relaxation was due to having something tangible to present to Ober. It might not be as earth-shaking as Ober desired, but it could be made to work, damn it. The restaurant was empty at eleven. Morry Marino came over and sat in the booth with him and

bought him a *strega* on the house, and for a little time
they talked together about old friends and other times.

Craig was yawning as he walked to his car. By the time
he unlocked the back door of his house he felt drugged by
the need for sleep. Halfway across the dark kitchen he
paused and was suddenly awake and alert. There was no
sound in the house, but there seemed to him to be a different quality to the silence. It was an atavistic warning,
coming from far beneath any exercise of logic or deduc-
tion. He waited and listened and the feeling died away
and the back of his neck stopped prickling. Living alone,
he thought, is turning me into an old lady. Have to get a
cat, and look under the bed every night. He was sufficiently tired to be amused by the mental image.

He went up the stairs, suit coat over his arm, unknotting
his tie as he went. The soft yellow glow from the street
lights were enough so that he could see his way. He clicked
the bedroom light switch and nothing happened. Fuse or
bulb. No point in messing with it now. The bathroom
lights would be enough. He hung up his coat, took off his
shirt, headed past the bed for the bathroom. He caught a
drifting trace of scent that stopped him in mid-stride.
Very little light came into the bedroom. He looked at the
double bed and was suddenly startled by a small smothered
sound.

"What's that?" he demanded. His voice sounded too
loud.

She spoke from the bed. "I spoiled it, darn it all." Her
voice was dancing with amusement. "You were supposed
to crawl in and find yourself confronted with a bundle of
girl. I unscrewed the bulbs. Then I had to snicker and
spoil it."

"How the hell did you get in?"

"You don't have to roar. I kicked a cellar window in."

"Did anybody see you?"

"I'm pretty sure nobody did. You worry about that sort
of thing, don't you?"

"You're damn right I do. You're getting out of here,
right now. What are you trying to do?"

"Didn't I tell you I'd fix it?"

"What do you think this proves?"

"You just don't understand the Clementina Bennet system for handling a conscience. I've used it for years and

years. Here's the way it works. Suppose you do something and it kind of bothers you and your conscience itches a little. Then you use the system. You go right back and do it again, only more so. You just hammer your conscience into submission. You teach the darn thing it can't go around making you feel uncomfortable. That's what I'm here to help you do." She moved quickly, walked on her knees to the foot of the bed, took hold of his wrists and tugged at him. "With my help you'll find it absolutely painless, dear. Just like a shot of Novocain. And that old conscience will go away and leave you alone."

He pulled his hands free roughly. He went over and leaned against the bureau and lit a cigarette. "We've got to talk."

"Later. Do you know I've been here since five o'clock? This is a terribly grim house. Did you know that?"

"I'm aware of it."

"It's been a dull six and a half hours. But not as dull as it would have been without the game."

"What game now, for Christ sake?"

"He only uses me on the most delicate missions. The colonel, you know. He said, 'Miss Bennet.' No, he didn't. He called me Z-3. He said, 'Z-3, we have an operation where we can use your photographic memory, your intuition, your superb judgment of character. Go at once to 1109 Federal Street. The house will be empty. Gain admittance, unobserved. Find out every last thing you can about the occupants of that house. Take no notes. Leave no sign of your search. Report back to me.' "

"So you spent the time prying."

"Don't you see? Without the game, it would be prying. With the game it's investigation. If I wasn't Z-3 I would have felt real queasy about reading Maura's letters. But it didn't bother me at all."

He stared into the dark in her direction, utterly incredulous. "Why, God damn you!"

"Shush, now. You shouldn't mind at all. She writes a very lovely letter. Intelligent, and a nice sprinkling of humor, and a very ladylike whiff of sex."

"But you have no right!"

"Well, it's sort of like in that joke about the doctor and Marilyn Monroe where he says to her, 'Gosh, I shouldn't even be doing this.' "

"I just don't understand how you can act as though this is a big jolly deal."

"You know, I do have one mystery for the colonel. It's about you. I found a lot of college stuff and army stuff and so on—by the way, that's a perfectly darling medal—but nothing at all about you before you went to college. Just one frighteningly perfect transcript of a high school record. A pure monotony of ninety-sevens and eights and nines."

"Would you—could you shut up for a minute and listen?"

"Of course, dear. Anything you ask of me."

"This is my home. It's on the grubby side, but it's mine. Actually, it's only half mine. Both our names, Maura's and mine, are on the deed. We've done what we could with it, but there wasn't a great deal to start with. Are you following?"

"Yes."

"We have lived here for many years. In our own corny middle-class way, there are things that are known and dear to us here. Little private things that couldn't mean anything to a third person. At heart I am a very stuffy and conservative guy. I am in favor of apple pie and Mother's Day and the innocence of childhood. That double bed you are in. The inner springs and mattress were new last year, but it is the same bed where my younger daughter was conceived. Maybe, in a sense, Maura and I are a little like hermit crabs. This house is a part of us. That bed is a part of us. The clothes she didn't take are in that closet. This house is full of things she bought me and I bought her. It makes me feel actually, physically ill to have all of this violated by somebody who apparently doesn't give the least damn about my feelings. Or hers. It sickens me. I want you to get up very quietly and get dressed and go home. You've just made a hell of a bad estimate of what I am, and what I'm capable of. Okay, so I got carried away for a time. I was ready, or vulnerable, or whatever the right word is. And I'm over it. This isn't a game. You're attractive in a quaint, ferrety, fidgety, juvenile way. You're half fourteen years old, and half a thousand years old. As far as having you around, I'd rather have a comb in my pocket. You're a strikingly accomplished performer in bed. But it isn't that necessary to me. The fact that you could think for a minute that I'm capable of climbing in with you, here, in this house, in that bed, is the damnedest insult to my sensitivity, or what I call my sensitivity, that I've ever heard. Now, get out!"

"I guess my mood was wrong," she sighed.

"Everything is wrong."

"That was certainly a . . . a staunch speech, Fitzfellow. You make me feel as if I took my bongo drum to a funeral." Her voice was dreary.

"Are you going?"

"With one quiet little word of defense. I'm beginning to know you. And I made a very good guess as to what this would have done to you—if it had worked. It would have been a very nasty bit of deliciousness, and vice versa. In retrospect, it would have shocked you right all the way down to your honorable core. It would have shocked you so badly, you would have had to turn one whole part of your psyche numb just in self-defense, almost the way a lizard shucks its tail."

"I didn't know you ever organized anything so carefully."

"Oh, I'm a plotter, Fitzcautious. It would have been the first big, healthy shovel-load."

"Of what?"

"Weren't you aware? I'm digging a grave."

"For whom?"

"For your love for her. A nice deep one. One day it will be deep enough and we'll have a simple ceremony and afterward you can help me pat the dirt smooth with my shovel, and we'll go off arm in arm. Then she'll be a stranger to you. Just a big, limey blonde going a bit to seed. Somebody you knew once."

"That won't happen."

"For the first time I'm not quite sure it will." Her voice seemed to choke. There was a shift of movement, half seen, a pat of bare foot on the rug, and then she was small against him, shivering and shuddering, and he automatically put his arms around her, his hands moving tentatively awkwardly, feeling the warmth and firmness of her back, the shifting velvety skin-sheath over the firm fibers, the pronounced crease between her shoulder blades that flattened as it neared the small of her back where he could feel the smooth rounded knuckles of the vertebrae close under the skin. She held her clenched fists close under her chin, and as she cried she hit him softly in the chest with alternate fists, each blow traveling no more than an inch. She seemed very small and curiously alone. He sensed that if he continued to hold her, he would, in a very few moments, become aroused. He let his hands fall to his sides. She held her breath and then backed away.

"That wasn't another device, Craig. Not really."

"I'll accept that."

"But there are other devices, second lines of defense. I hid my clothes. That was in case you got stuffy."

"Which I did."

"And then I was going to . . . the hell with it. Go in the bathroom. I'll fix the bulb and get dressed."

When he came out she sat at Maura's dressing table, using an old brush of Maura's to brush her hair. He made a mental note to inspect carefully for long shiny black hairs. She finished and tilted her head to the side. "An Italian hairdo would really suit me, you know. I've been tempted to fly to New York and have Caruso give me one. But there is no such thing in this world as a short-haired ballerina. And I've learned that when I can keep thinking of myself as a ballerina, I adjust a lot better to any number of things. I couldn't think that way with short hair." She turned a bottle around and looked at the label. "This Maura of yours goes for the flower scents, doesn't she. She doesn't seem to own a single ounce of tiger sweat. Give me the musky ones."

"Are you ready?"

She stood up. She struck a pose that he imagined was one of the basic ballet poses and said, "Look at me! Only a damn fool in love would put on clothes like these on a bake-oven day like this. I suffer just for you. Like the outfit?"

It was a curious shade, not quite peach, not quite salmon. The color suited her very well. There was a soft sweater in that shade, and beautifully tailored slacks, high-waisted, and so closely fitted he wondered how she got into them.

"It's a very . . . unusual outfit."

"I designed it. I'm a very talented child. Cashmere sweater and matching doeskin flannel slacks. You will note, sir, that the slacks prevent me from gaining an ounce where I least care to gain." She pirouetted, stopped, slumped, sighed. "What a hell of an empty routine! I feel like I was behind a cafeteria counter, pushing hard to unload all of the day's special. Does your brittle honor permit you to escort me to the door?"

"Of course, Clemmie."

She paused halfway down the stairs and looked back up at him. "It's *such* a dull house. I'm a horrid snob, I know. It doesn't suit you."

"What would?"

"You? A lot of paneling. Gun racks. Leather furniture. The sea beyond your windows."

"Too bachelor. Married people live in this house. And two small girls. Where's your car?"

"Down around the corner."

When he half-reached around her to open the door, she pushed his arm away and turned and put her back against the door, hands behind her. "I was wrong, Craig. I'm sorry."

"It's all right. Maybe I was too rough."

"You weren't. But I would like to make a counter offer. Will you listen?"

"I'll listen, but—"

"I said something once to you. About a summer affair. Then I tried to make more out of it. So I can't. I know this is a table stakes game. I thought a flush was good enough, but you have—a full house. And I lost my stake. But I don't think I can stand being dealt out of the game all the way. I don't think I can stand and watch."

"What do you want?"

"You won the pot. I want a small loan. Just enough to put me back in business. Back on the basis of the summer affair. I won't hurt you and I won't embarrass you, and I won't try to buck this full house again. I'll be—just a usable thing, disposable after a reasonable service period."

"Clemmie, I . . ."

"Begging isn't pretty to do, or pretty to listen to. I'm abject and I'll stay abject. Slave girl. When you purchase me, Mahster, I hope you be kind to Fatima. I hope I be house girl, not work in fields. I be perfume for you, and all love, asking only food, and to work for you. I am daughter of many kings, Mahster. In my own land I had slaves. Now you own me and always I do as you tell." She bowed deeply, gracefully, almost to the floor. "Come now to slave girl tent," she whispered. "This night."

"Clemmie, I don't . . ."

She came up quickly, fiercely. Her voice was harsh, and her pale blue eyes seemed more bleached. "What *harm* is there in it? What *harm* can it do? For the love of God, stop your posturing. You've won. You've picked up all the money. Do you have to grind me down to nothing? I'll be at my place. Come if you want to. If you don't you can stay right here and compose little odes to the superb texture of your righteous little soul, you damn superior hypocrite."

The door banged behind her with a force that rattled the living-room windows. He moved to a window. She walked swiftly down the block, head high. Soon he could no longer see her.

He turned the light out and sat down in the dark living room. She was quite right. He had won. It had been a very close thing, because he did not know if he would have been able to win had he gotten unsuspecting into bed and then had her slide over against him, her strong arms around him. And there would have been no more vicious thing he could have done to Maura. There was a curious wisdom in Clemmie. He sensed that had he done that to Maura, the shame would have been so great that the only possible adjustment would have been to invent some way of resenting Maura. It is so easy to despise those we hurt, and those who help us.

But he had been strong. He had handled it well. Yet strength should not be an inflexible, unforgiving thing. Small mercies should be possible. Now the relationship was on a new basis. He was in command. Since that had become established, the potentialities were not as dangerous as before.

He shifted in the chair, scratched his bare chest.

In a sense he had cured himself of her. Or she had cured him, by trying to trick him. What could be the point in grinding her down all the way? A man could become entirely too fond of his own righteousness. The major battle had been won last night. The war had been won this past hour. From now on there might be minor skirmishes with the remnants of the defeated army, but those could be easily won.

Why not? What harm is there in it? There could be more harm in an artificial denial of need. It might cause curious tensions that could affect his work. A normal man was not physiologically capable of spending a celibate summer without strain. Her fangs had been pulled.

She had seemed so small, so hurt and so helpless. She was there to be used. It would be no defeat to go to her now. Actually, it could be thought of as an affirmation of strength—proof that this new confidence was well founded.

Do you have to grind her down to nothing?

What harm could there possibly be in seeing her one more time? And that would give a good chance to explain more gently than he had explained tonight why he could not see her any more.

It was the kind thing to do. The fair thing to do.

As he walked toward the metal door he thought he heard something move in the impenetrable shadows beyond the unused loading platform. He waited and listened, looking toward the shadows, but heard nothing more.

He put the key into the lock, and it turned easily and silently. When he stood outside her door he could hear, in his own ears, the coursing of his blood. It was like hearing, in the night, the roll of distant surf.

He opened her door and walked into the darkness and pulled the door shut behind him.

CHAPTER TEN

THOUGH APPREHENSIVE of his interview with Ober, he was in good spirits on Friday morning. Betty showed him the folders she had borrowed from accounting. Helen was making good progress on the tabulation. He made a point of being particularly cordial to Bucky, to make up for yesterday's snarls.

Betty brought the four copies in at five minutes of

eleven and stood beside his desk as he looked the original copy over.

"Okay?"

"Nice work."

"Don't forget to sign them. How many will you give Mr. Ober?"

"Three, I think. He'll probably want to send at least one to New York with his own comments. Maybe two. What do you think of it, Betty?"

"You must have worked terribly late."

"Until after ten. Are you trying to hedge the question?"

"Oh, no. I thought it seemed—very well thought out and well said. But—well, I don't know anything about these things."

"Skip the false modesty, Betty. You've got a good head and you know the work. If you see anything wrong, for God's sake let me know before I have to go see Ober. I'm perfectly aware that there may be factors I've overlooked."

"Well, just one thing. Some of these nuisance orders, don't they come from firms that give us good orders too?"

"Yes."

"Isn't it sort of easier for them to use one supplier for several items. I mean the billing and shipping and all. So if we won't take the orders we don't like, maybe we won't get any."

"That's covered in the report, Betty."

"Clearly enough?"

"I think so. Don't worry so much."

She smiled crookedly. "I guess I can't help it. Anyway, I can make good potato salad."

"What?"

"For the picnic. Gosh, you didn't forget, did . . ."

"No, I didn't forget."

"If you can, pick me up at nine o'clock Sunday."

Miss Commerford said, in her robotic, electronic voice, "You may go right in, Mr. Fitz."

"Thank you, Miss Commerford." He paused outside the office door, knocked twice, turned the knob and went in. There were four men in the room. Three of them were laughing heartily—Ober and two strangers. L. T. Rowdy sat by the window, barely smiling.

Ober got up and the two strangers stood up slowly. L. T.

Rowdy did not move. He had the knack of being inconspicuously apart from every group.

"Thanks for coming up, Craig. I want you to meet two young men who are good friends and ex-students of mine. May I present Bud Upson and Charlie Montgomery. Boys, Mr. Fitz is my assistant in charge of the grief department. Nobody has it exactly easy in this antediluvian sweat shop, but Craig is on a hotter spot than most."

Craig shifted his report to his left hand and shook hands with the two men. They were both in their late twenties. Bud Upson had a crew cut, the open rugged face of an ex-wingback, alert eyes, and an easy smile. Charlie Montgomery was taller, blond, with a face that was at once ugly, likable and satanic. His eyes were set at a slant, and blond tufted eyebrows slanted up even more sharply above them. His nose was long and large, and his smile was wry and inverted. Both men, though casual and respectful, were dressed in a way that gave them a curious air of importance. Lightweight suits, dull gleam to expensive shoes, gold glint of cuff links and tie tack, conservative yet interesting ties. Haircuts, shaves and fingernails had the gloss of barbershop attention.

Craig saw himself in them, the way he had been, polished, easy, confident, avoiding both the too casual and the too formal. He wondered what had happened to himself along the way, why now he should react like a clerk to Paul Ober's easy charm. He wished he had remembered to get a haircut, and he wished he had not tried to get another few days out of the suit he wore.

They all sat down. Craig was not close enough to Ober's table to casually lay the three copies of the report there. He put them on the floor beside his chair, propped against the leg.

"These two agnostics," Ober said, "were unfortunately in the same class. Very distressing to their instructor. They had no mercy."

"That's funny," Montgomery said. "I sort of remember it being the other way around, don't you, Bud? I recall being flayed in public. They used to claim Paul bound his lecture notes in human skin. And if you could give up sleeping, which of course is a time-wasting habit, you could almost get all of the assignments in on time."

"I used to wake up dreaming about that course," Upson said in a tone of nostalgia. "Screaming."

"Craig, Bud and Charlie work as intermediate consultants with Baylor and Killian. You know the firm?"

"Industrial management, isn't it? Offices in Chicago?"

"That's right. They work as a team. Right now we're going to have them conduct a preliminary survey. It may take a month; it could take six months. Our contract with Baylor and Killian has no termination date. I hope that when their survey is over, they'll come up with some miraculous recommendations. We've decided the first thing to do is split them up. Charlie is going to concentrate on the paper end, accounting, personnel records, reports, and so on. And Bud will be under your wing, Craig. I warn you, no six-year-old ever asked more questions. But he has one advantage over a six-year-old. He never asks the same question twice. I want him to get the entire production picture. He is to have access, naturally, to all records, will attend all pertinent conferences. And they're both ready to start now. All set?"

Ober, Montgomery and Killian stood up as though on signal. This time Rowdy stood up also. Craig got up, then remembered his report, stooped awkwardly and got it. "Paul, you asked me for . . ."

"Yes, of course. Your own recommendation. How many copies have we? Three? Excellent. Charlie, you and Bud each take one copy. Here you go. I'll keep one. We'll go over it independently, Craig, then put it in the suspense file until Bud and Charlie are ready to come up with their formal report. Then, I assure you, your suggestions will be given consideration in conference, and we will bounce them around and see how they fit into what these boys come up with."

"My report is pretty informal, Paul."

Paul laid his hand gently on Craig's shoulder, subtly moving him toward the door. "I realize that. I realize that, old man. It's the integrity and originality of the idea that counts, not the presentation. You see, you and I are two old hats and we're too close to our own problems. These two young moderns will set us on our corporate ear. Someone said that if a man is overly fond of the existing order of things, to invite management specialists in is as unthinkable as lending your wife to the Navy." He gave

Craig's shoulder a little pat, and enveloped him in an aromatic cloud of pipe smoke. "Don't let Bud grind you down."

"*Illigitimi non carborundum,*" said Montgomery.

"Smile when you call me that," Bud said.

Once they were clear of the glacial area around Miss Commerford, Bud Upson said, "Unless you've got to get your hands back on the reins, Mr. Fitz, coffee is indicated. Have you got a cafeteria that's open?"

"The name is Craig. There's a thing down the street."

They got black coffee in heavy mugs and carried them over to a plywood booth. Upson dumped in sugar and stirred it and grinned across at Craig and said, "We're always on a spot when we first come in."

"How so?"

"Young jerks, full of theory. We alarm all the cliques, and thus unite them against us. That makes information hard to get."

"You won't find cliques."

Bud raised one eyebrow. "No?"

"All right. You would have found some before Paul Ober came in. He served that purpose before you got a chance to."

"All united against Paul?"

"I don't mean that. I would say everybody is anxious to work with him, for him. Pick your own word. A certain reputation preceded him. I guess you would know that. The suspense, waiting for him to jump, has been a little wearing."

"I can see that."

"We can't—I better say, I can't figure out what kind of a man he is."

"He's quite a guy." It was obvious to Craig that a fishing expedition was useless.

"You won't find information hard to get."

"It's a relief to hear that."

"Will you need secretarial help?"

"Maybe later, but then we'll have somebody sent down. About all I'll need is a corner somewhere, out of the way. Could you take me around and introduce me to the key production people?"

"I could take you on a tour of the whole setup."

"I don't want you to take time doing that. I'll just drift

around for awhile. Paul says it isn't something you can cover in an hour. It'll take me a long time to get it straightened out in my head. I'm the plodder type. Charlie is the bright half of the team."

Craig knew there was nothing stupid about Upson. He would say nothing unguarded. His face and expression were without guile, yet there seemed to be very little change of expression. His eyes were quick. For a moment Craig was puzzled, and then he knew exactly what the expression was. It was that of a man in a poker game who has been dealt his cards, but feels there is more to be gained by watching the way the others pick up their cards and sort them. His cards are always there. He can look later.

As they left the booth, Craig looked back and saw the copy of his report on the table. "Forget something?" he said.

Upson went back quickly. "Pretty stupid. I wouldn't want to lose this."

"It's easy enough to make another copy."

He could not escape the feeling that Upson had left it behind on purpose, and had gained something by analyzing his reaction.

As they walked back Bud said, "Paul says your family is in England for the summer."

"It seems strange to have them away." In a sense Bud had jabbed him again, probing. It was clear they had talked about him in Ober's office. And if they had gotten as far as the detail of Maura being away, the talk had been more than casual. Though the sun was hot on his forehead, he had a sense of chill. Ober had been too elaborately casual about his report. He could hear Ober's voice. "Here's a man who's been in the same slot too long. My guess is that he's stale. And he acts as if his nerves are a little shot. My instinct says get rid of him. I don't think his recommendations will be worth a damn. Bud, instead of putting you with Terrill, who satisfies me completely, I'll put you with Fitz. Give me your best judgment." Then Bud had asked questions, and it had come up about Maura being away.

And all the time L. T. Rowdy would have been sitting there, larded and owlish and still, waiting for the questions from Ober, and then he would take out his dime-

store notebook and turn immediately to the right page and
say in that thick choked little voice, words dripping like
wet pastry, "The suspect drove last night to a warehouse
area and, using his own key, entered the studio apartment of a woman known as Clementina Bennet at exactly
twelve twenty-three last night. The apartment lights were
turned off at twelve fifty. The suspect emerged from
that apartment at seven twenty this morning, made one
stop at his home for a change of clothing, a second stop
for breakfast, and arrived in his office at four minutes of
nine."

It was entirely too easy to see L. T. Rowdy down there
in the alley darkness, with the faintest gleam on heavy
lenses, motionless, tireless, inhumanly patient. Or Rowdy
behind the screen of lilac bushes, listening to the scene
with Floss, then writing pertinent notes.

The power of negative thinking, Craig thought. Take it
another step. Ober, Upson and Montgomery, watching
with their cold Martian eyes, while Rowdy and Miss
Commerford demonstrate, enacting the parts of Floss and
Craig, Rowdy, blindfolded, laying his wax hand on the
narrow gray belly of the arched Miss Commerford, her
skin puckered by the air conditioning, her bandeau and
bikini improvised of letterhead and transparent tape so
that across one buttock which, exposed, would have the
look of a half cantaloupe, there is inscribed QUALITY
METAL PRODUCTS DIVISION.

"So that was how it was," says Ober, and all three nod
and repeat in unison, "So that was how it was."

Rowdy strips off his blindfold, Miss Commerford rises
effortlessly, hauled erect by the piano wires spot-welded
from steel socket of hip to knee, concealed under the
clever forgery of the neoprene thighs. They link arms and,
in sideways rhythmic shuffle, exit to outer office with duet
—wet baritone against steak-knife soprano—"That was
how it was, we swear. That was how it was." After final wave of blindfold, door closes with a Chase Bank
click and Ober, standing, removing pipe, mustache, hair,
plastic nose and lenses of eyes, is exposed as an egg-thing
from Galaxy Q which says, "Now you know what we must
put up with."

"I beg your pardon?" Craig said.

Bud Upson gave him a puzzled glance and said, "I just

said you must get as much heat here as we have to put up with in Chicago."

"It gets rugged. The hills aren't high on either side of the river, and the valley, if you can call it a valley, is fifteen miles across. But there's just enough contour here to cheat us out of breezes. So we sit and steam and bake. Have you got a place to stay yet?"

"Paul arranged it. He got us two rooms with connecting bath at the Downtown Club. It's old-fashioned, but it's comfortable, and damn cheap."

"Are you married, Bud?"

"No. Charlie is closer to it than I am. It would be a hell of a life to wish on a girl. I've been living out of a suitcase for five years, Craig."

He took Bud into his outer office, introduced him to the staff. Craig asked Betty to arrange to get a desk and chair for Mr. Upson. He offered to rearrange things to put Bud near the windows, but Bud stated firmly that he would be perfectly happy in the corner half behind the door. Craig was aware of Betty's curiosity and her instinctive wariness. He took Bud around and introduced him to key production personnel. By that time he had fallen behind in his normal routine, so when Betty came into his office, obviously anxious to hear the score, he sent her out to get him a sandwich and coffee. That gave him a few moments to think of his curious flight of fancy, so like a nightmare. Unlike most thoughts of the same nature, the continual fleeting grotesqueries that infest the mind of every man, this had had a vividness and a continuity that had, for a time, blocked him off from conscious awareness of where he was and who he was with. It half amused and half disturbed him. This would indeed be a peachy time to go nuts. He knew that he would never again be able to look at Ober, Rowdy and Commerford in precisely the same way. There was something tantalizingly familiar about the unexpected mental aberration, and he groped cautiously for it. With a feeling of slight shock he realized what it was. Though such a weird tableau was alien to him, it would come naturally and almost automatically to Clemmie. Knowing all the people and all the facts, it was just what she would come up with. He wondered if there was any contagious aspect to the uncontrolled imagination. She, last night, had so expanded and embroidered the slave girl motif that it had been impossible to talk in any realistic and serious way.

When Betty brought the sandwich she said, "His desk is all set, Mr. Fitz."

"Thanks."

"Who is he?"

He looked up, leaned back. "Half of a team of two management specialists. They're conducting a survey."

"Why does he move in with us?"

"Why shouldn't he?"

"I don't like it."

"I don't think I know what you mean."

"He's a pretty suave-looking article, Craig. And what was he doing with a copy of your report? How did Mr. Ober like it?"

"Mr. Ober didn't look at it. Upson and his partner both got a copy. Later, God knows when, they're going to 'bounce it around.'"

"I don't like that, either."

"For God's sake, Miss James, maybe you could type a list of what you like and what you don't like. I do my work the best way I know how. If you're trying to infer I'm incompetent, say so. You act like I was being trailed by assassins."

She blinked and swallowed, backed a half step away and said, "Are you sure you're not?"

"The word is chopping out dead wood. You've heard that, I presume. You're afraid I'm dead wood."

"If you weren't upset you wouldn't snarl at me, Mr. Fitz. You're not dead wood or incompetent or anything like that. I could even explain how I feel if you'd be patient for twenty seconds."

"Go ahead, Miss James."

"There's a story about a bad thing happening to the bearer of bad tidings. This is sort of like that, if you know what I mean. Suppose instead of you in this job they had a man who is, say, the world's greatest administrator, and an engineering genius, and he worked twenty-four hours a day seven days a week. He *couldn't* do the job right because the job can't be done right, because the job is to go around patching and fixing and adjusting. It's like a terrible old car—a headlight falls off and while you're putting it back on a tire goes flat and while you're changing the tire the other headlight falls off. That's just the way it is. It makes them nervous upstairs. When you and John Terrill try to explain, they think you're making excuses. So it's a lot easier to get nervous about you than it is to try to listen to what you think ought to be done. And I don't want them *doing* that to you." Her voice went strange and she whirled and left the office.

A very dandy boost for my morale, he thought. But she has it pinned down very neatly. Maybe that's what's been happening to my nerves. That's where the confidence went, maybe. That's why I'm beginning to feel and act like a clerk. They say that if you train a rat in many mazes, and then put him in an insoluble one, he'll finally roll over, squeaking, and chew his paws in a curiously human way. My maze lends itself to about an eighty per cent solution. If I worked an eighty-hour week, I might conceivably boost it to eighty-one or two per cent. If I worked a ten-hour week, it would drop to maybe fifty per cent. So I balance my energies against a predictable degree of imperfection. If Upson is as shrewd as he appears to be, this may be the best thing that could have happened to me. My special problem, the problem that has kept me trapped in one job too long, will be presented objectively.

The other possible result is a not-too-glowing letter of recommendation and the quick heave back out into a world that each day seems more disconcertingly full of bland, wise, promising young men such as Upson and Montgomery.

The hell with it. Get to work.

But there is a change coming. It can be smelled from afar.

Al Jardine phoned Craig at five minutes of five.

"How about joining me for a knock at Nick's after work? When can you make it?"

"Quarter of six okay?"

"We'll be in the back room in a booth."

"We?"

"Yes. Brace yourself, wolf. Me and Steve Chews."

"Oh dear Jesus!"

"Did you think nobody noticed?"

"Al, it wasn't like . . ."

"Save it until later, Craig."

The bar at Nick's was crowded. The back room was
dimly lighted. He had to pause a moment until his eyes
adjusted, and then he saw Al and Steve in a corner booth,
drinks in front of them. Al hailed him and Craig walked
over and sat down. The waiter took his order for a tall
Scotch.

Steve was a colorless and apologetic man, and he looked
ill at ease, and not at all friendly.

"What's this all about?" Craig asked.

Al said lazily, "I'll summarize. At the party Wednesday
night you and the Westerling woman were making what
my Irene calls a spectacle of yourselves. Her husband was
aware of it. She was loading his drinks. That's why he
made the scene. Jealousy. Everybody saw you and Floss
go down by the tool shed and come back looking all
primed. She left and you left fifteen minutes later. She
was out all night. Lollie kept phoning your house. You
were out all night too. Yesterday Floss phoned Dave from
a hotel. He went down and got her. He checked at the desk
and found out she'd checked in at about eleven yesterday
morning. He took her home and he and Lollie went to
work on her. They broke her down. She says she was so
drunk she didn't know what she was doing. You took her
to a motel. She implies it was very close to rape. Then you
drove her into town and dropped her off. Dave is torn
between murdering you and divorcing her. Lollie is all
for divorce. I think we better have the story, Craig."

Craig put down half his drink. "My God, if there's any
implication of rape, it was the other way around. She told
me to leave in fifteen minutes and she'd be waiting down
by the playground. She went home and changed and
picked up a small suitcase. I didn't go home with her and
force her to change."

"She covered that," Steve said awkwardly. "She claims
you agreed to drive her into town and leave her at a
hotel. She said she was just going to punish Dave for kicking her in front of everybody. But instead you took her to
a motel."

"That's a damn lie. My God, Al, she drove the car. I
was in no shape to drive. She even found the motel."

"Can you prove she drove?" Al asked.

Craig thought for a moment and said, "No."

"Did you have relations with her?"

"I guess you could call it that. I'm pretty vague about it. We didn't wake up until ten. She was scared stiff. She hadn't intended to fall asleep. Listen, Al. This isn't a new deal with her. She's a tramp."

"But it's the first time she's been caught," Al said.

Steve seemed a little more friendly. "Dave is my cousin, Craig. Lollie has never liked Floss. Floss is trying to lie out of it, I'm sure. Now that I've heard your side of it, I have the feeling you're telling the truth. But Dave doesn't know what to believe. He's damn near out of his mind. I tell you, it's hell around that house. I hate to go home any more."

"What should I do?" Craig asked Al.

"It's pretty delicate. If he wants to try for a divorce and name you corespondent, it could clobber you nicely. Maybe we can pull some of the rug out from under him. Where did you stay?"

"A place called Pine Tree Cabins, out on Route 80, just this side of Forrestville."

"Nice place?"

"God, no. Sordid. It was the sort of place where they'd welcome—the sort of business we took there."

"Did you sign the register? What name?"

"Wait a minute. Now I remember. Jonathan Johnson. I don't remember what I put down for an address."

"On a registration card?"

"No. In a notebook."

"I'll pay a call. It shouldn't be hard to get that back, or cost too much."

"Then what?" Steve asked. "Where does that leave everything?"

"Then," Al said, "I see Dave and I give him my man-to-man lecture number twelve. The need for love and tolerance. Let him who is without sin and so forth. I tell him that in a sense it might have been Floss's fault, but really the fault is in the life we lead. Decay of moral values, too much strong waters. And so on. Give the girl another chance. It may strengthen the marriage instead of weaken it. Blah, blah, blah."

"Floss told me that Dave isn't the faithful type."

"If true, that will help. Can you shed any light, Steve?"

"I know there was some bad trouble a while back. Something about Dave and a waitress." He looked at his watch. "I've got to run along." He looked at Craig. "I'm just damn sorry this had to happen. I wish to God Maura hadn't gone away for the summer. It just doesn't seem like you, Craig. Damn it, it doesn't."

After Steve was gone Al said, "We certainly put on a lovely party, didn't we?"

"I didn't know I was being so damn obvious."

"You haven't had enough practice, maybe. I think it will blow over. But, my friend, you are not going to get away unscathed. You know Lollie. She is her own news service. By the time this week end is over, everybody you know is going to have the juicy details. And when Maura comes back, it is inevitably going to get back to her. And, knowing Maura, it's going to hurt her."

"What the hell can I do about it?"

"There isn't going to be much you can do. Jesus, Craig, why did you get mixed up with one of those? How was she?"

"I wouldn't know."

Al shook his head. "Irene is furious at you. And so are Jeanie and Alice. The great idol has tottered and fallen smack on its face. Let's get another round here, waiter."

"I don't know why I drank so much, Al."

"I've never seen you hit yourself so hard and often. I'm no psychiatrist, but are you trying to hide from anything."

"How do you mean?"

"Are you in any kind of a jam. At the plant? Financial? A woman? Health? Got any bad worries?"

Craig thought of Ober and of Clemmie. "Nothing I can't handle."

Al studied him for a moment. "Make sure of that. We've been friends a long time. I always had you cased as somebody who'd never make much of a client in the kind of law work I do. But I've been wrong about some others I cased the same way. A man is a pretty delicate organism emotionally. And a crack-up can come when you least expect it."

Craig forced a smile. "I'm not fixing to crack up, Al."

"Why don't you get a complete physical check? I don't like the way you look and act. You seem tightened up. You don't have that old control. You seem a little blurred around the edges, and frankly, and don't take offense, you're looking a little seedy."

"Lay off, Al!"

"I won't lay off until I scare you a little, ole buddy. You know about accident prones. In my work I get a different kind of prone. I don't know how to describe it. Call it a self-destruction prone. The tensions of the kind of life we lead pile up without our being aware of it. Then something gives. And you start a long ride down the chute. Or a short ride. The chute can be women or horses or liquor. But in every case it's a way to hide from the tensions, a way of sticking your fool head in the sand."

"For Christ sake, Al!"

"How come this is making you so uncomfortable? Am I hitting too close to home?"

"No. You're swinging wild."

"Okay. Is it like you, is it typical of Craig Fitz, to take a jump at that big, young, whining housewife?"

"No, damn it, but I was drunk."

"Okay. Is it typical of Craig Fitz to get so boiled?"

"No. I had no intention of doing so. I—I was making myself a drink. I was making it light because I'd had two that Chet had made me. Then I just reached out and took the bottle and slugged it good. I don't know why the hell I did. Maybe I'm lonesome. Maybe I'm worried about our new plant manager. Maybe I'm bored with my work. Does a man have to be completely logical in every single action?"

Al stood up and clapped him on the shoulder. "I've got to run, fella. I'll let you pay the check. I hope I've started you doing some thinking. If there's something chewing on you you haven't told me about, get to work on it and find a solution. And stop at the house when you can. I'll get Irene cooled off, and we'll sit around and tell lies. Hell, why don't you come along right now. You can keep her company while I go out and get that registration."

"Thanks, Al, but I think I better stop around another time."

"Be sure you do."

After Al had gone he sat and finished his drink. Maura was going to hear about it. There was no way to keep her from hearing about it. It made him sick to think of how it would be for her when she heard. He could deny it, and that wouldn't help much, or he could give her the full reason why he had decided to do it, why, with drunken logic, he had thought of Floss as an antidote to Clemmie.

The waiter came over and picked up the empty glasses and said, "Another, sir?"

"Please," he said. When the waiter was ten feet away he said, "Waiter!"

He turned. "Yes sir?"

"A double this time."

"Yes sir."

He drank the double slowly. Al was wrong. There was no danger of a crack-up. That was foolish melodrama. A stupid episode with Floss. The marriage would survive it. Marriages had survived worse. Much worse.

Seedy.

That could be fixed. Should be fixed at once. But why should Al try to make a big deal out of it? It was under-standable, certainly. A man's wife is away. So he gets a little careless.

What big problem?

The Clemmie problem was under control. Well under control. A summer affair. Nothing more. Discreet. And, anyway, the damage was done, wasn't it? That Floss thing fixed it. Once you bought your ticket, you might as well see the whole show.

He paid the check and left. The car was in a lot three blocks away. Dusk was over the city. He walked and swung his arms and felt very good, light on his feet, and half-smiling and leanly co-ordinated. He had an inexplicable feeling of anticipation. He knew he had had very little sleep, and it would be wise to eat and go home and sleep the clock around. But it was a summer dusk and he felt nimble and quick and he could hear music. He smiled at a pretty girl and winked a monstrous wink, and grinned inside when her face froze and she turned her head quickly to look the other way. The music was behind him and lost, and he hummed the melody and snapped his fingers in time to it.

He stopped in front of the parking lot and looked down the street and saw some white and elegant neon that spelled out, expensively, The Belle and Bottle.

He left his hat with a Botticelli virgin in the foyer, went in and sat in dim light at a padded bar stool, rested his arms on the padded edge of a freeform bar, sipped his Scotch and watched a tawny lass in a mirrored niche, in a black and silky sheath, in a pink spotlight, finger a pallid piano and sing, into a golden mike, with a husky and sinuous sensuality, "Lush Life," rocking her rounded silken hips on the bench in tempo.

He pulled a dime of his change to him and found the booth and dialed the number and heard her answer and heard, beyond her, the tinsel and rumble of party.

"Where have you been?" Her voice curled and whip-cracked.

"Am I supposed to be there?"

"You promised. You promised faithfully."

"I forgot."

"Get here," she said and hung up.

So he went back to the bar and took his time and listened to the questing lyrics and watched the red mouth make the words and told himself he would not go, even up to the time when he got into the car, right up to the moment when he had the final choice at the stop light, and turned right toward the river.

CHAPTER ELEVEN

IT WAS nearly nine when Craig drove into the alley beside the warehouse. The shadows were blue-black. He looked up and saw the light that came from the big window. There were cars parked by the loading dock, and a man in a chauffeur hat sitting on the dock, a pink glow on his face when he drew at his cigarette.

The big metal door was unlocked. When he pushed it open he heard the music from above. It was one of her records that she had played for him last week end on her high-fidelity equipment. Strange music, a stirring, eerie thing by a man named Chavez entitled *Toccata for Percussion*. She had played other music for him and had been amused and slightly contemptuous of his lack of knowledge of them. Bartok, Stravinsky, Sheldon, Stotl. Odd music, full of jagged edges and prolonged discords that seemed to set up a sympathetic resonance in his teeth. And since so much of that music had been a curiously apt background for the decadencies of their experimentations, that music, as he climbed the stairs, awakened specific memories, hollowing his belly and greasing his hands.

He looked up and saw Clemmie at the head of the stairs talking to a man. They stopped talking and looked down at him. Clemmie wore a white linen shirt, white tailored slacks, a gold mesh belt. Her hair was piled high on her head. She looked dainty, fragile and virginal. The man was elderly, stocky, brown as an Hawaiian. Crisp gray hair curled close to his head. He looked fit and forceful.

"Hello, Craig darling," Clemmie said in a caressing voice. "I was afraid Daddy was going to have to leave before you got here. Daddy, this is Craig."

They shook hands. The studio door was shut. Party sounds came from behind the door. George Bennet's handshake was hard and warm, and he looked at Craig with pale blue eyes startlingly like Clemmie's.

"I had about all of that group in there that I can take, Craig," Bennet said.

"Now, Daddy."

He released Craig's hand. Sighed. Looked at Clemmie. "Kitten, I'm no fool. I haven't led what you would call, in any sense of the word, a sheltered life. With a few exceptions, those people in there are degenerate trash. You claim they amuse you. I believe you collect them and expose me to them just as a part of your tiresome persecution of me."

She pouted. "Now, Daddy, really. No parlor psychiatry. They're creative people. That's why they make you uncomfortable. You're being too self-conscious about it."

He turned her around gently, slapped her across the back of the slacks and said, "Go on back into your snakepit, kitten, while I talk to your Craig."

She went meekly in and closed the door. Bennet offered cigarettes and Craig took one, lighted Bennet's and his own. He felt most uncomfortable.

"Clemmie's had a lot to say about you."

"I—I suppose she has, sir."

"George. Call me George. You're at Quality Metal Products."

"That's right."

"You look mature enough to know what I'm talking about, Craig. Maybe you're mature enough to handle her, maybe even understand her."

"I hope so, sir. George."

"She's my only child. I had too much money. I've always had too much money. I wanted all the fun and all the games, and the money was nice because I could put her in good schools and tell my conscience I was doing well by her. I rejected her, Craig. And that rejection drove her into a horrible experience when she was fifteen. I won't go into details, but she had to be institutionalized. And since then she's never been—completely stable. She needs stability. And maturity. And understanding. I can't control her."

"I . . . understand."

"I like you, Craig. I like the look of you. I've been hoping she would . . . form an attachment to somebody with his feet on the ground."

Craig dropped his cigarette and ground it out. "Maybe you don't understand. I—I'm married."

There was no expression on Bennet's face. "She mentioned that."

"Well, I . . ."

"I've got to get along. I'll give you a ring. We'll have lunch one day." Again the firm handshake, and George Bennet went down the stairs, holding himself and moving like a much younger man.

Craig waited a few moments and then went in. The big studio seemed crowded with people, a confusion of areas of bright light and deep shadow, talk and motion, glitter and change. Clemmie came swiftly to him and her fingers were cool around his wrist as she drew him over to the bar improvised from the large painting table. He fixed a drink for her and one for himself.

"Take care of my poor bewildered, precious little girl," she said, making her voice deep.

"Something like that."

"Well, are you?"

He touched his glass to hers. "In one way or another. Do I get dragged around and introduced?"

"Gawd, no. Come over here, Fitzhoney. Now this is a lovely vantage point. Get set for an intensive briefing. The barefoot and raddled blonde doing the strenuous interpretive dance is named Hildy. She used to do it for a living. The powerful young man who looks like an Indian is her husband, Rick Kelly. He paints. They live out in Belson Village. Rick is about twelve years younger than Hildy. They can't actually get married or the alimony would stop. Over there on the couch and on the floor by it is the intellectual set. The big pasty one with the ginger hair, the one sounding off now, is Fletch Harrikon, probably refuting Barzun. The small fussy-looking man trying to interrupt him is an essayist named Morton DeVell, and that bored-looking young boy with the curls and the salmon pants is Morton's latest acquisition. Derivation, pure gutter American. The other member of the group, the mean-looking man with the gray butch cut, is Jake Romney. He's a collector. He's fondling his latest acquisition."

Craig, looking across the room, saw the girl who sat on the floor at Romney's feet, her head against his thigh. Romney, while listening to Harrikon, rubbed the nape of her neck. She had a coppery skin, a sullen and vital face, a ripe body so precariously confined in a light cotton dress that it looked as though she could burst it with one indolent stretch. Her eyes were half-closed, her feet broad and bare.

"Jake was in Guatemala dickering for some ancient gunk, and he found Esperanza and brought her back on some sort of a tourist permit. He could get in trouble, but probably won't. She's only sixteen. Now look over there. That woman in boy clothes, with the silver hair and the Viking face, smoking the little cigar, is Gretchen McRory. She came uninvited. She's very tiresome. She has a crush on me. The frumpy little overdressed matron type talking to Gretchen is a nothing named Mrs. Hudge. Bernice Hudge. Let me see now. Oh, that businessman type standing alone and looking bored and uncomfortable is Dan Bradley. And the tall, slim, blonde, lovely young thing over there talking to the man in jeans is Taffy Bradley, Dan's second wife and one of my most long-term friends. The man in jeans, with the beautiful body and the El Greco face, is Raoul Caprichos. He's a dancer, a true dancer, not a fake like Hildy. He could be a great dancer if he weren't so lazy. And that's the lot. Have I missed anyone? No. Daddy thinks they're terrible unwholesome, all but Dan Bradley and poor little Mrs. Hudge." She laughed and when he looked at her he saw that she had had more to drink than he had guessed.

"It's—an unusual group," he said uncomfortably.

She gave him a tilted and hoyden look and said, "Poor stuffy Craig. You look as disapproving as Daddy. I'm almost tempted to shock you right out of your socks, darling."

"Go ahead," he said, attempting to sound casual. "I might be tougher to shock than you realize."

"Let me try then. I'll tell you the wheels within wheels. Young salmon-pants is getting bored with poor Morton. I just hope that when he decides to leave he won't beat Morton up like the last one did. The center of tension tonight is Raoul, though. When male dancers aren't queer they're almost desperately male. Raoul is all male, and he's been zeroed in on that Indio girl, Esperanza, all evening, without having to say a word to her. Esperanza is aware of it, and so is Jake Romney and so is poor Bernice Hudge, and so is Taffy. Bernice is Raoul's current means of support. See her look at him with all that naked yearning adoration. Raoul is working her for all he can get. But right now he wants Esperanza. Bernice is alarmed about Esperanza, but actually she should be alarmed about Taffy. Our Taffy has Raoul squarely in her sights, but Raoul isn't aware of it yet, and Dan Bradley certainly isn't. And Taffy generally gets what she goes after. It's an interesting operation to watch. Shocked yet?"

"Not yet."

She looked up at him with an odd expression. "Then try this, dearest. Taffy has been angling for Raoul ever since I gave her a full report. He's very virile and practically tireless, dearest. And I take it Dan isn't."

He felt his face get red and his muscles tighten. He looked down at her incredulously. "You mean you . . ."

"But, darling! I wasn't alone with him! He brought a friend. A little Pole named Yancha with the most incredible breasts I've ever seen. It took us days to exhaust him. But does it matter, dear? That was before I knew you."

He knew his face was contorting. He wanted to smash his glass against her eyes. "You're sick!" he said.

"Hush, baby," she said, touching her finger to his lips. "Taffy is giving me a signal."

She left him. He made a fresh drink. Clemmie and Taffy stood together in a corner, talking earnestly, the tall blonde, the tiny brunette, both fresh and poised and lovely and utterly evil. He looked at all the others, and walked over to where Dan Bradley stood and introduced himself. Bradley was fifty, large, soft, redfaced, an older version of the same physical type as Bill Chernek and Chet Burney.

"Where have I seen you before, Fitz? General Lighting?"

"No. I'm at Quality Metals."

"Hell, we do a lot of your short haul stuff. B and L Trucking. I owned it. I sold out a while back for a fat capital gains. A man's a fool to work his ass off when they take it away from you fast as you can make it in salary and profits. But I rigged a consultant deal out of it so I'm still on the old expense account. You known Clemmie long?"

"Not very long, no."

"Taffy—that's my wife over there in the blue—she and Clemmie are old buddy buddies. So I have to come to these things. Taffy thinks they're the apex of glamor or something. These jokers give me a pain. I'll bet we're the only sound people in the place, Fitz."

"They're different."

Bradley had a deep laugh. "They sure in hell are. I'm sorry to see that McRory woman here. She always makes some kind of a pass at Taffy. It makes my stomach turn over. That Kelly guy doesn't seem so bad, but did you ever see one of his paintings? Like somebody threw Easter eggs into an electric fan. My God, if one of my kids ever got mixed up in a crowd like this, I'd blow my stack. But there's no danger, I guess. They're good kids. Jimmy is taking aeronautical engineering at M.I.T. and doing damn well. Kit got married her second year of college. I raised hell but it didn't do any good, I guess. She's happy enough, she says. The kids are by my first wife, Marge. We broke it up three years ago. Agreed to disagree, like they say. Then I married Taffy. She's a great girl."

"She's very beautiful."

"She's got a real sense of humor and a lot of life. Good head on her, too. My friends wondered what an old joker like me was doing getting mixed up with the young

stuff and breaking up my marriage, then marrying a
twenty-one year old kid, but when they meet her, they
catch on fast. But we don't see much of the old crowd
any more. They're pretty dull for Taffy. She likes to
travel. You know, she's got friends all over the world. Her
people had money, but Taffy got screwed out of her in-
heritance when she was twenty-one. I'm glad to have the
business off my neck. You got to have fun while you're
still alive, Fitz. Next month we're flying down to São
Paulo and have a time. God, you couldn't even get Marge
on an airplane. If I'd stuck with Marge, I'd have spent
the next fifteen years easing myself into the coffin. A
young girl like that keeps you young, Fitz, and don't you
forget it." He nudged Craig heavily and winked broadly.

Taffy and Clemmie came over to them, arm in arm,
smiling.

"What have you two been cooking up?" Dan Bradley
asked. Clemmie introduced Craig to Taffy. Liquor had
softened Taffy's mouth and slightly glazed her eyes. As
soon as he could Craig got Clemmie aside.

"You were making that up, weren't you?" he said.

"Of *course*, darling," she said, too blandly. "Now I
have the most delicious little ending to what I was telling
you before. Taffy was talking to Raoul and Bernice. She
took a big chance and switched to French, and fortunately
Bernice has no French at all. So, right in front of the poor
little lamb, Taffy set it up with Raoul. So tomorrow, dear, I'm homeless from two to five."

He looked beyond Clemmie at Dan and Taffy Bradley.
Dan had his big arm around the girl's slim waist. His
thick hand was at the indentation of her waist, his fingers
working as he smiled down at her. Taffy, with mask
face, was looking across the room, her stare locked with
Raoul Caprichos, her underlip swollen.

The evening continued. He drank. He blurred the
voices and the movements with drink, but he could not
blur the sick and vivid little images in the back of his
mind. Raoul and Clemmie. He tried not to look at Raoul.
He had a startling breadth of shoulder, lean waist, belly
and hips. His dark hair was long, his face pale, his nose
sharply beaked. His eyes were flat, green and feline. He
had a look of cruelty, humor, and complete and arrogant
maleness. Craig knew that Clemmie was ignoring him be-

cause of his sour mood. The intellectuals had switched to French. Morton and the boy in salmon pants were having a bitter, whispered quarrel. Dan Bradley kept trying to make conversation with him. The others ignored him.

Once, as he was making another drink, he looked over at Raoul who leaned against the wall, thumbs hooked in the waistband of the jeans. The Indio girl was standing close to him, talking to him. Craig saw Jake Romney walk quickly over, spin the girl around, and hit her in the stomach with his fist with great force. The girl doubled, gagged and fell. There was a sudden hush in the big room. Then the conversation began again, and did not stop when Romney pulled her to her feet and struck her again. Raoul restrained him and spoke quietly to him. Romney nodded, his face chill. He went over and said good night to Clemmie and nodded at the others. Raoul had pulled the girl up. She was crying silently, hands pressed to her stomach. Romney took her by the arm and left with her. He did not notice DeVell and the boy leave. Harrikon made a florid ceremony of his departure, bowing low to kiss Clemmie's hand.

He overheard a private conversation between Dan and Taffy Bradley. He was pleading with her to leave.

"Get me one more big stiff drink, lover, and then I'll go."

"You've had enough, baby. You'll pass out again, honey."

"I faithfully promish—promise I will stay awake long enough to fulfill my wifely obligash—obliga . . ."

"That's a hell of a thing to say."

"Get the drink!"

He moved away so as not to overhear more. He saw them when they left, right after the Kellys. Taffy gave one last glance back at Raoul. It was not a sensuous look. It was a quiet look. Young girl contemplating death. The dancer yawned. When he left, walking lithely, Bernice Hudge trotted busily at his side and got to the door first and opened it for him.

Gretchen McRory was the last. She sat on the couch and lighted a small cigar.

Clemmie went over to her and said, "Dearie, you're not going to outwait Craig. He's what you might call a house guest. So clump away, dearie, silly cigar and all."

McRory's face turned dark red. She gave Craig a look of virulent hatred. She stomped to the door, slammed it shut behind her. Clemmie laughed. "She's so tiresome. She does illustrations. Children's books. She's really very good at it, but she despises children."

She pirouetted, then spun into Craig's arms, hung against him for a moment, then pushed away and looked up at him and wrinkled her nose. "You are dronk, Baron."

"Need any help?"

"A faithful Swede will be in in the morning to hoe the place out, dearest. But you could make us a special nightcap. I think a very tall, tall brandy and soda. Look in the kitchen like a dear. There are some enormous glasses. Then I'll let you go. And if I forget it, please remember to put the latch on down below. Gretchen might be lurking around down there."

As he made the drinks, she went around and turned out most of the lights, then collapsed on the couch, propping herself up on the pillows. She looked small and drained, and when she yawned she made a little sound at the end, like the lost yowl of a kitten. He sat by her feet and they touched the glasses together.

"Like my friends?" she said casually.

"Is it required?"

"Of course not. I don't like them. All but Taffy. Why should you? But you seemed to be hitting it off with Dan. Did you boys compare Rotary buttons or something? You looked as if you were trying to disassociate yourself from all the rest of us, including me. This is a tiresome drink, lover. Go put some brandy in it, please."

As he walked over to the table he said, "Dan kept following me around."

"Poor old Dan. Taffy shot him on the rise. He looks frightful. She keeps him going at a dead run. When he drops, she's got it made. It isn't like her to be so calculating because actually she's kind of warm and crazy."

"Warm for that dancer. I think the whole thing is sordid."

She looked at him round-eyed. "But of course it is!"

"Clemmie, I just can't imagine you and that . . ."

"Hush now! I will not stand for any obligatory emotional scenes. I'm much too tired and you're much too drunk. You seem to want it between the eyes. All right. I slept with Raoul. It didn't mean anything to him or to me. He's as vain as a show horse. If you want to be real stupid, ask me for a complete personal history some time. I might give it to you."

"But these people . . ."

"They amuse me. There's always something going on. There's always emotional tension. They take their little re-shufflings in such dreadful earnest. And all evening you looked like a man in a parade trying to pretend he hadn't stepped in anything. I have other groups, you know. One group will talk of nothing but sailing. Then there's a horse group and a dog group. They amuse me less. And, my dear, you don't seem to be amusing me at all right now. Not at all."

"I don't understand you, Clemmie."

She sat up. "What's this fetish people have about understanding other people. Do I ask to be understood? Do I beg for it? There's nothing significant to understand. I want to be alive. I want to feel alive. I want to take my single turn around the track at a sprightly pace, lifting my knees high, baby. So I make things happen to me. Like Raoul. I wasn't impressed. Children walk on high narrow railings. It's the same motivation, probably. If I'm afraid of anything, my dearest, I'm afraid of going stale on life, of being grim, of losing all the magic of being sensuously involved in life. So why sweat something out that isn't important? Do I look shopworn or something?"

"Clemmie . . ."

"Kindly stop making moose calls at me, Craig, sir. If you want to be a love, make it your turn to be a slave. Will you be?"

"Anything you want."

"Let me see. First I want my face washed with a very cold washcloth. Then I want to be carried to my bed, and I want to be gently undressed. Then I want an alcohol rub on my back, and I want to fall asleep while that is happening, and I want to be otherwise left alone. And then tomorrow I will be all alive again, all for you. But now I am going to be a boneless doll. Can you stand one more request?"

"Of course."

"Don't go home. I'd like to fall asleep knowing you're going to sleep out here. Fix that latch thing downstairs. The Swede doesn't come until eleven. Tomorrow I am going to see that you get a haircut because you are shaggy.

And buy you a shirt I saw. Then something normal to do
with the day—so utterly normal that you can stop thinking about my horrible friends. Please stay here, darling.
Sleep out here. I'll sleep so much better if I know you're
close. Now go down and make sure the outside door is on
the latch or on the lock or whatever the hell it is when
you push that little button so you can't open it without a
key. Then the cold cloth. Wait a minute. I'm not going to
say another word, so kiss me good night now. There. Good
night, darling."

She was as relaxed and boneless as she had promised.
After he had undressed her and rolled her face down on
the cot, he located the rubbing alcohol in the closet in the
bathroom. Light came into the bedroom from the studio.
He rubbed her pale strong back, digging his fingers into
the muscles, tracing hard with his palm the clean lines
down to the small of her back. When he pressed hard she
grunted with sleepy contentment. As he worked he thought
of her with Raoul, imagined his use of her, and the thought
was a dull redness in the back of his mind. It was a curious jealousy, mixed with tenderness. After a long time he
seemed to feel a change, feel the texture of sleep under his
fingers, and he became gentler with her. Her breathing
became long and deep. He bent over her and kissed her
shoulder lightly, tasting the tartness of alcohol against his
lips, smelling the party smoke caught in her thick black
hair. He pulled the sheet over her.

Just as he reached the door she stirred and said in a
slurred yet understandable voice, a voice from the other
edge of sleep, "I guess you know I'm going to marry you."
He went back and stood by the bed. She was indubitably
asleep, with a faint snore of exhalation that was like the
purring of a cat.

CHAPTER TWELVE

BETTY JAMES had suggested the public camp ground at
Lake Eldon, nearly forty miles south of Stoddard. He
had picked her up shortly after nine at the small frame

house where she lived with her mother and her two children. Her mother was a heavy woman with a tragic face, a listless, whining voice. She scrutinized Craig very carefully. It annoyed him out of all proportion to be introduced as Mr. Robertson. And he was appalled by Betty's attitude, an entirely unsuitable elfin gaiety, coy and bouncy. It looked as though the day might be much worse than he had anticipated.

Betty's mother warned them about all the drunken drivers, and the treacherous lake water, and the danger of getting under a tree in a thunderstorm. She told them not to buy the children a lot of stuff they couldn't digest, and watch them every minute they were in the water, and don't let them swim for an hour after eating. She told Betty to stay out of the sun because she knew she never tanned but each summer it seemed as though she wasn't happy until she had to go to bed with chills and fever from a bad burn.

Though the two children were in practically a frenzy of excitement and anticipation, they seemed to be well-behaved. There was Dickie, who was six, a skinny, sandy kid with a peeling nose and hot blue eyes. And Sally, who was four, with darker complexion, somber brown eyes—chunky, square and placid.

While Craig carried the picnic basket to the car, Betty carrying thermos jug, bathing suits and towels, her mother plodded along with them, repeating all warnings, her tone of voice conveying her certainty that the day would most certainly end in some unimaginable disaster.

As they drove down the block, the kids and gear in the back, Betty beside him in the front, she gave a great sigh and said, "I thought we'd never get away from there. What did you bring?"

"Some beer in a cooler in the back end."

"And a swimsuit?"

"No."

"I guess you can rent one. Isn't it a perfect day. It's not so sticky. Yesterday was a horror, wasn't it?"

"It certainly was."

Once they were out of the city the miles passed smoothly. Traffic was heavy. The kids chortled in the back seat. At one point they started to quarrel. Betty swung around at once, kneeling on the front seat.

"All right, you two. Hold out your hand, Sally."

"But he—"

"Out!" There was a quick stinging smack, and Sally began to whimper desolately.

"Now you, Dickie." Another smack. "Don't snivel at me. Every time you start that, the same thing happens." She turned around and plumped back down into the seat. There was a dismal silence from the back seat for five minutes. And then they were as happy as before.

After one imperative gas station stop, requested by Sally, they reached the public camp ground at ten-thirty. It seemed to be packed. Craig pulled up beside the registration booth.

"Sorry, folks," the tanned attendant said. "We can't let any more cars in. There isn't a table or a locker or an inch of beach left. This is the biggest day we've ever had."

"But what do we *do?*" Betty demanded indignantly, leaning across Craig.

"I can't help you there, lady. I got my orders: no more cars."

Craig swung around and turned back out onto the highway. "Got any ideas?" he said.

"Nobody is going to spoil this day. Just follow this road. Go slow. It looks as though it goes all the way around the lake."

The lake was about ten miles long, three miles wide. They passed scores of summer cottages. Dun Roamin', Our Hideaway, Seven Pines, Nick's Nook, Sootsus. Betty sat well forward on the seat, her jaw clamped with determination. When they came to a place advertising beach cottages to rent, she said, "Stop here. You watch the kids."

She went into the store and office. She was gone ten minutes. When she came back a man was walking slowly with her. She was talking to him earnestly, with many gestures. He looked uncomfortable. They came up to the car.

She said, "Craig, he's completely rented, but on one cottage, the people won't arrive until tomorrow morning. He says it's all cleaned up and ready for them. It has a private beach. I've been trying to tell him that we'll only spend the day. We won't disturb anything."

"Lady, I just . . ."

"Do my husband and I look like the sort of people

who'll mess up your place? We understand the situation. Just tell us how much you want."

The man made a helpless gesture. "Sure you won't let those kids run loose in the cottage?"

"Of course."

"I guess I could let you take it. How about twenty dollars?"

She opened her purse, took out a ten dollar bill and handed it to him. "You know perfectly well this is ten dollars you wouldn't have otherwise. I certainly am not going to be gouged."

"Lady, I can't . . ."

"You've accepted that money. Now don't try to give it back to me. Just get us the key, please."

The man looked as if he wished he could break into tears. He sighed. He put the bill in his pocket. He trudged back to the store. Craig pulled up beside the store. He came out and handed the key to Betty. "It's the last one on the left. Honest to God, lady, please don't mess it up. I got no help here until tomorrow afternoon."

"You worry too much," she said. "Let's go, Craig."

They drove down to the cottage. It was directly on the lake shore. There was a small screened porch, a tiny rustic living room, a primitive kitchen and bath, two bedrooms with unfinished walls, the studding showing. It was shining clean throughout.

"Imagine him being so nervous about *this!*" she said.

"Betty, you astonish me."

"I know," she said, with a grimace. "I've heard it so many times before. They say, 'I couldn't do that. I couldn't get away with that. I wouldn't have the nerve.' For goodness' sake, we'll never see him again. And here we are, with a private beach, instead of driving around and ending up eating in some farmer's field. Let's get the stuff in."

"Let me split that fee with you."

"I wouldn't think of it. Kids! You can get your suits on now." They brought the stuff onto the screened porch. Craig opened two beers. The children raced up and down the beach. It was the sort of day when the water is very blue. There were fast boats, and many water skiers.

"I'll look around," she said. "Maybe there's a pair of swimming trunks you could wear."

"Actually, I'd just as soon skip it. I'll be comfortable right here. You go ahead."

"I'll go change," she said. "Keep an eye on the kids. Yell if Dickie tries to go in alone."

She came out in a tightly fitted one-piece aqua suit with V-slits laced with white at the sides of the thighs. She moved in a self-conscious way and said, laughing, "Here goes nothing."

She ran down the slope of beach. Craig, watching her, thought the most grotesque thing a woman can do is run when you can watch her from the rear. Her body was acceptable, waist just slim enough to make a proper contrast to hips and breasts. She was chunky but not soft. Her skin had a rough, reddened texture, particularly on the tops of her thighs. He sensed that she wanted him to be pleased with her. She swam clumsily, with a great deal of splashing, but with respectable speed—a determined kind of swimming—stolid as a tug. She came back to shore and took the yelling kids in.

He sipped his beer, looking out at them but not seeing them. Clemmie had talked about having an utterly normal day. If he could imagine himself married to Betty, this was a normal day. Clemmie could not achieve this kind of normality.

Yesterday morning he had awakened in the green pool of light that came through the draperies, awakened by the sounds she made as she exercised at the bar. She was unaware of him. For a time he watched her intent face, and the sweat-darkened leotard, and then slid back into sleep. When he awakened again, he could hear her shower. When he awakened the third time, she was sitting at the foot of the couch wearing a hip-length wisp of sheer black nylon lace that fastened at her throat with a red ribbon. She sipped her coffee and said, "Hello, sleepy you."

"Time is it?"

"Nine-thirty, darling. Sleep well?"

He said he had, and he yawned. She had a quality of briskness about her on this Saturday morning, the faintly patronizing flavor of a suburban housewife with a mental list of errands.

"Hungover, dear?"

"There is a dull thump in the attic. But bearable."

When he came back in his striped shorts after brushing his teeth, she had put the bedding away, opened the draperies, put juice and coffee on the low table in front of the couch. He asked her just what she had meant by the curious remark about marriage as she was going to sleep. She denied making it. She accused him of making it up because he was spoiling for a fight. They both became angry. Quite unexpectedly she slapped him. Her hand was hard. Spilled coffee stung his bare foot. He managed to grab her wrists. It took an astonishing amount of strength to hold her. When she sagged, exhausted, he released her, and found out it had been a trick only when she lunged at him again. He could not catch her wrist. He grappled with her, and in the midst of the ridiculous combat it turned, quite suddenly, into something else entirely. Later, in his arms, she sulkily admitted that she had made the remark about marriage, but it didn't mean anything. They showered together in the large stall, and had more coffee and were leaving just when a monolithic and impassive woman named Olsen arrived to clean up.

First came the haircut, and then they shopped and she insisted on buying him a shirt of Egyptian cotton styled in Italy, paying more for it than he had ever been willing to pay for a sports shirt. Then she found hand-tailored English slacks in a shade of linen he would never have bought for himself. They had coffee nearby while cuffs were being put on the slacks. Then he dressed in the new clothing and looked at himself in the mirror of the expensive shop and was pleased with the effect.

As he walked down the street with her, carrying the box with his other clothing in it, she said, "And next time you get a haircut, lover, I'm going to have a word with your barber. The way you wear it is utterly wrong for the shape of your head. I'm going to make you over, pet, and when I'm done you are going to look very casually distinguished, instead of like some kind of a clerk."

"I've been doing all right."

"Ho ho! You go around looking as if you're bucking for the ways and means committee of the Lions Club. I want you to look as if you're killing time while little men are servicing your private airplane. The look of success, darling, is a sort of calculated arrogance."

Just as they were nearing the car, he saw Jeanie Tribbler walking toward them. She carried an armful of packages and she was walking slowly, looking in the shop windows. He tried to keep looking the other way, but as they neared her he could not prevent a quick and cautious glance at her and, to his consternation, found her looking directly at him. He smiled and nodded and said, "Hello, Jeanie."

"Hi, Craig," she said, and half hesitated, willing to stop if he showed an indication of introducing them. He continued on. The fading smile felt stiff on his lips. He had not missed the intentness with which Jeanie had looked at Clemmie. He glanced at Clemmie, trying to see her through Jeanie's eyes. A small and arrogant looking young girl with white skirt, yellow blouse, white thong sandals, thin gold clasp on the lush black horsetail. Black burnished bangs curling almost to the line of black brows. Small pointed face. Sauntering, ungirdled walk, hips swaying the white skirt. She looked up at him with mocking amusement, and did not speak until they were in the car.

"You could have been wearing a sandwich sign, of course."

"What does that mean?"

"Let me see. White background, bold black letters. Something very simple. Like: I am sleeping with this girl. Sleeping could go in italics, I suppose."

"She wouldn't think that."

"Oh, wouldn't she now! Let me show you something, you lovable blunderer. Suppose you were alone. Suppose, thirty paces before we met that little figurine called Jeanie, one of the office girls had come out of a store and you walked along with her, all casual and innocent. What would you have done when you met Jeanie?"

He swallowed. His throat felt tight. "Stopped and chatted, I guess."

"Go on."

"Introduced them. Talked about the party the other night."

"See? But instead you stride on with a horrid frozen grin on your face, your ears bright red, both hands plunged deep in the cookie jar. Darling, you have all the knack for intrigue of a sheep-chasing Airedale. Stay loose. The next time that happens, pretend I'm an acquaintance and act accordingly."

"You, of course, have had a hell of a lot of practice."

"Now don't go all hairy. It comes naturally to women. Who is she? She's a stunning little thing. All ivory and rose leaves. But she looks as cold as a witch's aspirations."

"Jeanie Tribbler. She and Joe are friends of mine and Maura's. He's at National Lighting, assistant to the sales manager."

"And the four of you have jolly times together at the Rivergreen Country Club."

"Cut it out, Clemmie."

"Jeanie fixed me with a very beady and suspicious eye. She's very fond of Maura, I suppose?"

"She is."

"And that will give her a perfect excuse to conduct a full-scale investigation. Save Craig from himself. But just be thankful, honey, that I didn't follow my impulses. I had an urge to hug your arm, look up at you with sticky adoration, and say something gooey and incriminating when she came within range. Let's drop it right here. This is our normal day. I want something so standardized it will be quaint, darling."

"No county fairs."

"Of course not, pet. We *never* repeat. That's one of our primary rules of procedure. Let's do something indigenous. A segment of Americana."

So they went to Stoddard Stadium to a baseball game, and they played a variation of her game wherein they were married and she was a nagging and neglected wife who was seldom taken anywhere by her husband. They ate peanuts and hotdogs and drank beer. The sun baked them. The game was dull and they left in the bottom half of the seventh. On the way back she saw a big new bowling arena, and they went in and bowled several games and drank more beer from chilled mugs. She was a novice and she looked very cute and very provocative, switching her hips as she tripped up to the foul line to release the ball. She soon acquired a self-appointed instructor, a swarthy man with a gold grin who told them to call him Howie. She began to act so indifferent to Craig and so flirtatious toward Howie that he made an effort to move in, buying them beer and whispering to Clemmie, making her giggle. Craig felt the familiar dull-red glow of jealousy. When Clemmie started to get a blister on the inside of her thumb, she became tired of bowling and tired of Howie, and cut him off very deftly by telling him that she and Craig had to get back home to their three kids. If Craig hadn't been so annoyed with her, he would have been forced to laugh at Howie's stunned and incredulous expression.

They stopped at a small bar and had cocktails and, because he was still quietly angry at her, and because he wanted to hurt her, he told her the Floss episode, in complete detail. He wanted to make her feel rejected and jealous. But, when he was finished, after hearing him out with no change of expression, she broke into laughter, and laughed helplessly for a long time while he sat glowering at her.

When she was under control again, she patted his hand and said, "Poor beastie. Poor ole mixed-up monster. That little adventure must have had all the charm of a soap opera."

"Don't you give a damn? Don't you give a single damn?"

"Of *course* I do, baby. I treasure those little gestures of rebellion, I really do. Last Wednesday night. My, my! While I was waiting for you, you were out motelling with a mother of three. I certainly couldn't be annoyed, could I? Just think of how I benefit from the contrast. Try it any time, laddie. I encourage comparison shopping. And isn't it delicious irony that your limey lady will clobber you for that little clumsy adventure instead of all our giddy sins? For heaven's sake, kindly stop looking so black and sour. Smile at me."

"Just tell me why you have to rub yourself on a clown like that Howie? Tell me that."

"It's all jealous, isn't it? Suppose you call it Clemmie's quest for reassurance. I just love the way they get all hot-eyed and insinuating, and the way their hands shake and their mouths get dry and they keep congratulating themselves on this incredible stroke of luck. He had it all figured out how we could ditch you. Then, when he started to look smug, I let him have it. He's still talking to himself. So that's fine."

"Do you hate them?"

"A girl of my base instincts couldn't possibly hate men,

darling. Now could I? Really? Finish your drink. Clemmie wants heavy food. Bratwurst and kraut and black
draught beer, and there is a fine, fine kraut place on
Stafford Street, where all the waiters are sixty-six and
they all have bunions and they all despise the customers."

So they ate the heavy food and then she wanted to go to
a drive-in movie. They got back to her place at midnight and he felt as though he had never been so tired in
his life, but Clemmie was avid for him and weariness was
soon forgotten.

"Knock, knock," Betty said, standing in front of him,
sandy hair soaked flat to her head, water droplets on her
body. "What kind of deep thoughts are those?"

The kids were digging a hole in the beach. She toweled
her hair and sat beside him on the porch, with beer and
cigarette, in her damp suit, and, after many hesitations,
made the openings she wanted and told him the story of
her life, of a college marriage to one W. Browning James,
called Brownie. Two kids and a weak husband who resented the responsibilities of marriage and who, after losing too many jobs, became increasingly alcoholic until he
had to be institutionalized. Betty had earned a Florida
divorce and come back and gotten a job with Quality
Metals.

He felt remote as he listened to her. His mind would
wander and then he would hear her voice again and pick
up the threads of the long story. He knew that as recently
as a few months ago he would have been very interested
in hearing about it, because he had wondered about her.
But now it seemed like a very dull story indeed. And despite his previous curiosities, he had little interest in hearing it.

It disturbed him to be so indifferent, to have to pretend an interest he could not feel. It was as though he was
losing touch with life. Clemmie had introduced him to
such intensities that everything else seemed pale and colorless and rather far away.

"So I'm getting along," she said. "There's nothing at
home. Except the kids, of course. So that's why I put so
much into the job. Too much, I guess."

"Not too much, Betty."

"I've wanted a chance to talk to you like this. Oh, not about me. Not my ancient history. But about the job and where you're going."

"Do you know where I'm going?"

She looked at him steadily for long seconds, and said, "Out, Craig. Out on your ass. That's where you're going. I use that kind of a word because I want to jolt you. I have to jolt you."

He did not feel anger. He did not even feel very interested. There was a visceral quiver of alarm, easily stifled. "What makes you think that?"

"You're a nice guy. There are some little people around that shop who'd jump off the roof for you. You're too nice a guy for that outfit. It's too hard-nose for you. You could ride along all right until Ober came in. It's the wrong kind of company for you. You don't get along there on merit. You get along if you carry a sharp knife and know whose back to put it into."

"You're being pretty dramatic, Betty."

She touched his arm and drew her hand back quickly. "I'm not! I'm rough, Craig. I'm as rough as they are. I've tried to think of some way of telling you. According to the latrine-o-grams, you may last two months, and you may last six. Ober doesn't think you have enough drive. Chernek is knifing you every chance he gets. I don't know why. I thought he was a friend. But he is. And there's something else. You seem to be going along with it. Like you're giving up. You know that special report wasn't any good."

"He shouldn't have asked me to make it."

"He threw you a slider to see what you'd do with it."

"I didn't do much. I admit that."

"It's just the last few weeks. As if you don't give a damn any more, Craig. I've got something at stake too. I couldn't stomach being sent back to the steno pool. I want to protect both of us."

"So what do I do? Got any suggestions?"

She hitched the wicker chair closer to his. "You make fourteen five. I'm not supposed to know that, but I do. You'll be forty soon. If you're bounced out, and stay unemployed for sixty days, you'd be glad to get back in somewhere, anywhere, for eight five. Personally, I don't think you can salvage anything at Quality. It's gone too far. But if you handle it right, I think you can ease right out from under the ax. If you move fast. You've got contacts. Your present title has a nice ring to it. You've got a good excuse for looking for a new position. You're in a dead end job. Ooze confidence. You're loyal, of course, but there comes a time when a man has to think of himself. You would consider seventeen five provided the job has some challenge."

"For God's sake!"

"I'm not dreaming this up, Craig. You *must* take it seriously. You're going stale in that job. It's a crucial time for you. You've got to beat Ober to the draw."

"Are you trying to terrify me?"

"Don't you dare smile. This is important. If you move now, you can have twenty years of increasing pay and better jobs. If you don't move now, this will be the farthest you'll ever go. All the rest of the way will be downhill."

"To the inevitable bread line."

"I could kick you. You make me so mad I could spit."

"How do I look for a job and work too?"

"Cover the local firms first. National Lighting, Federated Tool and Forge, Alsco Industries, Donner Plastics, Hallohan Wheel Works. Any one of those could pick up the tab. Use your contacts. You make a good impression when you *care*. When you *try*. Set up lunch dates."

"Are you absolutely positive it isn't your imagination when you say I'm on the way out?"

"Oh, heavens! Just the little things. I used to have standing. Now I've got to fight to get an office requisition filled. I have to raise hell to get the mail as early as they used to bring it. We don't get the major policy memos any more. They leave you off the routing list. It makes me mad as hell. When I bring those things up to you, and you'll remember that I have, you just don't seem to hear me. Darn it all, Craig, you seem to think that damn jungle is some kind of a pea patch." Tears suddenly came to her eyes. "What's taking the guts out of you?"

She jumped up and went by him hastily and awkwardly, bumping into his knees. The screen door slammed shut behind her. He opened up another beer. She was being dramatic. It couldn't be that bad. Yet there was a feeling of stiffness in the back of his neck. They would give his thirteen and a half years with the company some consideration. Then he remembered how they got rid of Rollins, five years ago. And then he remembered that his last raise had come two years ago last month. He tried to compute what he had in the pension fund.

Say five thousand there. And maybe another nine in cash value of insurance policies. Fifteen hundred in bonds. Nothing in the savings account. Eight or nine hundred in the checking account. Car was free and clear and the house nearly so. Healthy enough situation unless. . . .

Quite suddenly he wanted to hurl the beer can through the screening, and kick the chairs over and yell. Why couldn't they leave him alone? Why couldn't all of them just leave him alone?

After a while he walked down onto the beach. Betty was sitting on her heels, helping the kids dig their hole. She looked up at him with eyes slightly red and a shamefaced smile. "Sorry, boss."

"Maybe you've got something."

"Will you think about it?"

"Yes, Betty."

"Don't take too long."

"Mommie, it's *my* turn with the shovel," Dickie said.

"Don't bend it this time," she said, giving it to him, standing up, dusting the sand from her hands. Sally peered down into the hole as her brother dug. Soiled water was seeping into the bottom of the hole. They went up to the camp and Craig helped her set out the lunch. Cold fried chicken, potato salad, pickles, cold ham and tongue, rye bread, and a thermos jug of lemonade. Craig had to pretend to be hungry. When he was finished the food was leaden in his stomach. After the lunch Betty put the kids to bed for a nap.

She sat out on the porch with him and then said she was sleepy and went into the living room to nap on the couch. The couch was against the wall just under the two open windows that opened onto the small screened porch. He heard the rippling clatter of cheap Venetian blinds as she darkened the room, heard the creak of springs a few feet from him, heard her sleepy sigh. He sat and looked out at the lake. He sensed that she had told him true things, and that he should be disturbed. It made him uneasy, but it was much simpler to try not to think of the implications of what she had said. It was simpler to sit and feel remote from all of it, unconcerned and unaffected.

"Craig?" Her voice was low.

"Yes?"

"I shouldn't talk to you the way I did."

"Don't let it worry you."

Then, after a long pause, "Craig?"

"Yes, Betty."

"Could you come inside a minute?"

He went inside, walked over and stood beside the couch looking down at her. She turned her head away and said, "I talk too much."

"No, you don't," he said, feeling awkward with her.

"It's all I've got. You can't build a life around kids. Mother whines every waking moment. Do you understand?"

As he started to speak she reached out and caught his wrist and tugged strongly, pulling him off balance. He managed to turn and sit rather heavily on the edge of the couch, his hip near her waist. The dim light had softened her face. She looked almost pretty. She was flushed and breathing rapidly. She kept hold of his wrist, and her fingers were cold with her nervousness.

"I've got so damn little," she whispered. "The kids won't stir for another hour."

He had a sudden strong feeling of empathy for her. He sensed all the strong and unrequited needs of the sturdy body, the endless hours in a lonely bed, the imaginings and the torments that had grown so strong that she could take this unthinking gamble.

"It—it wouldn't solve anything," he said.

"I know that. I don't want to help anything, or solve anything. I just want— Oh God, I don't know what I want." She turned her face away from him again and released his wrist and began to cry almost without a sound.

"I'm such a damn fool," she said.

"No, you're not."

"Just stop being so damn reasonable, please. Stop being so charitable and so patient and kindly go the hell out of here and leave me alone! Just go away. I'm a spectacle. I buy a new bathing suit and offer my all to my employer. How cheap and trite can you get? I just want somebody to look at me the way—a man looks at a

woman. I never thought I'd get this—hard up. So get out.
Go walk on the beach. Go look at the pretty little things
on their water skis."

He left without a word, and as he left the porch he
heard her begin to sob. He walked on the nearly empty
beach. He woke her at three. She was subdued, still-
faced. She woke the children. They had another swim. He
finished the last can of beer. They left at five-thirty,
turned in the key and he bought them a meal at a Howard Johnson's just outside Stoddard. He dropped them
off at her house at seven thirty. Betty thanked him a
little too politely, never quite looking directly at him.

As he drove home he sensed that her overt invitation
had destroyed any future chance of working together in
harmony. She would remember it as rejection and humili-
ation. Yet had he taken her there on the battered couch,
twenty feet from her sleeping children, their future relationship would have been just as impossible. He wished
she had not created such an insoluble situation. He could
think of no action he could have taken, of nothing he
could have said which could have repaired it after that
initial frantic tug at his wrist that had pulled him down
to her. It was forever impossible from that moment on.

The city was heavy with a sick heat. He went home. He
stripped and showered and stretched out on top of the bed.
When he awakened it was ten o'clock and he had a dull
headache and his mouth was sour. He had the feeling that
he had dreamed of horrors, but he could remember no fragment of a dream. He was sticky with sweat, so he showered
again and thought of trying to go back to sleep. Instead he
dressed and wandered through the empty house for a time,
and then went out and began to drive aimlessly.

And, after a time, he found himself driving up the
winding roads of River Wood. He had the feeling that he
was searching for something without quite knowing what
it was. There were lights in the Jardine house, and so he
turned into the drive and went up to the door.

Irene came to the door and opened the screen and said,
"Come in, Craig. Al should be back soon. Isn't it horrible?"

He walked in. She looked as though she had been crying. "What's horrible?"

"Haven't you heard about Anita Osborne?"

"What happened?"

"You know where everything is, Craig. Fix yourself a drink and bring it out on the terrace and I'll tell you about it. Oh, and would you make me a gin and tonic, please. A tall one."

He made her drink, and then decided on a Scotch and soda for himself. He looked down at his hand holding the bottle as he poured the Scotch. It was like watching someone else pour. It was like the night of the party, yet different in that the hand did not seem to belong to him. Neither the hand nor the volition. He poured the tall glass half full. After he added ice and soda, it looked much too dark. He wished he had selected an opaque glass. He picked it up quickly and drank a full half of it, drank steadily until his throat closed and he gagged. He added soda again. The drink was sufficiently pale. He carried the two glasses out onto the terrace and handed Irene hers. She was in a chaise longue, ankles crossed. He sat in the safari chair near the foot of the chaise longue.

It was evident that Irene was pleased to find someone who had not known about Anita. Ralph Bench had found her when he stopped by to take her to church. When there was no answer he became worried and forced his way in. She was nude in the tub, and the medical examiner established the time of death at about three in the morning, and established that she had been intoxicated at the time she had made the deep cut across the inside of her arm at the elbow. Her new denture was to have been ready the middle of next week.

Irene told the story well. She was a plain-looking woman with a pleasant expression, an animated face, cropped graying hair and a slim figure. They had all liked Anita. They had all felt sorry for her in her desperation. Craig made the proper sounds of surprise and distress, but he could feel nothing. It was like something you read in a paper about a tragedy that happened a long way away to someone you had never known. He felt as if he had somehow lost his ability to react, to feel deeply about anything or anyone.

"I've been sitting out here thinking black thoughts," she said.

"How so?"

"You were very naughty the other night, Craig. I was very displeased with you. It wasn't at all like you, not at all."

He shrugged. "The curse of alcohol."

The insecticide lamp made a yellow glow against her face. She looked at him somberly. "More than that, I think. Something has gone wrong with all of us, Craig. I'm not trying to excuse you. Something is changing the world. Ten years ago it wasn't like this. Oh, there would be some free-hand necking in the kitchen and out on the eighteenth fairway, but it was shallow. It was foolish, and there were spats, but it wasn't destructive, really. Somebody would pass out. We'd have our little scandals to talk about. We knew who was living beyond their means, and we knew whose kids got expelled from school. And we were shocked. We went around deploring things, and it gave us something to talk about."

"Isn't it still the same?"

"No, Craig. No, now things are colder and more cruel and more vicious. There isn't any unity. I mean people aren't living and hoping for the same things. Now it's all keyed to one idea. I've got to get mine before the roof falls in. People want sensation. They want money only because then they can buy more expensive sensations. I guess we're upper-middle-class. Before I go any further, I've got to give Al a credit line. We've talked about this. Al says that if you take a society and hang a cobalt bomb overhead and set up a tax structure that makes it impossible for them to accumulate anything, and then promise them that no matter what happens, they'll never actually starve or lack shelter or medical care, then you've got them in a real box. People seem to have—less dignity as human beings. I used to love to give parties. Now they scare me a little. Marriages go boom in front of your eyes. And maybe Anita started committing suicide right here the other night. And you going off with that Westerling person. It isn't like it used to be. This is getting too serious, Craig. Get yourself another. Your glass is empty."

"You ready?"

"Not yet, thanks."

When he came back she said, "Jeanie was over this afternoon as soon as she heard about Anita."

"What are the arrangements about Anita?" he said quickly.

"Funeral Tuesday. And Al is terribly afraid Anita never changed the will she made out when she was still married to Tom. So he'll not only get off the alimony hook, he'll get the house and everything. He'll be coming back here with that horrid, mercenary little pig he married, and I could gag when I think of her getting Anita's lovely emerald. First the little tramp got Tom, and then she got the marriage certificate, and now she gets everything else. It's too damn bad she can't take Anita's head to a taxidermist. She could have it mounted over her dressing table. I must be getting tight. That's a truly macabre idea. I guess I lose my sense of proportion when I think of all the sexy little harpies of this world lying in wait for good husbands to reach the restless years."

"The restless years?" he said.

"Craig Fitz, you know perfectly well what I'm talking about. The florid forties, or whatever you want to call them. We marry our men young. And we have to become budget experts. We paint the walls of shabby apartments and make our clothes last and last. We put on frantic little dinner parties for the boss. Oh, we can look back and think what a fun time it was. What a gay time. But an awful lot of it was a gray time. Then your man comes up in the world. Fool that you are, you think you had a share in it. If you fish long enough, he'll sometimes tell you you've been of help. So there you are, faded by the years, still trying to look your best, and finally able to enjoy some of the leisure and some of the luxuries you've helped him acquire. But then he gets the scent of girl flesh, young and fragrant and a hell of a lot more resilient than you are. She is all awed by the 'dweat big successful man' with the nice big thick wallet, and she can tell him he is *so* much more interesting and virile than all the silly young men. Which is just what he needs to hear so he can forget his sagging waistline and his bald spot. So he has to prove he is quite a guy. And if you are lucky, it will turn out to be just an affair and he'll come bumbling back, terribly ashamed, of course, but secretly pleased with himself. And you can try to pick up the pieces of your marriage and get it back on the rails. If you're a fool you'll be so hurt and indignant you'll punish him by consorting with your golf pro, art teacher or a friend of a friend. Then grandma and grandpa can have all the declining years during which they are not quite friends.

"If you're completely unlucky, like Anita, the fragrant chippy takes him away for keeps, and can henceforth sit on her piquant little can and enjoy the fruits of his success. If she springs for a baby, there will be nurses and maids and hundred-dollar bed-jackets. And she need only keep from looking too impatient until he receives that final cachet of success, the acute and fatal coronary. It's a pattern. The two-wife two-step. Change your partners. Dos-à-dos. One for the labor and the second for show. Anita got trampled in the dance. Do I sound very bitter?"

"It's—a little unexpected, Irene."

"I know. Placid Irene. Please do have another stuffed shrimp, Mrs. Flapsaddle. And tomorrow I *must* re-pot the geraniums. Don't look alarmed, Craig. It's one of my pet peeves. I'm not against men. They are fine things. But I wish they weren't so emotionally gullible. When they are at the height of their powers it only takes one overly obvious little sex-pot to plow up the pea patch. Jeanie and I sat here for two hours, snuffling and blowing noses and being bitter about men."

"Let me know the time and place of the funeral, will you? I want to go."

"Of course. By the way, Craig. Jeanie said she met you on the street yesterday and that you acted quite odd."

Now he knew the reason for the tirade. "Did I?"

"She says there was an odd-looking little girl with you. Quite attractive in an unusual way."

"Oh, I remember. I'd just run into that girl and I couldn't for the life of me remember her name or where I'd met her. If I acted odd it was because I was trying to keep from having to introduce them."

"Jeanie says she got into your car with you."

"That's right. She asked for a lift. She was parked about ten blocks away. It was too hot for anybody to have to walk."

Irene stared at him for a few moments and then seemed to relax. He felt that he had kept his voice bland, his manner casual, and he had avoided trying to explain in too much detail. He suspected that Irene and Jeanie, after they had worn out the subject of Anita, had done some speculating about him. Just as Clemmie had guessed. Take care of Craig. The poor dear is at loose ends, staying alone all summer. You know how men are. And he got into trouble with the Westerling woman already.

"I don't know what's keeping Al. He's working too hard."

"Are you taking a vacation, Irene?"

"Next month. Both kids are going to camp for the full month of August, and we've half decided to fly down to Mexico City. But you know Al. We'll probably end up with a week end in Montreal. You and Maura are taking an October vacation, aren't you? Where are you going?"

"We haven't decided yet. Someplace inexpensive, anyway."

"You can get acquainted all over again. You must miss her very much."

Suddenly, without any warning, he found himself on the verge of unexpected tears. He got up quickly, his eyes stinging, and said in a thickened voice. "You're ready for a refill." He took her glass and his own into the kitchen. When he came back he was all right. But he knew he was getting tight. The floor had a far-away look. And when he sat and looked at Irene he experienced a curious distortion of vision. One moment her face would look very close, enormous. Then it would be far away, a pale little blur. Her voice sounded as though she spoke in an echo chamber.

Al arrived at midnight. He acted very tired. He sat with them and there was some desultory conversation about Anita, about how hot it had been today and how hot it would be tomorrow. Irene went to bed and Al fixed Craig one for the road, and a nightcap for himself.

"You can relax on the Westerling thing, Craig. They're leaving in the morning. I had my talk with Dave. They're going to try to, quote, make it up to each other, end quote."

"Thanks."

"You'll get a bill. You'll pay for it."

"Okay. I'll pay for it."

"Are you as loaded as I'm beginning to think you are?"

"Maybe. Yes."

"Remember me asking you about trouble?"

"Of course I remember."

"It's the job, isn't it? I heard something. I heard one

hell of a big shakeup is in the offing. Ober has imported a couple of young hatchet-men."

"I know. He put one of them in my section."

"Is that good?"

"I'm tight right now. But I can answer a question with a question. You know any outfit in town where something might be open?"

"That bad?"

"I don't read Ober. Maybe he's not going to push me out. But maybe it isn't a good gamble to hang around and find out. But I can't have any other outfit checking back with Quality after I apply."

Al thought for a time and said, "Ever run into Kyle Webb, president of Donner Plastics?"

"Slightly. I played in a foursome with him one time."

"He's both shrewd and lucky. He's got a rubber stamp board—until he starts making mistakes. Here is some confidential information. They've quietly picked up a tract of land on the Sanderville Road and next week they're going to announce a new plant to be built there. It'll be a big operation, a new product line. Employ a thousand people even with a lot of automation. There's a crash priority on plant construction. They'll keep the old plant going and detach certain key people for the new place. It'll leave them thinned out on the executive level, particularly in production, and I don't think they're having an easy time lining up people. I've got a good friend over there. Johnny Maleska. He's Webb's special assistant. If you want me to, I'll brief him and set up a date for you."

"I'll say yes right now. Go ahead, Al."

"No, boy. You phone me tomorrow and say yes or no. Major decisions shouldn't be made out of a bottle."

As Craig started to leave Al took him by the arm and said, "Are you in shape to drive home?"

"Always in shape, old Al."

"Let me get you a cab."

"I'm okay. I'll creep along."

"Go right home, Craig. Tomorrow is another one of those days."

He meant to go home. But it was like the night he had left with Floss. Consciousness flickered off and on. It was like a very amateur and unedited home movie.

He was aware of driving down the alley and of bumping into the shed when he tried to park.

He dropped the key and took a long time to find it.

And he was in front of her door, thumping the door and kicking it, his voice echoing hollowly as he called out to her and cursed her.

And he was alone in his own kitchen with the light on and he was on his hands and knees, being sick. . . .

CHAPTER THIRTEEN

CRAIG, DEAREST,

We arrived back here from London an hour ago, and it is now three o'clock on a dingy afternoon. The clouds are small and low and sullen and they are going by so close overhead you can almost touch them. The girls have gone scampering off to make full reports to their new friends, but I know those reports will be made in a carefully offhand way, as they have learned that obvious enthusiasms are contrary to protocol.

Darling, I am quite burdened down with *weltschmerz*. In a sense, that is our city, you know. Our place. And I should have been there with you. With the girls in Elizabeth's safe hands, I walked alone for a very long time, very dim and moony indeed, walking where we had walked. I seem to be so often wrong about things. I expected my sentimental journey to bring back a lot of vividness, but do you know I actually had difficulty locating the places that once, for me, were the most important places in the world. I did find the corner where we were both certain we had lost each other. There is a great ugly new building there, and a weedy little man smirked at me. I wanted to take him by his nasty little shoulders and shake him until his teeth rattled and say, "What do you know about this spot? What do you know about anything?" But I was a lady. Sometimes it is a great burden to remain a lady.

I tried to find us in the city, but I could not. There was no such couple, no American officer, bravely mustachioed, with a slight limp, walking a rather awkward young girl with a face too round, and body a bit bulgy with baby fat, a girl in a grisly uniform trying not to look at her officer with too much love because, after all, it is a public place. They were utterly gone, and I mourned them. The city they knew is gone too, and it can never come back. No other great city in the world will ever have that flavor again, because wars will never be that way again. No city in the future can be struck and struck and still endure. Now I can romanticize it, with a flavor of knights and heraldry.

All of that excitement is gone. It is a weary gray place sprawling for angular miles about a filthy river, and it is full of closed gray faces and dark threadbare cuffs and a kind of plodding hurry. It made me think of that book we read. *Cards of Identity*. There were so many identical little men, all with the same purpose, that I felt that if somehow the contents of their pockets could be switched, they would accept the new wife and flat and position without anyone being aware of the change. I do not mean to be so utterly grim, my dear. But I am constantly being struck anew by the knowledge this is no longer my country. It is a gray place, and grayer without you. The girls and I have quite violent discussions about who misses you most of all.

Please write us and tell me all the unimportant little details. Bore me with your misadventures at golf. Tell me what you eat and wear and where you go, and what other people wear and say and do. I do love you. Now I am going to be very diligent, and write letters to Irene, Alice, Jeanie, and Anita. If there is strength left, I shall add Bobby and Lollie to the list. And if the strength is superhuman, I shall include Bunny, though I have serious doubts as to whether she can read. There has never been such a long summer. The earth has slowed. Someone quite obviously forgot to wind it up. All of my love.

Maura

Craig refolded the letter and put it back in his pocket. He felt guilty about the letter. Evidently it had been delivered on Saturday and when it had been pushed through the mail slot it had fluttered to one side and was partially under the hall table. He had happened to notice it just before he left for work. There had been no time this morning for breakfast. Betty was due back any moment with

coffee. His hangover was severe. He did not like to think
of the picture of himself kicking Clemmie's door, shouting
—a noisy amorous drunk, devoid of dignity. And it
alarmed him to think how easily he could have fallen down
the steel stairs or piled up the car.

Betty closed the door when she came in with the coffee.
Her face was bright pink with sunburn. The awkward
episode at the cottage had apparently been thrust firmly
out of her mind. She was brisk and confident. "I slept
like the dead," she said. "But, darn it, my shoulders are
going to peel. Mother told me she told me so. She couldn't
understand why we didn't drown one of the children. That
Mr. Upson was already in when I got in."

"Was he?"

"He lounged over to my desk. Very suave and friendly.
I hardly noticed the pump he was holding behind his
back."

"What did he want to know?"

"Nothing specific. He isn't that obvious. He just
wanted me to start chattering. But I didn't. I put on a
Miss Commerford act. Have you—thought about what
we were talking about?"

"A little."

"It needs more than a little, Craig."

"Miss James, I'll give it careful consideration."

"Now don't get that way with me."

"Would you bring your book, please?"

"*Yes* sir, Mr. Fitz. Immediately, sir."

He did not want to phone Clemmie from the office. He
had a chance to use a pay phone at lunch time. He dialed
her number, and she answered on the third ring.

"Hello?"

"Clemmie. This is Craig."

There was a decisive click.

"Clemmie? Hello?"

He fumbled for another dime, called her back. He
counted twenty rings before he hung up. The dime rattled
down. He went to the counter and ordered his lunch.
This, he thought, is an ideal solution. It makes it very
simple. It takes it out of my hands. It ended right there
with that click, and now all I have to do is leave well
enough alone. Now I can feel an enormous relief. A great

weight lifted. It's over, and I have no more responsibility, and no more desire. She's too young and too erratic. She is trouble. Now the danger of trouble is ended.

Upson had questions to ask that afternoon. Searching questions that required complete attention and orderly thought. The session lasted an hour and a half. Several times his mind wandered to Clemmie and he would come back to see Bud looking at him curiously.

When he got home at five-thirty, he became very diligent. He took the laundry and dry cleaning out, and on the way back he stopped and bought the ingredients for a simple meal at home. He also bought two bottles of Scotch and a bottle of bourbon, and, after hesitation, two bottles of gin. There was really no reason, he decided, why he couldn't make a stab at entertaining. Not too many people. Say just the Tribblers and the Jardines.

He changed to work clothes and mowed the lawn, edged the walk, clipped the hedge, carried the small amount of trash that had accumulated out to the curb for Tuesday morning collection. He put the sprinkler out, then went in and cleaned the house, dusting, dry mopping, changing his bed linen, emptying a startling number of full ash trays. The weakness of hangover plus the stickiness of the continuing heat wave made him sweat profusely.

When he could think of nothing else to do, he rewarded himself by making a tall Scotch and water and taking it with him to the bathroom so he could sip from time to time while he showered and got cleaned up. He put a robe on and went down to the kitchen and fixed his meal. He set his place at the table very carefully, using the best dishes and silver. He found a book to read while he ate, a rather difficult book that he had been meaning to read for some time.

After he had washed and dried the dishes and put everything away, he made himself a weak highball and took it to his desk in the living room. He made a neat stack of unpaid bills, wrote checks and addressed them for mailing. He balanced the checkbook against the last statement, and put a blank check in the pocket of his robe. When those details were settled, he went up to the bed-

room, put the blank check in his wallet, planning to cash
it the next day, and took Maura's letter down to the desk.
He read it over, then typed her a long letter, four pages.
He read it over. It read well. It seemed to be a very good
letter. He had covered a lot of the aspects of the Jardine
party, and he felt that he had made it quite amusing. It
needed to be amusing to offset the serious part, the story
of Anita. Maura would be most upset about Anita. She
had been very concerned about her.

Four pages, single-spaced with narrow margins. A
hefty and most respectable letter. He put all the outgoing
mail where he would see it in the morning. He went out
into the night in his robe and turned off the sprinkler,
coiled the hose and put it away in the garage. He made
himself a third weak highball, settled himself in the living
room with book and drink and ash tray, and the lamp
properly placed.

The house did not seem nearly as empty if you kept
busy. And it was much better to eat with a certain style,
rather than gulp a ragged sandwich while you stood by
the sink. And the house looked better when it was neat
and clean.

This would make a perfectly acceptable routine. Eating
in would save money. There was some inside painting that
needed to be done. Maura would be very pleased to find
it done. Pick up some paint tomorrow. Good quality.
Brush it on carefully.

He regarded himself with satisfaction. There was such
a satisfying aspect to orderliness and routine. Some work
and dinner alone and make three mild highballs last
through the evening. Some constructive reading. Long letters to Maura and the girls. They would appreciate those.

He began to read again and found he had lost track.
He turned back three pages and began again. After some
minutes he began to be aware of a sound that annoyed
him, barely audible over the never-ending hushed sound
of the traffic.

He got up and went out into the kitchen. The faucet
dripped steadily. He tightened it. The drip was much
slower, but it continued. He gave it another wrench, but
it still dripped. Suddenly, without warning, he was violently angry, throat swelling, face hot, trembling. He

grasped the faucet with both hands and turned it with all
his strength. It hurt his hands. He stepped back, breathing hard. "Now drip once more, you son of a bitch!"

It did not. He went back into the living room. In a
little while his breathing had slowed down. He picked up
the book. He read without knowing what he read. The
individual words had meaning, but they would not fit
into any intelligible pattern. He dropped the book on the
floor. He sat for a long time. Then he got up and began
to walk. When he paused, he was by the phone. He rested
his hand on it. He picked it up and dialed slowly.

"Hello?" Clemmie said, her voice distant as though she
held the phone too far from her lips. He waited, not
speaking. "Hello?" she said, more distinctly, more crossly.
He put the phone back on the cradle. He walked back and
forth through the house. He went upstairs and lay on the
bed in his robe. And felt then a rising need for her,
a tingling and a stirring, as though a warm oil moved and
shifted in his loins. It was an addiction, too great to be
contained. He jumped up and ripped the robe off and
threw it aside.

He stood by the studio door. He felt as if he had run
all the way.

"I can't hear you," he said.

"I won't let you in." He knew she stood close to the
other side of the door, perhaps leaned against it. He
touched his fingertips to the door and imagined he
could sense the heat of her body through the plain blonde
wood panel. Her voice did not sound angry. It sounded
very tired and very sad. He wanted his hands on her, his
mouth on her lips.

"I have to see you," he pleaded.

She refused. He said he had something to tell her. She
finally agreed to let him in for five minutes, on the
condition that he would then go and promise never to call
her or try to see her again. He promised. He heard the
latch, but the door did not open. When he tried it, it
opened.

She had moved back from the door. Three of the small
low lamps were lighted, casting their white light down-
ward, leaving the ceiling heavily shadowed. Her hair was
down, falling in blackness to her shoulders. She wore a

pink cotton nightgown, prim at her throat, without a waistline so that it draped from the pointed thrust of her breasts to the floor where her bare toes were visible under the hem. She looked small and tired and depressed and, but for the obviousness of her breasts, no older than twelve.

"Sit over there, please."

He took the chair she indicated, some six feet from the couch. She sat on the couch, her legs curled under her, one hand clasping a slim bare ankle.

"What do you want to say to me, Craig?"

Her subdued mood was contagious. "I just want to talk to you. I want to know why you hung up on me. I came here last night. You weren't here. I was drunk."

"I don't think I have to give you any reasons. You have no claim."

"What happened? Why are you like this all of a sudden?"

She shrugged and turned her head and looked out at the wide slice of the city across the flat roofs of the lower buildings.

He had to strain to hear her when she spoke. "I've just been looking at myself. It isn't pretty. Like a frog I had to dissect in school. I cut him carefully and laid out all his hidden little colored parts so that he stopped being a frog or anything that had ever been alive. I've been doing that to myself, yesterday and today."

"What are you trying to say?"

"I became a woman when I was twelve. When I was thirteen Daddy took me along with him and his wife to Cuba and we stayed at the Hotel Ventura at Varadero Beach. The woman resented me. I was lonely. I was seduced by a drunken boy from Duke University and I can't remember his name. I'm twenty-three now. I've had ten years of living. Ten years of flesh. I think I've tried everything at least once."

"Why do you think you have to tell me this?"

She turned back and looked at him. "You asked for it, didn't you? There's always been the money, you know. When you get bored you buy a change of scene. And when you get a jaded palate, you use more spice on your food. I'm as coarse and jaded as any whore you ever saw, Craig."

"I can't believe that."

"It's true. I've been making decisions. I've spent two days thinking about myself. Gretchen is going to the Virgin Islands to work on some illustrations. I'm going along with her, I think."

"Aren't you feeling sorry for yourself?"

"Terribly sorry, Craig. Terribly, bitterly sorry. Because if I'd known you were going to happen along, I wouldn't be the person I am now."

"The person you are now is all right."

"Do you want a list? Careless, selfish, vicious, sensual, jaded, amoral."

"You're just in a mood."

"My God, how comforting that is. I'm not going to see you again. I keep telling myself that you've changed me, Craig, and that I can give you more love and more loyalty than anybody. But I keep hearing a nasty little laugh in the background. And I remember that I've felt this way before. I've felt sincerely, thoroughly, completely in love. And it always wore off, after a bit. Sooner or later. And then I'd despise the poor damn fool that kept hoping he could turn all my lights back on. I know, I agreed that this would just be your summer affair, darling. But my heart got involved. I'm in love with you. So I don't want crumbs. I'd rather starve. So get out. You're not committed yet. We're splendid in bed and I do amuse you a little, so I'm throwing you out. I'm not having mercy because you are a good and decent man, and a sensitive man. And believe me, I'd have no mercy on your jolly limey wife or your kids. I'm throwing you out because I love you and I don't want to hurt you and I inevitably will."

"Such melodrama, Clemmie."

"Is it? Is it really? I'm committed to you all the way down to the bottom of my rotten little soul, dearest. Leave while you can."

"You won't feel this way tomorrow."

"I *know* that. Don't be such a fool, really. Right now is one of the few times in my life when I'm capable of being honest. This place is finished for me. I'll be gone by tomorrow."

"You can't do that!"

"Why not? You don't give me orders. Nobody in the world has any claim on me or gives me any orders, ever."

"Clemmie . . ."

She uncurled her legs and stood up. "I'm really very tired, Craig. I'll pack your things for you. Then you must go, and we'll say good night and good-by very politely. We will close this deal up with all the politeness in the world, and all the regret on my side, thank you."

She made a wide half-circle around him and went into her bedroom. He stood up and walked slowly to the bedroom door. She had the small suitcase open on the bed, his things piled next to it. Perhaps if she had been hasty, tumbling the things in, snapping the lid, it would have been different. She bent over the end of the narrow bed, underlip caught behind her white child-teeth, trying to fold things neatly, but folding them very awkwardly and slowly.

He said, slowly, thickly, so that each word fell solid as a stone into the room's silence. "I can't let you go."

She straightened up slowly and turned toward him, her face very young, almost frightened. Her lips moved but she made no sound. He took one slow step toward her and she ran into his arms, sobbing and shaking, and he held the slight sturdy body very tightly, his own eyes stinging. They moved with a four-legged awkwardness to the cot, unwilling to break the embrace. They lay in each others arms and he spilled the suitcase to the floor with a sweep of his leg. She covered his face, his eyes, his throat, with small fluttering kisses, warm as spilled wax, and she made in her throat the crooning sounds of love. When he kissed her, her lips were salt. Then after a time she was content to lie still in his arms, her forehead hard against his shoulder, her lax fists against his chest, shuddering slightly with each deep exhalation.

"I'll try," she said in a small voice, faint as a whisper. "Oh God, I'll try. I'll be what you want. I'll always be as you want me. Demure when you wish it. Bawdy when you want that. I'll wait on you and serve you and love you all the days of my life. I love you so hard, my darling, my heart is way too big for my chest. No woman has ever been happier than I am this minute. Don't . . . start anything for a while, my dearest. I just want to lie here and hear your heart and be happy through and through. Help me make it last this time. This is the best love of all, and help me keep it so I can keep feeling this way forever."

He held her for a long time, and each time his mind turned toward the implications of the commitment he had made, he was shocked and frightened. But he could force it out of his mind by thinking of the long warmth of her body against him, the feel of her under his hands, the fragrance of her hair and her breath.

"You will write her soon, won't you, darling?" she said.

"What?"

She pushed herself back, tilted her face up at him. "To Maura, darling. Write to her soon. It's the fair thing to do you know."

"I think it would be better to wait."

"No, dear. You'll tell yourself that it is better to tell her face to face, but you're only rationalizing. If you want me to, I can help you with the letter. This way she'll have a chance to adjust. Maybe she'd like to stay in England with her people. You will do it soon? You'll feel so much better when we drop it in the mail."

"But . . ."

She closed his lips with her fingertips. "I won't nag you about it. You do it in your own time. But do it. And now Miss Clementina Bennet wants Mr. Craig Andrews Fitz very much indeed—very, very much indeed."

She got up with him early and made breakfast, refusing all offers of assistance. She was alight with love and laughter, flushed and lovely, with a walk like dancing. He tried to give the impression of matching her mood of gaiety, but he felt apprehensive. He could not understand exactly how it had happened so quickly. It was a most awkward situation to be in and, looking across the table at her, he did not see how he could tell her that it was all wrong.

He felt as though he had been a consistent winner in a poker game with a limit on bets and raises, and suddenly, without warning, it had become a no-limit game. He told himself not to think about it. Not for a while. There would be a chance later. Perhaps a quarrel. There would be a chance for him to gracefully change his mind.

He went directly from her studio apartment to the office. As he left she said, "I begin sulking at five thirty, darling. If you aren't here by six I'll be unbearable, and it will take hours to soothe me."

It wasn't until Irene phoned that he remembered that

this was the twenty-third, the day of Anita's funeral. It was at two thirty at the Congreve Funeral Home. He told Betty where he would be and said he doubted whether it would be worthwhile trying to get back to the office.

He arrived at Clemmie's at a quarter after four, after going home to change again. The somber aftermath of funeral faded as he climbed the steel stairs. The door was locked. After he called to her through the door, she unlocked it for him and flung herself, laughing and naked into his arms, chiding him for being early so that she'd had no chance to take a beauty nap and dress so very carefully for him. She'd gotten back a little while ago so the sparkling burgundy wouldn't really be cold enough yet, but it should be cold soon. Never, never had there been enough, but this time there was enough to bathe in, should the fancy strike them. And they would eat late, because it had to be dark enough for the candles. Clams in aspic and a shameful number of the most enchanting little squab. And if we move the couch away from the window, we can put the table there.

During the morning, in the office, when he thought of how she had acted the night before, he had wondered uneasily if it hadn't all been just another of her games. He thought of it again later in the evening and across the table and told himself it couldn't have been a game. No. By then they were gay and blurred by burgundy, and wearied by lovemaking, but the mood of celebration was still upon them.

And later, after they'd put the couch back, he sat on the couch with a half-empty bottle of burgundy between his bare heels. She sat on the floor facing him, so close he could look down into her upturned face. Her bottle was beside her, and she sat in one of the positions of Yoga, legs interlocked, the soiled soles of her bare feet upward. She wore nothing but a pair of vivid orange shorts, harsh as sailcloth, and he could not remember when she had put them on. She was talking and smiling up at him and he realized he had lost track somewhere and made a heavy effort to concentrate on what she was telling him.

". . . was perfectly, perfectly crazy. Because, and this is the thing Marvin didn't know, it was the ski instructor all the time. Hans or something like that. Eyes like a great sad cow. Well, he would take Delia off for these very expensive lessons, individual instruction. Marvin was paying him fifty dollars a day for those lessons for Delia. Then Delia and Hans would spend the *entire* day up in one of those rescue cabin things halfway around the mountain. And this is the funniest part. Hans, or whatever his name was, was a very nervous type. And so he *insisted* that when he'd bring Delia back to the lodge, she'd have to look as though she'd spent the day on the trails instead of in a bunk full of pine boughs. She told me the last hour was absolute hell, every day. Hans would make her charge up and down the slopes, and he'd knock her into drifts and rub her face with snow and then make her schuss down into the flats and run all the way back to the lodge. She'd come back utterly exhausted, and once with a wrenched ankle which made it look better, of course. She said that nobody, but nobody, ever had a more athletic affair. Between the bunk and the skiing, she lost eight pounds in the three weeks we were there. Toward the end it was all she could do to drag herself out of bed and crawl up the mountain in the morning. She said that if it had lasted another week, they would have found her in May when the snow melted. Of course, she was absolutely no use to Marvin, but what she didn't know and I didn't tell her was that Marvin and I were having such a mad time every afternoon when we were supposed to be taking naps, so I imagine they were equally exhausted. I even thought I was in love with him and I used to have the most delicious quivers waiting for him to come tippy-toe down the hall. But he got very demanding and very dull indeed, and when I tried to brush him off he kept hanging around, whimpering and tearing his hanky and threatening to kill me and then himself. Somebody has been drinking out of my bottle, said the little bear. You ready, darling?"

"Not just yet," he mumbled.

She wavered away and he heard the cork pop in the kitchen. Who the hell was Marvin? How many Marvins had there been? Sounds like a hell of an unwholesome three weeks.

When she came back and sat in front of him as before, he said, leering at her. "How was old Marvin? Good as Raoul?"

Her mouth changed. "Don't start getting dull. What possible difference could it make to you?"

"Hey, now!" he said, hurt by her quick viciousness.

Her face slowly softened again. "Didn't mean a thing," she said. "Not a thing. And you're drinking too slow, Fitzbaby. Lean way over now and you can kiss burgundy lips for free. On the house."

CHAPTER FOURTEEN

CRAIG found it easier not to think. He began to spend every possible moment with Clemmie. He went to his house to get his mail, to pick up changes of clothing. When he went there he spent as little time inside the house as possible. Day by day the job became merely hours that had to be endured. He worked mechanically, doing what had to be done, impatient for five o'clock when he could leave. He found he was able to turn off any thought of the future, the way a light can be turned off. He fended off Betty's attempts to speak seriously to him about his future in the company. When Al called him at the office to ask him if he should set up the appointment with Johnny Maleska, Craig said he hadn't made up his mind yet. He'd let Al know.

Jeanie Tribbler phoned him at the office to invite him to a party. She said, with a teasing edge in her voice, that it seemed impossible to catch him at home. He made up an excuse which he knew was clumsy and would probably hurt her feelings, but it didn't seem worthwhile to devise either a better excuse, or to go to the party. He let Bud Upson corner him as infrequently as possible.

Clemmie filled the nights and the days and the week ends. He knew they were both drinking too heavily, but that was something he didn't care to think about too directly. He made a habit of going to the roadhouse for lunch, and soon it was no longer necessary for him to place his order for vodka on the rocks. The bartender placed it in front of him when he sat down. Three of them were generally enough to steady him and get him through the afternoon.

She had stopped her exercises at the bar. A new softness came around her middle, and when she got tired she became querulous. When her eyes were closed the lids were darkly shadowed. When she was gay it was a hectic manic gaiety. They played her games often, and many of the roles were highly inventive. Yet sometimes she would break off in the middle and turn sullen.

They did strange things at strange times on impulse. Roller skating at a pavilion at a lake eighty miles away. Once, at her insistence, and with her money, they flew to New York. They arrived late on a Saturday afternoon. When he awakened on Sunday morning, he could not remember registering at the hotel, nor could he remember buying the cheap suitcase in a drugstore as they had come without luggage. They flew back on Sunday night and she had slept the whole way.

He was often very drunk, and he was never entirely sober. He knew that he was showing the effects of continual dissipation. His weight was dropping and his face was gaunted. Betty James spoke to him very formally, and with an undercurrent of disappointment and contempt. There were fewer and fewer conferences in which he was asked to take a part. He was listless in his approach to work. The only brightness was Clemmie. The only times of feeling alive was with her. His sexual energies were undiminished. She seemed able to arouse him as completely as in the very beginning, and was herself as easily, as thoroughly aroused. They spent most of the time in her studio apartment. Twice they went out together, on invitation. Once to a very odd party at the converted barn where Hildy and Rick Kelly lived, and once to Jake Romney's hotel apartment. He turned down all invitations from his former circle of friends, with just sufficient rudeness so they would not be likely to ask him again.

Once, because Clemmie was too scantily dressed and too obviously intoxicated, there was a particularly nasty brawl in a bar, and he got her out moments before the police arrived. Another time, coming home from a curious picnic, driving through thunderstorms, he fell asleep and smashed the front end of the Speedster into an elm tree. She got a bruised lip and a cut on her knee, and it was a great joke to walk through the drenching rain, singing. She had it towed in and traded it on a new car the next day, a pale green Austin-Healey.

She never stopped demanding that he write to Maura.

She said that if he didn't, she would find the address and write to her herself. He could not quite bring himself to do it. Once he told her he had mailed the letter. Later, when he confessed the lie, she had been more angry than he had ever seen her, yelling and stomping her feet and striking at him, and finally flinging herself on the floor and drumming her heels and screaming a flat endless shriek that scared him.

He moved through a misted world, and he moved aimlessly, indifferent to direction. The only clear light in the world was Clemmie. And yet there were moments of a curious vividness. There seemed to be no continuity in them. Quick flashes, as though a bright light went on for a few moments in a dark room.

Once, while dictating to Betty, he had looked down at his hands on the desk top. He saw the grimy knuckles, black-rimmed nails, two inexplicable scabs on the backs of his hands. And he grew suddenly aware of his own body odor, a smell of perspiration, soiled underclothing. He put his hands out of sight.

Another time while walking through one of the production areas in mid-morning, he had a sudden attack of weakness and nausea. He had moved to one side and leaned heavily on the bed of a lathe, hands flat on the bed, head bowed. Within a few moments he felt all right again. He had straightened and looked around and, near an assembly operation, he had seen L. T. Rowdy standing and watching it. He was making notes. There were high windows. Light reflected from the lenses of his glasses, from the gold pencil. Craig could not tell if he had been watched.

And there was a moment in a bar. He could not remember which bar, where it was, what day it had been. But it was night and they sat at a turn of the bar near a piano being played very loudly. Clemmie was at his left. The back bar mirror was tinted blue. He had tilted his head back and drained a Scotch old-fashioned, the ice clicking against his teeth, and then had lowered it and looked at the blue image of himself, at collar that looked too big for his lean throat, at necktie shoved over to one side, at loosened mouth and sunken eyes. He could see Clemmie in the mirror, beside him. She wore a strapless dress. Her face was turned away from him, turned up and talking animatedly to the man who stood half behind her, a large

man. The piano covered the words she was saying. Then he
had turned and looked down at her bare right shoulder, so
close to his. The man had his hand on her shoulder. The
hand was very vivid, very memorable. A big, coarse, tanned,
thick-fingered hand cupping the ivory shoulder. There
was a seal ring with a ruby in it on the little finger. Flesh
bulged around the ring. There was coarse reddish hair on
the back of the hand, and in patches on the backs of the
fingers. The nails were heavy and ridged, but immaculate
and freshly polished. The hand was six inches from his
eyes. He could see the flexion of it, the rhythmic change of
muscle tension as he squeezed the unprotesting shoulder.
He had looked for a time, and then knocked the hand off
her shoulder. He could not remember what had happened
after that. There had been some sort of trouble, some waiters who came around.

And he could remember when it was raining very heavily and he sat on the floor in his own front hall, sorting a
big accumulation of mail. At least a week of mail.

And a glimpse of Clemmie's hands, her small, square,
thick, short-fingered hands. She held a stack of blue chips
in the palm of her left hand, fingers curled up around
them. With her right hand she slowly picked up the stack
and let it clatter down again into the palm of her left
hand. Out of the corner of his eye he could see the flicker-
ing spin of the wheel, the marked squares on green felt.

That had been at that place upstate she knew about.
She had won a great deal of money, but it didn't seem important to her. What had happened to it? Oh, later they
had been in the big kitchen of the place with the owner,
who was a friend of hers, and he remembered watching her
imitation of a punchy fighter he had once managed and
they had both known. There were men there who laughed
loudly at her. And he had fallen asleep with his head
on a table and when he woke up it was gray daylight and
his neck was stiff and she sat playing gin with the owner,
their faces grave, speaking in a low tone only when necessary. Slap of cards, and gray light over the stainless steel of
the kitchen equipment. Down for three. That's where most
of the money had gone back, but enough left over to buy
him the wristwatch, a Swiss thing, incredibly thin, actually
the size and thickness of a silver dollar.

Clemmie naked by moonlight, wading into a lake somewhere, wincing over the sharp stones, then diving forward,
slow arm lifting in moonlight in the perfection of an effortless crawl, going so far out that he could no longer see
her and then the fear came and he looked at the black
emptiness of the lake and finally went back to the car for
the bottle. She drank from the bottle, dripping in the warm
moonlight, head tilted, throat working as it had at the
barn dance.

The men were always there. They always drifted over to
her with an animal casualness, a knowingness, and they
created violence in him, so they stayed in the apartment
more than they would have otherwise.

Clemmie, standing in the big shower stall, hands braced
against the wall, saying, while he scrubbed her back with
the brush with the blue nylon bristles, "Harder, damn you!
Harder!"

An evening of marvelous half-drunk strength and miraculous co-ordination when she had sat behind him at
the driving range, and he had hammered out bucket after
bucket of balls, sending them soaring far out, arcing,
winking white in the floodlights while she said Aaah at
the longest ones, like a kid watching fireworks. Finally
blisters had broken on his soft hands and the grip of the
club became greased with blood.

And, repeated so many times, one great wide eye an inch
from his, a pale blue eye strained wide, with red tracery on
the white, with flecks of a different color in the iris near
the pupil. The anthracite pupil shrunken by the strength
of the light over her face. A great blue eye filling all of
the world, then beginning to shift back and forth in aimless pattern, faster and faster, and then focusing hard on
some far strange place, then suddenly, violently pinching
shut, lids deeply wrinkled, staying shut through the eternal
seconds, and then a relaxation that smoothed the pinched
wrinkles and the eye opening again, sleepily, lid moving up,
but not far, eye turning down to find his eye, then a little
pinching at the corners to show the mouth was smiling.

And her hands again, in another mood, moving with
precision. The fingers held the pale gray airweight envelope and he could see the British stamps. Then some
question had been asked, and he did not remember the

question, nor his answer. The letter was torn in two, then
the halves in two, then again and then once more. He knew
only that the letter had not been opened, had not been
read. She had found it in his pocket where it had been,
unopened, for a long time. There were others at home,
unopened. She went off to throw the bits away. One
square fluttered down and he picked it up and found only
a fragment of one word in that familiar hand. ". . . ident-
ly . . ." He rolled it into a ball between thumb and finger,
and snapped it into a corner.

He drifted through a shadowed place, marked with
these bits of vividness. It was like a long tunnel which,
once you had entered it, would bring you out into the light
again at some unimaginable destination. Or the tunnel
might have no ending. That was not important.

He came out of the end of the tunnel, opening his eyes
and sensing that the sun was high. He did not know where
he was. He kept his eyes open, unfocused, and waited for
the onset of the needle pains behind his eyes, the slow
uncoiling of nausea, the driving urge of thirst. But these
did not come to him. He felt dulled and listless. He had
slept very heavily, he knew. Somehow it was like awakening
in hospital. He could remember having been very sick. His
stomach felt sore from the continual vomiting. That had
happened when? Yesterday? Last night? Whatever it was,
it had drained the alcohol out of him and now there was
no hangover. Just weariness. But a vision formed in the
back of his mind. It took shape and clarity. It was a shot
glass held up so the sun came through its amber depths,
filled precisely to the brim. His own fingers held it steadily. It moved closer to his lips. Saliva flowed into his
mouth.

Directly in front of his unfocused eyes there was a dark
area. He was on his right side, knees bent, one hand under
the pillow, the other hand resting near his chest. The sheet
was down across his thighs. His body felt sticky. He focused
his eyes and saw Clemmie's hair, black, thick and tangled.
She lay facing away from him, the sheet at her waist. Some
strands of the dark hair were under his cheek. Her hair
did not have a clean scent. The texture of the skin of her
left shoulder was directly in front of his eyes, in perfect
focus, so that he could see the almost invisible imperfec-

tions of the skin. Her hip made a curiously high mound
under the white sheet. Not a very white sheet. It had a
grayish tinge to it.

He lay there too enervated to move, and gradually the
smell of her hair became more unpleasant to him. He lifted
his head and pushed it away, sank back again. He began
to wonder dimly about time and place. Double bed. Some
hotel or motel or something. God knows there had been
plenty of those. Saturday? Sunday? He listened and he
heard the city sounds, the murmur of a busy arterial street.

Suddenly the placement and intensity of those sounds
became all too familiar. He sat up abruptly. His own bedroom. His bed. His and Maura's. Her clothes were draped
across the dressing table bench. His clothes were on the
floor. There were two glasses on the dressing table with
dregs of drinks in them, another on the bureau. Printed in
big clumsy letters across the dressing table mirror was,
"Keeryst, Oliver! Not that way!"

He slid his legs out of the bed. There was a gray and
flattened cigarette butt in the bed, tobacco crumbs, a
scorched place on the sheet. When he put his left foot
down, he put it on the edge of an ash tray. It tilted and
clattered and spilled gray ashes over the top of his foot.
He brushed the ashes off, bent and picked the butts up
and put them back in the ash try. He saw where cigarettes
had been mashed against the hardwood floor, and he
found a glass tipped over with a piece out of the rim, and
the varnish white where the drink had spread.

He got up and went into the bathroom, into the stale
odor of dried vomit. He took a yellow plastic sponge from
the closet, got down with bare knees on the cool tile and
cleaned up. Only when the place was presentable did he
wash, brush his teeth vigorously, comb his hair. He needed
a haircut and his teeth had a yellowish tinge. He went
back into the bedroom. There was room on her side of the
bed to sit beside her. Her face was sallow in sleep, her
breath sour, her hands grubby. He put his hand on her
hip and shook her.

"Wake up, Clemmie. Hey!"

She opened drugged eyes, focused on him and scowled.
"Lemme sleep, damn it."

"Wake up!"

She grumbled and complained, but finally she hiked

herself up onto her elbows and looked at him unpleasantly. "Just why are *you* so bright-eyed and bushy-tailed?"

"What the hell has been going on here? What are we doing here anyway? I told you I didn't want you to come here!"

"Here? To the shrine? To the temple of love? We back on that? Lover, it's too late now. We've been here a long time."

"How long? What day is it?"

"Give me a chance to think. Oh God, what a head. Is blood running out of my eyes?"

"What day is it?"

"Don't shout. It hurts. I'm thinking. We've been here one, two, three, four. That's it. Four nights. Today has to be Monday, little chum. Blue, blue Monday."

"The office!"

"That's right. The office. We got here Thursday night. We came over from my place. I wondered if you shouldn't go to work Friday, but you said it wasn't at all necessary. You phoned the irreplaceable Miss James and you were very lordly with her."

He stared at her. "I can't remember."

"Can't you remember even coming here? That is one very long blackout. As your friend and advisor, I recommend you lay off the sauce. By the way, what *did* dry you out? Oh, I remember. Tummy trouble. How do you feel now?"

"Tired and confused. And sober."

"I'm sorry you missed your own house party. People say we had a wonderful time. God, I'm a ruin, completely. I'm dirty and I itch. Get out of the way like a good boy. I'm going to use that tub of yours. Maybe I'll use some of dear Maura's lavendar bath salts."

"What people? Was anybody else here?"

"Just an expression, darling. We were all aloney."

"What did I say to Betty James?"

"I couldn't possibly remember. Now will you *please* let me go get into that tub?"

He started to ask another question but the bathroom door closed firmly behind her. She seemed so damned— at home. And why not. The fourth day. He and Maura had little to do with their immediate neighbors, but this little arrangement would certainly not go unmarked. He heard the flush of the toilet, then the thunder of water into the old fashioned tub. He padded down the stairs to look at the rest of the house. The living room was not too bad. More glasses. A bowl of water that must have once contained ice. Two very sheer stockings laid over the back of a chair. He picked them up. They were as insubstantial as cobwebs. His legs had felt very weak when he had walked down the stairs. Suddenly they started to tremble and a cold drop of sweat ran almost simultaneously from each armpit down his naked ribs. He sat down, leaned his head back and closed his eyes for a moment. When he opened them he saw, through the window, some object close to the front of the house that he couldn't immediately identify. He stood up and walked to the window. The pale green Austin-Healey was parked in the front yard, close to the house. He could see the skid marks where it had ripped up the turf in a skidding stop.

Why not hang out a sign, he wondered. Clemmie sleeps here. Jesus! The top was down, and had probably been down for the four days, and it had quite probably rained during the four days. When it gets full of water, she'll trade it. As he turned from the window he saw records on the floor by the record player. He went over and looked down at them. Old 78's, one laying in two pieces, splintered in the middle where a heel had come down on it. He squatted, twisting his head to read the label. Fats on an old Decca. A piece of the melody went through his head, off key. If it isn't Bartok or Chavez or Whoinhellski, you break it.

When he stood up he stepped on one of the halves with the ball of his right foot, pressing down until he felt it snap under his foot. He went out into the kitchen. He looked around slowly. You could not see it all at once. You had to pan it, he thought, like a documentary movie.

Plates with congealed food. One gas burner lighted, turned high, nothing over it. Glasses and bottles. Garbage smell. Butts tramped into the floor. A pair of red shoes with heels hooked neatly over the back of a kitchen chair. Faucet dripping. Back door open. A new and inexplicable hole in the top panel of the screen door. Broken glass swept into a corner, the broom standing beside it. He turned off the gas and went to the screen door and looked out through the hole. There was an unbroken Scotch bottle in the middle of the backyard. The grass was high and scraggly, half concealing the bottle, but after going through the screen and clearing the railing, it had landed label-up.

He turned and looked helplessly at the kitchen, wondering where to make a start. He heard water start to roar into the tub again. He looked up at the ceiling. He crossed over, knelt in front of the cupboard where he kept the liquor and looked in. One bottle. Gin. There should have been a lot more bottles. He seldom drank gin. He stood up with the bottle in his hand and looked around the kitchen. He broke the plastic with his thumb, unscrewed the cap. Get right back where you came from, Fitz. Go right on back to never-never land where maybe this hasn't even happened, and if it has, it doesn't mean anything anyway.

He tilted the bottle and opened his throat and drank deeply. He drank until he started to gag. He lowered the bottle, made the sink in two strides, threw the gin back up and clung there retching, his eyes streaming. When he was able he washed his face, he rinsed his mouth.

Too much, he thought. Moderation does it. Slow absorption. He took one half-swallow. It stayed down for perhaps twenty seconds, and the spasms lasted longer. He thought of trying again, but he could not get the bottle to his lips. Limit of tolerance, he decided. Built-in safety switch for the aspiring alcoholic.

He heard her calling him. She called again and again as he went up the stairs. He went into the bathroom. It was hot and muggy, the windows steamed over. She had it very full and she lay back, her chin above water, dark hair afloat. At the other end her feet were braced between the faucets, pink toes in alignment. Her face was flushed. He never liked to look at her toes. Ballet had malformed her toes.

"I had to drain off the first batch, Fitzlamb. It was like gruel, truly. What have we been doing? Rolling in your cellar?"

"I haven't looked down there yet. I've seen the kitchen."

"Ghastly, isn't it. I'll send Olsen over. Where did you go? I called and called. You look absolutely green."

"I feel green."

"I have been offering up a prayer. A very important prayer. If it comes true, there is going to be at least one more can of beer in that antique box of yours. Be a lamb, will you?" As he turned toward the door she said, "And put coffee on, if we have any."

There were three beers in the refrigerator. He opened one, started to open another but felt his stomach knot, and put it back. When he came in with it she sat up and reached for it, eyes alight. She held the chill metal against her cheek and said, "Mmmm. Ambrosia. No, that's solid. Nectar? Hardly. That's sweet and icky. Mead. That's a good word."

She tilted the can up and drank deeply. She paused for breath, drank again. She finished it at the third try and, without warning, flipped him the can. It startled him and he missed it and it clattered off the tiles.

"Bad nerves, dear? You know this hanging over is cooking out very well indeed. I thought I'd have it all day, at least. But Clemmie comes bouncing back again, hooraw. For God's sake, Fitz, go put something on. You look like a litter case. All ribs and hip bones and strings. And try to stand up straight."

He looked down at himself, and was shocked. The bathroom scale was in the corner near the closet. He pulled it out with his foot and stood on it. The needle wavered and steadied at one fifty-eight. From one eighty. Twenty-two pounds.

"Dearest, you look like somebody just told you you were going to lose the baby."

He looked at her. "It's Monday, you say. This sounds like a damn fool question. What Monday?"

"No piker he. No crummy little one lost week end. This boy loses big gobs of time. Wait a minute. This will require computation. Maybe I'll have to whip out the trusty sextant. Today, sir, is Monday, the twelfth day of August."

He put the lid down on the toilet and sat down, face in his hands, trying to figure back. "That Monday you wouldn't let me in your place. Wasn't that the twenty-second of July?"

"Correct. Three weeks ago today."

"It seems like longer."

"I've never been so complimented, sir."

"Have I missed much work?"

"Not one day, until Friday last. But you have not been setting off in the best of shape lately. You're probably the talk of the industry. Face it, old Fitz. It's been a three-week binge, and I'm getting old before my time."

"Clemmie, I've lost twenty-two pounds. Haven't you noticed? Or worried or something?"

"I've tried to make you eat. Waiters have tried to make you eat. Husky waiters have tried to make you eat. Oh, no. Not Craig Fitz. No food for him, boy. Maybe just one mouthful of the steak. You could get your calories from the liquor, but too often, my friend, just when you have a nice snug load of calories aboard, you have to run to the side of the road and go whoops."

"Jesus! I've got to straighten it out at the plant some-how."

"Stop being a scared little man. I hate that. It's de-grading."

"All right, degrading. It's just filthy money."

"Don't shout, dear. And *do* go put something on. Put your robe on or something."

"How long are you going to soak? I want a shower."

"You're going to have to wait. This is Mother Clemen-tina's home cure for the trembles. But I could be bribed."

"How?"

"Is there just *one* more icy beer?"

"Two left."

"One more will do it, and I can get out that much quicker. And could you possibly find a real scratchy towel. A big rough one. The kind that makes you glow?"

"I'll look."

"And I can't possibly get back into my clothes. Do you think you could find something of Maura's that wouldn't be too grotesque on me?"

"I don't think so."

"There must be something around here. Panties with an elastic top. Any kind of wrap-around skirt. A white shirt of some kind. I could just fold it over and tuck it in."

"I'll look."

He got his robe, got the beer, found a big towel, went through the things Maura had left behind and picked out things that might suit her, and took the things into the bathroom. Her eyes were closed. She took the beer and said, "Just leave the towel here. The steam will melt those clothes."

"Do you think they'll do?"

"How can I *possibly* tell until I try them?" she said. "Put them on the bed. And see if you can find my shoes."

"They're in the kitchen."

"I don't think I'll be much longer, darling."

He went down and pulled a chair over to the phone table, dialed the plant and asked for his office. Betty answered, saying, "Production Control Section, Miss James speaking."

"New way of answering the phone, Miss James?"

"Good afternoon, Mr. Fitz."

"Betty, I'm sorry about that phone call on Friday."

"There's no reason for you to apologize to me, surely." Her voice was very formal.

"Frankly, I was drunk."

"I gathered that, particularly after the third call."

"My God! Did I do that?"

"Yes, Mr. Fitz."

"What's this deal on Production Control Section?"

"I believe that was arranged in a conference in Mr. Ober's office Friday morning. You were supposed to be at the conference."

"Did I know that?"

"You certainly did!"

"What happened?"

"Whenever you report back to work, you are to go immediately to Mr. Ober's office. If he isn't in, you are to wait there until he comes in."

"What does that mean, Betty?"

"I'm sure I don't know."

"Look, come off it for a minute, will you? I've been in a tail spin for three weeks."

"Longer than that."

"I'm trying to pull things back together."

"I think it's too late for that, Mr. Fitz."

"Betty, for God's sake!"

"All right. I'll tell you something, Craig. Listen good because I'm going to tell you good. I took it. I took it right between the eyes for those three lousy weeks because I'm a sucker. Now I don't give a damn if the main switchboard is listening in. I took it and I tried to cover for you. I worked like a lousy dog trying to keep it at least a partial secret that you were floating around here in a big fat alcoholic dream. I wrote memos for you. I did a lot of the things you should have been doing. I was worried sick about you. I couldn't reach you. I couldn't find out what was happening. You wouldn't let me make a doctor's appointment for you. You scared me on Friday. I was still your loyal dog. I was sick with fright. So I came from work right to your house. Anybody who comes to your front door can look right into the living room. I didn't quite ring the bell, thank God. I stood there for thirty seconds, probably, and then I left. I stopped in a bar and took on a load myself, and carried it home. Mother damn near died of shame. I'm through, Craig. When I'm through I'm all the way through. I'm not tying my little red wagon to an anchor. If there's any way I can knife you, I'll do it, just to prove that I'm off your leash. I hope you have a big happy time with that little black-haired slut, whoever she is."

Dazed by the tirade, he said, "Her name is Clementina Bennet."

"You're still drunk. Miss Bennet is a lady, not a half-naked, leering, cavorting, drunken slut. You're on your way to the gutter, right where you picked her up, and the faster you go, the better I'll like it."

The phone snapped in his ear. He put it down gingerly. He thought for a long time and then dialed the plant again and asked for Mr. Ober's office. Miss Commerford answered.

"Miss Commerford, this is Mr. Fitz. I understand that Mr. Ober is anxious to see me."

"I can connect you, sir."

"No, please. I understand he wants to see me in person. Would you give him a message, please. I've been having a nasty bout of intestinal flu. I thought I might be able to make it by tomorrow, but the way I feel, it's going to be at least Wednesday before I can get in."

"Please hold the line one moment, sir."

She came back on the line very quickly. "Mr. Ober asked me to tell you not to come in until you feel fit, sir. He'll talk to you when you come in. There is no hurry, he says."

"Thank you very much, Miss Commerford."

He went back up to the bedroom. Clemmie was out of the bathroom. She had put on the pair of panties. They were light blue. She snapped the elastic experimentally against her middle.

"Who were you talking to?"

He sat on the bed. "Miss James."

"And how is the gentleman's gentlewoman?"

"She blew my head off. Things are in a mess. My job has been switched around somehow. Ober wants to see me."

"What upset Miss James, pray tell?"

"This is pretty awkward. She came here to see me Friday night. Standing by the front door she could look into the living room. I guess it upset her. She said she stood there thirty seconds. She called you a cavorting slut."

Clemmie grinned broadly and then gave a sharp yelp of laughter. "Cavorting slut. That's pretty good. And I bet you it was closer to thirty minutes than thirty seconds, if I've been able to guess right from what you've said about her."

"Aren't you sore?"

"Why should I be? Maybe an eyeful of riotous gaiety will do her some good. Friday. About sixish? My memory is fogged over, but I think I was doing some dancing about that time. You look licked, guy. Get that damn office off your mind, will you?"

"It's only the way I earn a living."

"Nuts. How long do you think I'll let you keep that job after we're married? I will *not* be tied to this grim town. I've told you that. You're going to be a kept man, my friend."

"But . . ."

She moved closer to him. She put her hands on her hips, and bent forward slightly from the waist. Her body was pink from the heat of the bath. Her hair was still damp. She glowed with health, with emotional intensity. Her naked breasts were like weapons aimed at him.

"Now look you, Craig Fitz. Now that this has come up, there is something that I am getting damn sick of. And we are going to finish it right here, and right now. Nobody is going to do a single thing until this is settled. Do you understand?"

"What do you mean?"

"The letter! The letter! I'm sick of all the stalling.

You are stone cold sober right now, and you can't get out of it. You are going to do it right now. Is that clear?"

"But, Clemmie, don't you think—"

"The letter. Write the letter. We'll go right down to the desk."

"Clemmie, I . . ."

She bent backward from the waist, legs spread, hips thrust forward, head tilted back. She squeezed her eyes shut, opened her mouth, and yelled as loudly as she could, "WRITE THE LETTER!"

"Honest to God, Clemmie. I'll write it, but right now I can't seem to think clearly and . . ."

"WRITE THE LETTER!"

He got up and she followed him down the stairs. He opened the typewriter and rolled paper into it. He looked blankly at the paper.

"Come on," she said. "Dear Maura. You've stalled long enough. Write!"

He typed Dear Maura. And looked blankly and hopelessly at the paper. "You type then," she said. "I'll write it. Let me see now." She began to stride up and down the room behind him. There was an oval mirror with a gilt frame over the desk. He could see her in it each time she passed behind him, frowning. The blue panties were too large around the waist. They would slip lower with each stride and when they were almost gone she would jerk them up again impatiently.

"Dear Maura. This is the most difficult thing I have ever had to do. I do not expect you to ever forgive me. All I can hope for is a little bit of understanding. Got it?"

"Just a moment. Okay."

"All right. I guess the most merciful way is to do this quickly. I have fallen deeply in love with another woman. I cannot imagine spending the rest of my life apart from her."

"Isn't that a little—"

"Just type it, mister." When the typing stopped she said, "Ready? I did not look for this. It happened. And now that it has happened, there is nothing that can stop it. Our love had—make that *has* changed to contentment. What I feel for this girl is love. You must believe that. It is not infatuation. Going too fast?"

"Hold it a minute."

"Ready now? I do not expect the children to understand. I must have a divorce, as soon as possible. You may have custody of the children, of course. And I will make as generous a financial arrangement as I can manage."

"All right."

"Now we have to wind it up. I will confer with my attorney as soon as possible, and move my things out of the house. I will leave the keys with—with who?"

"Irene."

"And we might as well leave her that dismal car of yours too. No need to put that in the letter. Believe me, it would be easier to cut off my right hand than to do this to you, but . . . uh . . . circumstances have made it inevitable that I do this thing. There! Now what do you put at the end of this kind of a letter? Cordially? Hell, no. How about regretfully. That will do."

She leaned over his shoulder. When he had typed the last word she ripped the sheet out. He turned in the chair. She stood and read it, half frowning, chewing her lip. Then she smiled at him.

"Was at so awful, honey baby lambie?"

"I don't think . . ."

"At this point you are not supposed to think. Just do it. Just sign it and stuff it in an envelope and turn it over to the intrepid airmen. And it's over. So eeeeasy. Sign right there, sir. I assure you, you will never regret this move. It's a sound piece of property. Can't help but increase in value. That's a good lamb. Now go take your shower, *please*. You look all fingerprints."

After he had showered and shaved and dressed, he came down stairs. Though the skirt was far too long, she did not look grotesque otherwise. He recognized the skirt as one that Maura had made for herself.

"Now you look better, darling. Feel better?"

"A little."

Her soiled clothing was wrapped in her dress, making an untidy bundle. She smiled at him. "We better not lean on that sauce so hard, Craig. You look sickly and I feel all shaky. It isn't good for us. Fun is fun, but not this much fun. I'm going to run along now and get gallons of sleep. I'll send Olsen over right away. Then you better fold too. Going to work tomorrow?"

"I don't know yet."

"Why don't you just take a run over and dictate a letter of resignation to that nosey Miss James?"

"I don't know what I'm going to do."

She came over and kissed him lightly. "Poor old dissipate. Get your rest, dearest. Lots and lots of it."

He glanced toward the desk. "Where's the letter?"

She patted her purse. "Right here. I found stamps in the drawer and I typed the envelope. I got the address from one of her envelopes in the same drawer. I'll take care of it. I'll mail it on the way home."

"Let me see it."

"Now why in the world do you want to see it? It won't do any good. It's all sealed and everything."

"I can reseal it with tape. I never did get a good chance to read it over."

She sighed heavily and patiently and handed it to him. She sat on a chair arm, swinging her red shoe. He slit the envelope and pulled it out and read it. It did not seem right. It was not the way he would say things. It was too blunt.

"I'm sorry," he said. "I really can't send this to her."

She jumped up. "What do you mean?"

"Don't get angry. I just mean that I can do a better job if I'm alone and I have a chance to think."

"All right then. All right. But do it. And when you come to my place tomorrow, you have your version with you. Unsealed. I want to read it and then I am going to mail it. I have the address memorized. And if you don't show up before six o'clock tomorrow night with a letter ready to go, I swear I'll write her, and it won't be any pink tea letter either. If you don't have the guts, I do."

He heard her heels on the porch, then on the steps, clacking quickly and angrily. A little while later the motor of the car burst into life. She cut around through the yard, bounced over the curb and bullied her way into a solid lane of traffic while horns blew in protest.

After she had gone he turned on the radio and as soon as he heard a time signal, he turned it off and set his watch. Exactly two o'clock. Another wave of weakness came upon him and he sat down quickly, sweating, shaking.

He sat with his eyes closed and let his mind range back over the past three weeks. He could remember so little. Quick sharp fragments. Most of it blurred. What are people saying about me? It's so easy to see them. Knowing nod and smirk. There he goes.

He remembered an amusement park from his childhood, and a huge disc like a phonograph record. You all got on and got as near as the middle as you could and braced yourself as best you could, and soon the wheel started, and the women screamed. It went very slowly at first and you laughed when the first ones went, sliding ludicrously off, sliding on their backs, kicking their arms and legs like a bug. The wheel went faster and more slid off, yelling. Then you didn't laugh so much because you felt the strain on your hands and wrists, and felt an uneasy micrometric skidding of the seat of your pants. The amusement park whirled around and around the wheel and quite suddenly you were gone, sliding, spinning, being carried into the scuppers to pile into a man who pushed you away roughly and angrily, as if you had done it on purpose.

There he goes. There goes Fitz. Had a good grip for years, but the seat of his pants started to slide just a little, and then it goes fast. But he's carrying enough anaesthetic. He won't feel a thing.

Is that why I did it? To stop thinking? To stop having to think? After the seventh drink nothing in the world is seriously wrong, or terribly important. It is a superior grade of Miltown. It is a thunderous cure for the anxieties and neuroses of our times.

What were they all saying?

CHAPER FIFTEEN

OLSON arrived at four, a square, strong woman whose only detectable expression was that of faintest contempt.

"Miss Bennet sends me."

"Oh, I thought you'd probably come in the morning, Mrs. Olson."

"Just Olson. I stay until all is finished. Just show where are cleaning things, please."

He showed her and said, "Please do the bedroom first, Olson. I think I'll be taking a nap. The house is a mess, I'm afraid."

"Yes sir."

As she went up the stairs, he bent and picked up all the crumpled balls of typing paper he had thrown on the floor. He dropped them in the wastebasket beside the desk, kept one in his hand and opened it at random. "Dear Maura, There is no excuse for what I am about to do to you, and to our marriage. I have met a twenty-three year old girl named . . ." That was all to that one. The others were as fragmentary.

He knew he should eat. These attacks of weakness were probably partially due to malnourishment. He looked in his wallet and found that he had a little over a hundred and eighty dollars. He looked at the checkbook. Five checks were missing, with no notation on the stubs. He called up the stairs that he was going out for a little while.

He learned within one block that it was a mistake to think the walk would do him good. After two blocks he had to stop in the shade of a tree that grew close to the sidewalk. He leaned against the trunk with his eyes shut, his shirt soaking with sweat, his heart stuttering.

When he arrived at the small restaurant, he was too exhausted to eat. He sat hunched over coffee for a long time. Finally he was able to eat a small steak, potatoes, salad, and drink milk. The day was still as hot when he walked back to his home, moving very slowly, carefully and fragilely. He could hear Olson working in the kitchen.

"I'm going to take a nap now. I may sleep a long time. Can I pay you now?"

"All paid," she said.

The bedroom gleamed. Clean sheets were crisply white, the bed made up without a wrinkle, and turned back for him. There was no sight or scent or sound of Clemmie left. He sank, sighing, into the softness of the bed.

He awakened violently in the middle of the night, sitting bolt upright, eyes staring, trembling, mouth working, with the echo of a scream seeming to remain in the far corners of the upstairs rooms. He could not remember the dream. He wanted a drink. There were dry little fingers in every cell of his body, moving like cilia, waving in every direction, searching for a drink. He lay back to wait until his heart stopped thumping with unremembered fear—and awakened again in a gray world and could not tell if it was dawn or dusk.

It was not long until the sun came up and he knew it was very early. He felt hungry, ravenously hungry. He went down in his robe and searched the kitchen. He toasted stale bread, found a can of chili, heated it and poured it over the toast and ate greedily until, just before he finished, hunger left so completely he could not touch another bite. After a time he was nauseous, but not for long. Olson had been most thorough. He inspected the house. Furniture was not exactly in the same position as before. The changes were subtle, but enough to give the living room an alien look, a look of strangeness. It had changed. The house had changed. The four nights had changed the house; it would never be the same again for him, nor could it be the same for Maura. It had been an ugly house, always, and he had not felt any special fondness for it. Yet it had been marked by living.

He sat in the living room. Morning traffic on Federal Street was light this early. He contrived those pictures in his mind which, through contrast, could give him the highest flood tide of sick shame. When the girls were smaller, they would come bounding in on cold Sunday mornings in winter and burrow down into the warm bed. Maura would tell them not to awaken their father, but their whispers would be stage whispers, their gigglings inadequately muffled. Later, after Maura had gone down to start breakfast, there would be the ritual of the funny papers, one solemn golden child on each side of him while, propped up, he would read, and stop to answer questions when the action was confusing.

And in that same bed there had been hair not clean spread dark over the pillows, ashes and tobacco crumbs and spilled liquor and the sour-sweet odor that was a lingering byproduct of nights and days of sweaty, drunken love.

After this, no matter what happened, he knew he would

have to go through with it. He had lost any right to even think of any reconciliation with Maura. He had done a filthy thing to marriage, to Maura and himself. Guilt made the separation inevitable. It was the only clean thing he could do for Maura. He realized there were tears running down his face. He had not been conscious of weeping. He wiped them away with the sleeve of the robe.

The letter was finished by eight o'clock. It was longer than it had to be, and it was not a good letter. In it he tried to explain the feeling of restlessness which had made him vulnerable, and the chain of coincidence which had caused him to meet the girl. He had tried to describe her, and had scrapped that page. A description would accomplish nothing, and he was not at all certain he could describe her. She had seemed, in the beginning, small, rather quaint, amusingly uninhibited. Somehow she had grown in the past month so that she even seemed physically taller, stronger, and more dominant. In darkness her body, once so taut and tiny, felt swollen and luxuriant, the hips monolithically fleshy, as though she had gorged on his strength as she took dignity from him.

He had coffee in the kitchen and more toast while he read the letter over. The letter would fall into her life, come crashing down through all the shining things that had looked so durable, and come to rest lodged very deep, shifting the very foundations so that the structure could never again be true or strong. He tried to see her holding it, reading it. He tried to see her face and he could not.

And he would have to think of moving out of this place, taking his things away. Books, clothing, records. He looked at the record shelf and went over and knelt by it and began to pull the records out. Which were his? She had bought some for him. He had bought some for her. Many they had bought together. And it was that way with the books. Was there anything aside from clothing that belonged to him? That was exclusively his, unmarked by her?

He wandered through the house. There were so few things. Three pipes which, at least once a year, he tried to substitute for cigarettes. The gesture never lasted over two weeks, despite Maura's contribution of telling him he looked wonderful with a pipe. Tool box. But there had to be basic tools around a house.

He remembered the attic. There would be things up there he should take away. It wouldn't be too hot up there yet. He put on khaki shorts and went up into the attic.

Two hours later, in the baking heat of the attic, sweat running down his back and chest, Craig sat quite still, surrounded by the contents of the cartons he had opened. He had been sitting very still for a long time, arms resting on cocked knees, head lowered. At first he had started making a small pile of the things he would take away with him, but soon he had forgotten his purpose. He went through cartons and boxes, taking objects out, looking at them, remembering. He held the textures of their life in his hands. In his weakness, in the attic heat, he achieved a clarity of recall that was like a kind of delirium. Each object brought back a scene, a dimensional picture.

A green rubber duck with celluloid eyes—and he remembered the day Penny was three and wandered away, remembered the frantic search of the neighborhood. They found her sound asleep under a bush. That night, after she was asleep in her crib, he had stood with Maura looking down at Penny who slept with the green duck in the curve of her arm, and when he looked at Maura he saw she was crying without making a sound.

A piece of stone half the size of his fist, marked with the delicate traceries of sea shells from a different eon—and he remembered a picnic day when they swam in a deeply shadowed pool, in water so cold it took your breath, while the girls napped in the car parked in the shade. When Maura swam nude under water she was a wavering green paleness. When they came out to get warm in a patch of sun under pines, they had made love in that place, brazen before chipmunks and blue jays, and then went back into the water to wash away the brown pine needles and stains of leaf mold. The stone had come from the edge of that pool. Maura had saved it.

Each object had its special history. He stopped his aimless search when he came across the beret, the ugly and ridiculous hat with the pompom, hat which she had detested and had been forced to wear as a part of her uniform. He fingered the roughness of it, held it to his face and caught the scent of dust and attics and, so elusive it could have been imaginary, the light clean scent of her hair. And he remembered how, when she would come into the London flat, she would hang it on the back of the gray chair near the door and fluff her hair with her fingertips and, quite often, make a horrible face at it.

With the beret still in his hand, he went down into the relative coolness of the second floor. He sat on the bed, his body sweaty, and phoned Clemmie.

She answered the seventh ring and when she knew it was he, she complained about being awakened, sounding cross.

"Have you written the letter?" she asked.

"Yes. I wrote it."

"Do you want to bring it over now? You sound so odd."

"I . . . I'm not coming over. And I don't want you to come over here. I'm not going to send the letter. I can't do it."

"Craig, you are so incurably and infuriatingly tenderhearted. If you had to cut off a puppy's tail, you'd take it off a bit at a time. Can't you see, darling, that the quick, clean blow is the kindest?"

"You don't understand. You don't know what I'm trying to say. I'd rather have her than you. I want to stay with her."

The line was silent. "Clemmie?" he said.

"I'm still here. It's just a little too late for what *you* happen to think you want. I know what's best for you. I'm holding you to this. I'm going to write her and tell her we've been living together and you want a divorce but you're too chicken to ask for one."

"You'd better not do that, Clemmie."

"Are you warning me?"

"Just don't do it."

"There's no way in the world you can stop me from doing anything I want to do."

"Clemmie?"

The line hummed. He hadn't heard the click. He hung up. He looked at his watch. Ten thirty. He called Al Jardine.

"This is Craig, Al."

"What can I do for you?" The tone was curt.

"I want to talk to you. Can I come to the office?"

"I'm pretty busy these days."

"What's wrong?"

"You apparently don't need friends, Craig. You don't want friends. You should know what I'm talking about. I don't like the way you talked to Irene on the phone."

"Try to believe this, Al. I don't have any recollection of talking to her. I've been—drinking more than enough."

"She's pretty damn sore about it. Why haven't you been writing Maura? She's frantic."

"Al, I've got to see you."

"All right. I'll see you when you get here. Make it by eleven?"

"I'll try."

He took a quick shower and dressed. The car battery was dead. He had no idea how long it had been since he had used it. Yet it wasn't likely Clemmie would have been driving him to work. The taxi took a long time. He was fifteen minutes late getting to the old brick office near the County Court House where Al had a corner office on the third floor front.

Al's girl was not at her desk, and Al called to him to come in. He walked in.

Al stared at him over the tops of the heavy glasses. "My God, you look like hell!"

Craig sat down, tried to smile. "I feel worse."

"Are you sick?"

"This was the result of some plain and fancy dissipation. Now—I'm really jammed up."

Al got up and closed the door, came back and laced his fingers across his stomach. "You better tell me about it."

It was past twelve thirty by the time Craig finished. It was a painful story to tell. He found it hard to look toward Al as he told it. It sounded a good deal more crude than it had seemed while it was going on.

"Questions. Are you cured of her?"

"God yes. I think of how she was when I woke up yesterday and I feel physically ill. But after what I've done, it isn't fair to Maura to . . ."

"Don't bleed on the floor, Fitz. What's good for Maura is to keep the marriage going. There's no way to keep her from learning a lot of what you've told me, and filling in the rest. I don't know how good the marriage is going to be after this, but it's going to be better than being apart, maybe. In this, my friend, I'm on Maura's side. I don't dig you. You're not too God-damned noble to go take a quick hack at Floss who was practically saying pretty please. There was no special harm done. Then, with all your morality, you get yourself all fouled up with a very dangerous trollop, take her into your house, into your own bed. In this deal, I'm working for Maura."

"I'm trying to."

"You've acted like it. All right. You're cured of her. But she's going to write Maura. You want me to stop her."

"Yes."

"I can't. Some shopgirl, yes. That would be easy. I've got cop friends who could pick up that kind of a girl for soliciting, take her in, scare hell out of her. If she was stubborn, I could make sure she got the roust, right out of town. But you, my friend, are dealing with Miss Clementina Bennet. She's named after her grandmother, you know. The old lady met the robber barons on their own terms and beat hell out of them. Any little push I try to give Miss Clementina, she can push back twice as hard. If you've been factual, and I don't think any man would make up stuff that makes him look this silly, I don't think you can stop her. She'll write. Let her write. Tell Maura some psycho girl is trying to foul you up and she may hear from her. Then do an awful lot of rehearsal on the story you'll tell Maura when she gets back."

"There's the job . . ."

"Skip the job. Maura first." He pushed a button on the side of his desk. The door opened and a girl came in. "Dotty, I want you to get a Mrs. Craig Fitz on the phone. Person to person. Give her the address, Craig."

"Talk to her!"

"Why not? She's your wife."

Craig gave the girl the address.

"Buzz when you've got her on," Al told the girl. When the door was shut Al said, "That'll look imposing on the phone bill. This Jardine is a wheel. Talks to people all over the world. An international practice, by God."

"Will—you apologize to Irene for me?"

"No. That's something you have to do for yourself. Just drop by. She isn't hard to talk to." He shook his head.

"The last guy in the world to get in a mess like this one."

"All right. I'm ashamed of myself. Just stop patronizing me."

"Touchy, too. Miss Clementina must be a very special item indeed. Craig, you know what this makes me think of? Damned if I know why. It's like when the reverend runs off with the soprano in the choir. A terrific fall from grace. You've been around. You should have been able to take a chippy like that in your stride."

"Maybe I haven't been around enough."

"In a way, it's too bad you've got a conscience."

"What do you mean?"

"Plenty of people would give a left arm for the chance. Marry into the Bennet clan and nestle right down into the feathers. No more exercise except a languid gesture when your glass is empty. Are you certain she wants you to marry her?"

"She's made it pretty definite."

"Twenty-three and cute. Pretty flattering to a morose old goat like you."

"I know that Ober is going to . . ."

"One thing at a time, friend. One thing at . . ." There was a buzz. Al pointed at the phone. Craig picked it up gingerly. Al walked quickly out of the office and shut the door.

"Hello!" he said. "Hello! Maura?"

And he heard her voice, heard her say his name. It was a long way away, and came through a singing and humming of wires. She said something he couldn't make out.

"I can't hear you! Can you speak louder? Can you hear me?"

"Yes. What's wrong, Craig?"

"Wrong?"

". . . answer my letters . . . worrying . . . three weeks . . . wrong . . ."

"I'm sorry about the letters. I was sick. I'm better now."

". . . been awfully sick."

"Have you been sick?"

"No. You. Too sick . . . somebody could write . . . tell Irene . . ."

"Listen, darling. Can you hear me? You're going to get a letter soon."

". . . you?"

"Not from me. From a girl. You don't know her. Pay no attention to the letter. I'll explain everything later. Pay no attention to her letter. She's . . . crazy."

"What kind of a letter?" She came through clearly for a moment.

"A lot of lies. I'll write too. Don't worry."

". . . try not to."

"How are the girls?"

"Fine . . . little homesick . . . not here now . . . very disappointed."

"I love you."

"What?"

"I said I love you. And give my love to the girls."

". . . raining here . . . not much longer . . ."

"Good-by, Maura!"

". . . darling . . . soon."

He hung up, took out his handkerchief, mopped his face. There was no way of telling if Maura had heard enough to understand. Al came back into the office.

"Work out all right?"

"I don't know. It wasn't a good connection. I don't know if she understood me or not."

"You could have phoned her before. You could have phoned her when things started to go sour."

"Maybe I . . . wanted things to go sour."

"That's a damn strange thing to say."

"It isn't clear in my mind, not yet. Maybe it won't ever be. There's a fascination in—I've got to use a pretentious word—in evil. Maybe not evil. Recklessness. Disregard, for once, of consequences. Everything has always been so planned. Like that story you told once, about the man jumping. Part way down I wanted to yell stop. Maybe there's a law of gravity in emotion. I'm pretty damn incoherent."

"Don't look at me in that pleading way, Craig. I am not, for Christ's sake, going to write you out a permit. I'm not going to tell you how many times to go count your beads. I see this all the time. You want to roll in your own guilt. A dog who's found some lovely nastiness and gets tired of it and wants a bath. I see different degrees of this sort of thing all the time, and I can be objective, but not so damn objective with you because it usually doesn't hit this close.

It's like a disease, a special virus that infects the righteous. And your little deviation is not exactly world-shaking. It's closer to pathetic. Sometime you should get a look at somebody who has gone all the way down to the bottom. I spent a nasty hour in a hotel suite one time. It took them that long to come and get the body, the body of a dead girl. She was seventeen. Alive, she had been close to the borderline of feeble-mindedness. Not bad enough to put away, but just barely bright enough to earn a living at something requiring no thought. Even dead and bloodless she was a provocative-looking kid.

"She'd gotten into some kind of trouble. The Juvenile Court Judge, after questioning her, realized it had been inadvertent. He was a good and understanding man in his early fifties, respected, hard-working, even brilliant. A philosopher as well as a judge. He had her placed in a foster home and arranged for her employment in a laundry. He took an interest in her, and it seemed no greater than the interest he had taken in other kids.

"The cops stood around, very uncomfortable, and while we waited for them to come and get the body, I tried to talk to the judge because he was my friend. But there wasn't anything left of him. There had been a very clumsy attempt at an abortion, and some futile attempts to staunch the hemorrhage, and when he realized it couldn't be stopped he didn't have the courage left to put in an emergency call. So he sat in that mean little suite while she bled to death, while everything that he had been and could have been went away from him, turning him into a trembling old man, a gray sniveling old man on his way to prison. So don't expect me to punch *your* card, Fitz. The money gave your fling a better flavor. You could at least pretend it was romance. Let's go get some lunch and we'll talk about the job next, because that's the next thing that has to be fixed, and it should be fixed because it will be necessary to Maura and the kids. Come on."

They sat in a booth in a back corner of a restaurant near Al's office, and Craig told him exactly what had happened to the job, and to his own performance on the job.

"It's a good bet that Ober is going to bounce you out of there, wouldn't you say?"

"Yes. He certainly knows I've been drunk on the job. And he knows I've been brushing Upson off instead of cooperating. And I haven't been doing the work."

"So we can't salvage anything out of that."

"I wouldn't think so."

"But, as of this moment, you are gainfully employed as assistant plant manager. That condition will exist until you go back in and Ober ties a can to your tail. How long can you stay out?"

"I'll have to go back in Friday."

Al pursed his lips, rattled his fingers on the table top. "If this was the first time I ever saw you in my life, I'd say here's a guy whose nerve is shot. You've got a twitch in your cheek and your voice trembles when you talk and you can't keep your hands still. This is Tuesday. Forty-eight hours might do it, if you do exactly as I say."

"I'll do anything you say."

"I'll bet you don't have a suit that doesn't hang on you like you borrowed it. And all your shirts are too big for your neck. You go right from here and get a suit and a shirt that'll fit you. Don't try to save money on it. Insist on delivery by tomorrow afternoon. Conservative and impressive. Then you come back to the office and by then I'll have some pills for you. Some are going to be sedatives for tonight and tomorrow night, and I'll have a tranquility pill for you to take Thursday morning. You are going to be relaxed and confident when you talk to Johnny Maleska. On Thursday morning you are going to go to a Turkish bath and get the works. Then you are going to a barber shop for the final polish. And then, in your new suit, with some color in your face, all calm and confident, you are going to do a snow job on Johnny, and you are going to be employed by Donner Plastics. Just one thing. Will you do a job for them?"

"Yes, Al."

"Between now and then, don't think about a damn thing. Don't think about Maura or the Bennet woman or being unemployed. Eat and sleep like a vegetable. Get yourself pulled together."

He was to meet Johnny Maleska for lunch at the City Athletic Club on Vine Street. It was an old, gray stone building, with ten stone steps up to a wide door flanked by stone half columns. It was the third or fourth time Craig had been in the club. The lounge was to the left of the entrance, the desk to the right. The small bar was at the end of the entrance hall, and the dining room adjoined the lounge. It was a place of leather chairs, dark paneling, masculine talk. Political meetings were held there, with policy and strategy determined by the hearty red-faced men who wore cigars. The card rooms were upstairs. Downstairs was the pool, the gym, the handball courts.

He arrived at twelve-twenty and stopped at the desk and asked the attendant to tell Mr. Maleska when he arrived that Mr. Fitz was in the lounge. He went in and sat near the windows, with the latest issue of Fortune in a red leather binder in his lap. He felt rested, almost relaxed. At eleven he had taken the Dexamyl spansule Al had given him. It made him feel very clear-headed, keyed up, yet not shaky. It had given him a conviction of confidence and power. This was a poker game. After a long run of steady losses, there had been just enough left to stake one good hand. The cards had been dealt. He knew he would pick them up and sort them and find a pat hand, unbeatable.

Everything had gone just the way Al wanted it to. There had been no attempt by Clemmie to contact him. And he had not let himself worry about that. He had not conjectured about what she might be doing. He was as ready to meet Maleska, he felt, as he would ever be.

He turned the pages of the big magazine, half seeing the industrial photographs.

The desk attendant came in and said, "Mr. Fitz, Mr. Maleska just phoned and asked me to tell you he'll be late. He suggested you go in the bar and have a drink and he'll meet you there in twenty minutes."

"Thank you."

"The bar is at the end of the lobby on your left, sir."

The small bar was crowded, the air smoky, the single bartender very busy. He nodded at two half-familiar faces. A group left the bar to go to the dining room and he was able to find space. He ordered a vodka on the rocks, and as he sipped it he listened to the fragments of conversation, full of key words, option and wait-listed and write-off and dealer stocks and zoning board and sales picture and bogie on the stinking twelfth hole.

He felt a part of it, and yet apart from it. It was as though this was a language he had once known and spoken fluently, but now, hearing it again, he knew he had forgotten the syntax and the grammar.

When Maleska came up behind him and spoke his name, it startled him so that he spilled some of his drink on the back of his hand when he turned around.

Maleska was a stocky man in his thirties. His hairline and the pyramidal shape of his face reminded him of Richard Nixon, but his hair was white-blond, his eyes pale green, nose and forehead sunburned and peeling. He wore a cotton cord suit, pale blue shirt, dark knit tie. His handshake was firm. He apologized for being late and ordered dry vermouth on the rocks, steered Craig over to a small table.

The bar was beginning to empty out. They sat at a table with a top of pale waxed wood. Maleska said, "The old man is really something. I swear he works a twenty-hour day. God knows when I get my vacation this year, if I get any. Last year we drove up to Maine and two days after we got there, the old man sent the plane after me. Betty and the kids spent the vacation alone, and then I flew back up and had one day before we had to drive back. Al says there's a chance you might want to come to work for us. Want to fill me in on the background? Education, experience and so on."

Craig told him.

"So U. S. Automotive is the only outfit you've worked for."

"That's right."

"They're sharp people. Why do you want to get out now?"

He had prepared himself carefully for that inevitable question. "I could explain how I worked myself into a dead-end job at Quality Metals, Johnny. That's part of it, but it isn't the whole truth. Quality Metals is the headache division of U. S. Automotive. Plant layout is uneconomic and inefficient. They've brought a new broom in."

"Ober, eh?"

"That's right. A shakeup is on the way. I believe they'll transfer key personnel. You know, a change for the sake of making a change, just to see what happens."

Johnny Maleska nodded. "I see what you mean. There'd be no criticism of you, or of the others shifted, but you would always be the boys Ober moved out. Sort of a stigma on your record."

"Exactly. And there's something else. If they'd moved me around the way they do others, I wouldn't kick about a move. But they've left me here ever since the war. We've put our roots down deeper than we should have, I guess. We'd like to stay here in Stoddard."

"I appreciate your frankness, Craig. What would you have to get?"

"By leaving them, I'm cutting myself out of accumulated retirement benefits. In order to get back to even, I'd have to make seventeen five. Frankly, that's more than I'm making now."

"It's not out of line. There's a couple of flaws, though. The old man doesn't believe in raiding local industry."

"You didn't come to me. I've come to you. I want a change."

"I think he'll take that into consideration. The other thing is that our problems aren't the same as the ones you're used to."

"I'm assuming I'll be given a chance to learn. Basic policy should be pretty much the same whether you're making locomotives or clothes-pins."

"That's true, Craig. And another thing, plastics and chemicals are moving so fast, we can't get executive personnel out of our own field." New drinks were placed on the table. Craig hadn't seen the signal when Maleska ordered them. He felt wary of the third drink. There seemed to be a curious inter-reaction between the pill he had taken and the two drinks he had consumed.

"How do you think it looks?" Craig asked, hoping his anxiety was sufficiently concealed.

"I couldn't make a definite commitment. I guess you know that. But I'd say it looks pretty good. I realize the situation is a little delicate. We can't make the sort of investigation we'd normally make. Al vouches for you, and the job you hold in the outfit you're in is a pretty sound recommendation in itself. All I can do is present it to the old man. He'll want to have you stop in for a talk with him. Just between us, I think it should be okay. We're getting damn hungry for people with your qualifications, with production experience and supervisory experience. We're going to be spread awful damn thin before we get the new plant into operation."

Craig felt enormous relief. It had gone far easier than he had dared hope. The drink was no longer a threat. He picked up his glass and finished half of it and set it down.

"One thing the old man will want to know. How soon can you make the move?"

"Immediately," Craig said.

Maleska looked at him curiously. "No notice? Don't you have to break somebody in?"

Craig felt confused. "I—I guess that was the wrong word, Johnny. I mean I can give notice as soon as I hear definitely. I'll leave it up to them, up to Ober, as to how long he wants me around. But things are changing pretty fast there. There may be no need to break anyone in. I mean I *may* be able to leave right away. I don't know."

"Would they eliminate the job you're doing?"

"No. That would have to be done." He suddenly saw an out, and regretted that he hadn't thought of it before. "I've naturally been thinking of a change for some time. I've organized my own section so that it can carry on pretty well."

"Then the work is pretty routine?"

"No. There's plenty of decisions to make."

"If you left immediately, who would make them?"

"I might not be able to leave immediately."

"I don't think it would be very good policy to leave them in a jam over there. We wouldn't want that done to us."

Craig felt that something had slipped away from him. Johnny Maleska seemed to have become cooler toward him. A quick and logical answer would repair the situation. The seconds seemed very long. He sipped his drink, lit a cigarette, tried to smile in a relaxed way. Maleska seemed to be watching him very closely. "Ober put a man in with me a while back. His name is Upson. I suppose you could say that I've been breaking him in on the job."

"Did you ask for additional help?"

"No, I didn't."

"What was Mr. Ober's reason for putting this Mr. Upson in with you?"

Craig regretted opening up that subject. "He explained that it's a survey of the plant. An industrial management survey."

"Then Upson isn't actually an employee of Quality Metals?"

"No. But . . . well, the fact that he put him in my section . . ."

"I'm not following this very well, I guess. You sound as if you think Ober plans to have Upson take over your job."

"I admit that I've thought of it as a possibility."

"If you thought of it, why didn't you go to Ober and ask him?"

'I don't believe I would have gotten very far."

Maleska waited a few moments and then smiled and said, "Let's go in and eat. Want a drink at the table?"

"I—I guess so, thanks."

They found a table for two in the dining room. Craig's drink was brought. He noticed that Maleska was not having another one. He was about to remark on that, and then thought better of it. He decided to leave his own drink. He thought he could leave it untouched without making it too obvious.

Maleska seemed unwilling to get back to what they had been talking about. They ordered. Maleska talked about the continuing heat wave, about a swimming pool his neighborhood was building, about the improved airline service into Stoddard. Craig felt that he was saying the right things at the right times to Maleska, but he felt uneasy. This was not the way the conversation should have gone. Now, at lunch, it was more logical that Maleska should talk about Donner Plastics, about the expansion plans, about company policy. This was more the sort of conversation two strangers would have on a train in the dining car.

The more he thought about it, the more uneasy he became. He had ordered liver and onions. It was stringy and he found himself chewing pieces interminably, swallowing them with difficulty. Until he had given one incautious answer, he had gotten along very well with

Johnny Maleska. Damage had been done somehow, and
it was necessary to retrieve the situation. Obviously Maleska had become dubious of him. And no small wonder.
If any plant executive could leave immediately, it meant
either his job was of no importance, or he planned to have
no consideration for the firm he was leaving. It would
have been so much better to have shrugged and said, "As
soon as I can get away without leaving them in a jam."
Then when the offer came, he would have had the opportunity to explain he could report sooner than he had expected.

If the situation was going to be repaired, it would have
to be done now. Johnny Maleska was saying, "They figure
on finishing the new school before Labor Day. Betty and
I feel a lot better with Karen out of that fire trap. She'll
be in second grade this year."

Craig reached for his drink and found the glass was
empty. He did not remember finishing it.

"Johnny," he said, and his voice sounded odd.

Maleska looked at him curiously, and glanced at the
empty glass.

Craig smiled. "I'm not drunk. But I can feel the drinks.
I've been taking some cold medicine, and I guess it doesn't
go too well with alcohol."

"It'll do that sometimes."

"Johnny, I want to go back to the way we were talking
before. I mean I want to be frank with you. I sensed that
somehow I got my foot in my mouth. And this is important to me. I want to make the right kind of impression.
I know I can do a job for you. That's the only important
thing, isn't it?"

Maleska looked ill at ease. "Yes. I suppose that's right."

"That's the important thing. Nothing else matters. I'm
loyal, Johnny. I'm a loyal son of a bitch. I lay it on the
line. I put out. Al will tell you that. John Terrill can tell
you how I've performed on my job. I don't want you wondering about me because I said immediately and then
talked about Upson and so on. I'm loyal and I can do a
job."

"Certainly," Maleska said, and Craig felt he wasn't getting to him.

"That's why it would be a good thing for you to hire
me. John Terrill can tell you the job I've done at Quality

Metals. You've got to talk to somebody in production to understand. I'm loyal, and I put out."

Now he wanted to stop, but he could not. He sensed that it sounded as though he were whining and begging, but he could not stop talking. He knew he was making Maleska very uncomfortable, and that he was hurting his own chances, but the repetitious phrases kept pouring out. He felt divided in two. The rational part of his mind wanted to turn the other part off, but the switch was just out of reach. He knew his voice had begun to tremble. Now he had begun to tell Johnny Maleska how they didn't understand or appreciate the job he'd done for them over there. Maleska looked down at his cigarette, his face like stone.

Finally he was able to stop himself. He drew a long shuddering breath, and wished he was dead. In the silence Maleska stirred his coffee slowly and intently.

"I'm sorry," Craig said. "I guess I've torn it, haven't I?"

Maleska shrugged.

"Just don't blame Al. He was trying to help out. My nerves didn't hold out. The sad part of all of this is that I would have made you a good man."

Maleska looked at him directly. "They letting you go?"

"I think so."

"I didn't think so at first, and then from the way you acted . . ."

"I started botching it in the bar, didn't I?"

Maleska gave him a startled look. "Botched it? No, it was okay until you started all this funny-sounding quack. Why are they letting you go?"

"I went off the deep end. I botched things up. I'm back on the rails now, but a week from now I could have handled this better. I couldn't wait that long. Anyway— it nearly worked. Thanks for the lunch."

Maleska offered him a cigarette. "What are you going to do?"

"I don't know. I've got a few contacts. Try to work them."

"If you don't make out, stop around. Ask Personnel to give me a ring when you come in."

"What would it be?"

"Not seventeen five."

"How much?"

"It would depend on what's open. Maybe five hundred a month."

"That isn't much."

"I'd keep an eye on you." Maleska sighed, leaned back, looked at the burning end of his cigarette. "We lose a lot. It's a funny kind of tension. There's a mythology in business, in manufacturing. The ladder is supposed to end at the top. Be bright, clean and industrious and you get to the top. But you don't get there. The top is the top. Your picture in *Time*. Stock deals. Consultations in Washington. There are about four hundred men at the top, and no room for more than four hundred. And there has to be forty thousand of us, Fitz. Company and battalion commanders. Top kicks. We've got everything but that final indescribable ingredient. We tell ourselves we've got it. I thought I had it until I started working close to Kyle Webb. You've got to eat, sleep, live and dream the work. You don't get a minute off. You have no mercy on yourself or on anybody else. I've tried. I can't do it. I can't keep that close a focus on attention and ambition. So I won't get into the real gravy. I'll get some good drippings, but I won't get hold of the plate. So my future is in conflict with the mythology. The ghost of Horatio Alger haunts the business schools. That's a tension that cracks men up. They get as far as they can go, and refuse to believe they've been climbing a short ladder. Then comes the persecution complex. Somebody is knifing them. They've been shunted into a dead-end job. The joker in the next step up is related to the Chairman of the Board. It's so damn much easier in the shop. Do your work, draw your pay and your fringe benefits. Bitch to the steward when the foreman leans on you. Protect your seniority." He looked at his watch. "I've got to get back."

They stood up, walked to the lobby and stopped by the door.

Maleska stuck his hand out. "Try to roll with it, Fitz."

"What will you tell Al?"

"You tell him. It ought to be easier that way."

After Maleska left he went to a pay phone in the club and caught Al at his office.

"Are you in?" Al asked.

"No. I botched it up good. I got on a talking jag. I

whined to him. I whined and snuffled. I showed him my built-in cringe. He knew the score. He's seen it before. I wasn't ready yet. If I was Maleska I wouldn't have hired me to empty trash baskets."

"You better come right over here. I'll wait for you."

"No thanks. I'm all prettied up. I've got a good color and I smell good, and I'm wearing a miracle fabric. I'll never be any more ready for Ober than I am right now."

"Have you been drinking?"

"Moderately. Isn't that what you write on an employment form?"

"Where are you now? I'll be right over."

"Thanks for everything, Al. It was a good try. But you didn't start with the right material."

He hung up. He went out into sidewalk heat, into the blistering afternoon of the fifteenth day of August.

CHAPTER SIXTEEN

WHILE HE WAITED, knees crossed, cigarette in hand, for Paul Ober to see him, he was aware of the way Miss Commerford was watching him. Whenever he glanced toward her, he had the feeling she had just looked away. He felt utterly calm. He wanted to attract her attention and then make some horrible face or some grotesque sound to see if her calm, which was that of an icy crevasse, could be disturbed.

John Terrill came hurrying out of Ober's office, a roll of prints in his hand. He glanced at Craig, glanced back again, eyes wide.

"Hello," he said, hurrying by.

"Hello, John."

Paul Ober had come to the open door of his office. "Come on in, Craig," he said pleasantly.

Craig got up, not too hastily, rubbed out his cigarette in the chrome stand and went in. Paul shut the door. Craig waited until Paul had gone around to the other side of his table and then sat down without an invitation.

"You look as though you're feeling better, Craig."

"Much better, thank you, Paul."

A side door to the office opened and L. T. Rowdy came in. He nodded at Paul Ober, crossed the soundless rug and sat by the windows, his face as empty as an insect's.

"During your unfortunate absence, Craig, we took the liberty of making some basic changes in the production control setup. I'm certain they would have had your approval."

"I imagine my approval would have been automatic, Paul."

"Hmm? Yes, of course. The setup has never been entirely logical, you know. I realize that you and John Terrill worked well together for many years. But your functions logically belong under Terrill, don't you think?"

"Yes, of course. But as I remember, that was the only way I could be given the title of assistant plant manager. I got that more because of the complexity of that job in this plant. In any other facility I realize it would require less ability and less pay."

"I'm pleased you've understood the situation so clearly. You understand, of course, that if your job and Terrill's job were held by two men who didn't see eye to eye, there could be a lot of confusion. The two men might be working at cross purposes."

"That's quite correct."

Ober took time out to knock out his pipe and reload it. He was ostensibly taking time out to think. The interview was apparently not progressing as he had imagined it would.

He lighted the pipe, smiled wryly at Craig and said, "I am now in the bad graces of Baylor and Killian. I made a change without waiting for the report of their two field men, and I have hired Bud Upson away from them. They're sending a replacement, but they aren't happy about it. That's the calculated risk in the industrial consultant field. Sooner or later your field man may find himself face to face with too much of an opportunity to turn down."

"Upson is very competent."

"I'm glad to hear you say that. He's working with John Terrill on a consolidation of section records, a simplification procedure, and a closer control of the work flow. He's also going to get quality control methods closer to the actual machine operations so we should eventually have a healthier reject picture."

"I believe I made that same recommendation over three years ago, Paul. It should be in the files. The expense of installation was thought to be too high."

"Did you? That was back in the days when Quality Metals was treated as a stepchild. Now I'm beginning to make them see that we're going to have to spend some money here to get healthy."

"I'm glad to hear it."

Ober nibbled at the edge of his mustache. He put the pipe in an ash tray, took out a handkerchief and cleaned his glasses, huffing on the lenses, holding them up and looking through them toward the windows.

"I haven't been happy with your performance lately, Craig. I imagine you've been aware of the fact of poor performance."

"For the last month, yes."

"Longer than that. Since I've been here. Maybe even longer."

"Possibly. I wasn't particularly aware of it, Paul, until this past month."

He put his glasses back on. "In a sense, it's the fault of management. You've been eleven years in substantially the same job. To me that would be a very dismaying thing." He waited, but Craig said nothing. "Last month I was seriously considering arranging a transfer for you. I felt your future value to U. S. Automotive would be enhanced by a —a change of scene. But now I realize that for it to have been effective, such a transfer would have had to have taken place earlier. Perhaps two years ago."

"Why, Paul?"

"I've been going over a file of your memos. It seems to me you've lost respect for the judgment of top management. Your view has been too narrow. You seem to have forgotten, or to have been unwilling to admit that the top management of this corporation is among the most dynamic and progressive in the country. The policy of horizontal expansion has been extremely successful. Now we have a much broader base for growth, for controlled growth. Yet in your memos I detect the fact that you feel you have been persecuted and misunderstood and that the decisions affecting your narrow area of responsibility have been asinine."

"Paul, if those decisions were so sound, would there have been any necessity for you to be sent here?"

"You make a good point. And I admitted this *was* the stepchild. But top management attention had to be directed elsewhere. You should have understood that."

"Perhaps."

"Lately you have been of no value to this organization. It's no secret that you've come back drunk after lunch. You failed to co-operate with Upson. You stuck Terrill with work you should be doing. You and I are both too intelligent for me to try to lecture you about responsibility and reliability."

"If you say so, Paul."

He saw annoyance, quickly concealed. "I've given this a lot of thought. I've been over your record. I deeply feel the responsibility of U. S. Automotive in this matter. We have a reputation for ruthlessness, but we don't let a man go without thinking of every possibility of salvage."

"And I'm beyond salvaging, Paul?"

"Not as far as your future in business is concerned. But as far as your future with U. S. Automotive, I'm afraid so. Your attitude is obviously antagonistic. But we do owe you something for over thirteen years of work, most of it good work. I talked it over with Gibbs in New York, and we feel the cleanest way to do this thing is to accept your letter of resignation, and give you, in turn, a letter of recommendation."

"What reason for resigning shall I give?"

"That's hardly pertinent. Health, better opportunity. Anything you like. You can dictate it to Miss Commerford. And I have this letter for you. It came this morning."

He handed it over. Craig took it out of the envelope. It was from the New York offices, and bore the signature of the president of the company.

It is with sincere regret that I accept your resignation from the executive staff of U. S. Automotive.

Your work, ever since you came with us in 1940,

has been more than satisfactory. We are indeed sorry to lose a man of your competence, experience and integrity.

Craig put it back in the envelope. "I use this as a letter of recommendation?"

"I should think so. After you sign the letter you dictate to Miss Commerford, you should see Mr. Gidney about cleaning up the financial details. We are paying you through October, by the way."

"That's very kind, Paul."

"I took the liberty of having Mr. Rowdy tell your secretary to take the personal things out of your desk. She packed them in a carton. Is your car in the lot?"

"Yes."

"Do you know his car, Mr. Rowdy?"

Rowdy nodded and got up and left the office. Ober said, "He'll see that your things are put in your car." He stood up and held out his hand. "Sorry things had to work out this way. I'm sure you'll find something very quickly, Craig. And you'll be happier than you would be if you stayed with us, I'm sure."

Craig shook his hand, released it quickly. "Can I ask a question?"

Ober glanced quickly at his watch. "Yes, of course."

"It's a personal qestion."

"That's perfectly all right."

"It might even be a clue. You know, something you can use for self-analysis, or self-betterment. What I want to know is, did you enjoy doing this?"

Ober stared at him, off guard for only a fraction of a second. "No! And the fact you could ask that question indicates to me how neurotic your attitude is."

"Then why not have somebody else do it? Rowdy could do it."

"It isn't my habit to leave the awkward things up to others."

Craig smiled. "I guess you ought to think about it, though. You ought to check yourself and see if you liked it."

"Do you, by any chance, happen to have another job lined up?" Ober asked.

"No."

"I've never seen you act more confident."

"Do I?"

"If you'd acted this way in the beginning, this might have had a different ending for you."

"Good-by, Paul. And thanks."

Ober walked out and instructed Miss Commerford to take a letter. He nodded and went back into his office. Miss Commerford used a scratchy pen. He dictated a short letter of resignation which contained no reason for resigning. She typed it quickly and without error on her electric typewriter, making two carbon copies. He had her predate it a week, to co-ordinate with the letter of acceptance. He signed the original. She gave him one copy. He put it in the envelope with the letter from the president and said, "Thank you, Miss Commerford."

"You're quite welcome, Mr. Fitz."

Gidney was ready for him. The checks had been made out and so had the withholding tax forms, and an itemized statement of contributions to the retirement fund. Gidney speeded him on his way with a quick, damp, limp handshake. The carton was in the car, on the floor behind the seat. He stood by the car and looked around and listened to the familiar sounds of the place. By now they would know it. All of them. He had a feeling they were watching him out of the windows. But when he looked he could see no one looking down into the lot. No ceremonial dinner. No matched luggage. No toasts. This was the other way out, on greased skids.

When he got home the phone was ringing. He let it ring. It could be Clemmie, or it could be Al. He did not want to talk to either of them, or to anyone else who might call. He put the carton on the desk in the living room.

When luck went, your timing went with it. He did not want to drink. He did not want to yell and kick the walls. He wanted to go to sleep and sleep a very long time. A very long time. He took off his coat and tie and sat down in the living room. When he leaned back he realized he still had his hat on. He sailed it across the room. The phone began again. He got up slowly and answered it on the seventh ring.

"Mr. Fitz?"

"Yes." It was a man's voice, deep, cultivated.

"George Bennet, Craig. I've been trying to get hold of you. Like to have a little chat with you. Can you come out to the house tomorrow afternoon at about three-thirty?"

"I . . . don't know."

"Clemmie won't be here, Craig. I'd very much like a chat with you. Of course, if it interferes with your working hours . . ."

"I won't be working tomorrow."

"Then you'll come? Splendid. I'm on Robinson Woods Road, on the right, about two miles beyond the village. And bring your swim-suit."

Though he had taken no sedative Thursday night, Craig slept from nine in the evening to after eleven the next day. He awoke with the feeling that he had not moved, that he was in the same position in which he had fallen asleep. There had been no dreams. It had been a very deep sleep, and yet when he awakened he did not go through a gradual process of recalling the events of Thursday. They were with him the moment he awakened, as though they had rested motionless in his mind throughout the long sleep. He was beyond feeling dismay, or fright, or self-contempt. He felt numbed and chill, like an automaton—felt so unreal that he might have been someone he had read about, without particular interest.

It was twelve miles to the village of Robinson Woods. A mile beyond the village he was in rolling country, in an area of large estates. No houses were visible. The hedges were high. He was traveling slowly when he came to the entrance to the Bennet place. There were two pillars flanking the driveway. They were of rough gray stone with an ornate iron light atop each one. A corroded metal plaque on one column said "Bennet" and the plaque on the other said, "Christmas Ridge."

The drive was a winding gravel road lined with poplars. It climbed, not steeply, for three hundred yards and then he could see the house. It was on top of a crest, a long structure of stone and redwood, with big windows that caught the sun, with steep pitches of shed roof. He parked near the separate three-car garage, near a battered old green M.G. and a new Ford station wagon. It was very quiet out here, and much cooler than town. He had put on lightweight slacks and a short-sleeved sport shirt. The gravel crunched under his steps. He could hear bird songs, and he thought he heard a woman laugh somewhere behind the house.

An old man wearing a white apron came to the door and when he asked for Mr. Bennet, he said, "Are you Mr. Fitz, sir? Mr. Bennet is expecting you. They're out at the pool. If you'd walk around the east wing, sir, that way, you will find them."

He walked on the thick green turf. When he rounded the corner of the house he could see the big pool in the ell made by the east wing and a continuation of the central part of the house. The water was brilliantly blue, and it danced in the sun as a woman swam the length of the pool. She paused and looked up at George Bennet standing on the curbing of the pool and he heard her laugh again. Another man lay on a wheeled chaise longue in the sun, a folded cloth across his eyes, his belly tanned and mountainous. Near the house ivy grew on a horizontal arbor, shading a small portable service bar where a young man in a white jacket sat in a straight chair, apparently dozing.

Evidently the woman saw him and spoke to Bennet. He turned and came barefoot across the grass toward Craig, smiling. "Hello!" he called. "Glad you could make it." Slabs of muscle moved on his bare chest and on his arm as he extended his hand. Bennet wore an ankle-length sarong in a faded blue and white pattern. It was knotted across his bronze belly, enhancing his beachcomber look, his island look.

"Come and meet my neighbor, Craig."

The woman had hoisted herself out of the pool. She had a brown and weathered fifty-year-old face, very alert eyes, a smooth brown body that looked twenty years younger than her face.

"Mimi, this is the young man I was telling you about. Craig Fitz. Mimi McGowan." Her wet handshake was as strong as a man's and her smile was charming. "You can meet my brother, Dick, after his stingers wear off, Craig. So nice to meet you."

"How about a drink, Craig? Rum collins taste good today." Craig said that would be fine and Bennet called the order over to the bar man, then turned to Mimi and said, "Dear, would you sit in on our little talk? I'm not very good at this sort of thing."

They moved over to a metal table with a center hole for a large beach unbrella. Craig and George Bennet sat on the shady side and Mimi McGowan sat out in the sun.

"Before George bumbles into his act, Craig," Mimi said, "You should know I'm practically a member of the family. And we're both disturbed about Clemmie."

The bar man brought the drinks. George said, "I went into some of this with Craig a few weeks ago. He knows I accept the blame for Clemmie's erratic behavior. I was selfish and I rejected her."

Mimi said, "You were just too pig selfish to be bothered with a child, so you packed her off to school, and your taste in wives wasn't calculated to make the child respect your judgment."

George winced. "Mimi is an outspoken woman, Craig. I suppose you could say Clemmie and I are estranged. She's a very strong human being, Craig. I can't control her."

"From her grandmother," Mimi said. "Clementina Bennet was a rare type. Clemmie inherited all her strength and none of her purpose. Her strength is misdirected. George and I do not approve of her friends or her habits. She's living fast and foolishly and immorally, Craig. For too long. And I hope you are as concerned as we are."

"I—I guess I am."

"Good!" George said heartily. "This makes it a lot easier all the way around. Clemmie came out here Tuesday and asked my help. It's the first time that's happened in years. She was pretty wrought up. More than I've ever seen her before. She says she's in love with you, and she wants to marry you, and she seems to have the feeling that this is her last chance to . . . live sanely and decently."

"But, Mr. Bennet, I . . ."

"We're not children," Mimi said. "We know you have a wife and two daughters. We know that you and Clemmie have been living together. We also know that the arrangement was pretty much Clemmie's idea. She said she's raised utter hell with you, and she's handled it all wrong, and she wants our help."

"But . . ."

"Give us a chance to go over the whole thing, Craig, and then we can discuss it. Clemmie says you are a decent

man, a man of kindness and a sense of obligation, and
she says this conflict between her and your sense of duty
toward your wife and children is tearing you apart. I don't
condone your relationship with her. But she's trapped by
a paradox. She has finally decided she wants a good man.
But because you are a good man, she can't have you.
Believe me when I say she desperately needs the kind
of stability and authority you could bring into her life.
She needs maturity, not some crazy erratic kid."

Craig felt he had gotten into some strange game with
highly clever opponents. Their skill was effortless.

"Give me a chance to say something right here," he
said. "I'm a wonderful catch. I'd be dandy for her. I've
been drinking so heavily I've lost my job, and I don't
know when or how I'll get another. My nerves are shot.
I'm not entirely certain what I'm going to do or say next."

"Let's be calm about this, Craig," George said. "Reasonable. We have a problem and let's face it. Are you in
love with Clemmie?"

"I don't know. Maybe that isn't the right word. There's
something that keeps dragging me back to her no matter
how hard I've tried to fight it. Maybe it's just sex. But
now I think I've got it licked. I don't think I have to see
her again."

George looked disturbed. "She is definitely in love with
you. There's no mistake about it. And you can't bring
yourself to hurt your wife."

"I guess that's right."

Mimi said, "Don't you see, Craig, how terribly you are
hurting Clemmie? She can't adjust to that kind of hurt
as readily as a mature woman could. This is the second
major rejection in her life. I don't want to be dramatic,
but this is the rejection that might destroy her."

"There's nothing I can do," Craig said uneasily.

"Look at this rationally, Craig," George said. "Clemmie
told me about the quarrel over the letter to your wife.
That was a foolish test of strength. She shouldn't have
tried to insist. But you turned out to be the stronger one,
and she lost the gamble. I think I can speak with the
authority of experience. It's never as hard as you think
it will be to ask a woman for a divorce. You dread it in
advance. Then there is a nasty scene, but all scenes come
to an end. I think the way to do it is face to face. I think

you ought to fly over and talk to your wife about this.
And you may find her a great deal more understanding
than you anticipate."

"I don't think so."

"Don't leave George out of your equations," Mimi said.
"Clemmie asked him for help. He's delighted she came
to him. He'll help her any way he can. It should occur to
you, Craig, that, through George, you might be able to
provide for the future of your wife and children far better
than you could otherwise."

"I'm afraid I don't understand."

George said, "Now I know you're a proud man, Craig,
and I'm certain you wouldn't accept charity, so I'm not
going to offer you any charity. I'm going to . . ."

"Let me do this," Mimi said. "You fumble so. Craig, I
know that one of the things that could put you off is
Clemmie's money. You're not the sort of man to enjoy
being kept. George has a great many investments, a financial interest in a great many companies."

"No controlling interest, actually," George said. "A lot
of diversification. I could really use a personal repre-
sentative, a man who knows management methods and
production methods."

"To do what?" Craig asked.

"My brokers give me advice, of course. But I feel a large
shareholder has other responsibilities too. If I had a man
who could go to the factories and spend time there and
advise me, in words I can understand, about the strong
places and weak places in the production picture, I'd be
in a position to give advice to management, or change my
holdings, as the case might be."

"I don't know if I'd be qualified."

"I had my lawyers look you up, Craig. So I know you'd
be qualified to do this. I could pay forty thousand and
traveling expenses of course. That wouldn't match Clemmie's income, but it would certainly make you . . . ah . . .
independent of her income."

Craig stared at the two of them, the amiable brown
man and smiling brown woman. The pool behind them
was like blue glass. There were twin rows of poplars on
a neighboring ridge. He moistened his lips. They can buy
the happy endings, he thought. When it doesn't come
out right, they buy a new ending.

"Through the looking glass," he said.

George looked puzzled, but Mimi laughed abruptly, a short harsh sound like the single bark of a dog. "There's no butter in the works, Craig. It seems to me I've spent half my life explaining George to other people. His mother was monstrously efficient. George wants so badly to be of use, but the poor dear can't even read a balance sheet. He wants a man Friday."

"But forty thousand," Craig said faintly.

"It isn't all it seems," Mimi said. "George, just what was your income from dividends last year? Don't put in any capital gains or interest. Just dividends."

George frowned and waved a muscular brown hand. "Harvey could tell you exactly. Before taxes it must have been somewhere between two and three hundred thousand. There wasn't much left after taxes."

"I have a head for figures," Mimi said. "Your salary and expenses would be a direct charge against that dividend income, Craig, and so it couldn't possibly cost George more than five thousand a year to pay you fifty thousand."

"But, by God," George said, "I would expect diligence."

"This is all pretty fantastic," Craig said.

Mimi reached over and patted the back of his hand. "It's certainly worth giving serious consideration. And, since you're not working at the moment, it makes it easier, doesn't it? Your wife is English, isn't she? You know, she might very well want to stay there with her own people. And her alimony would have more buying power over there. Then your girls could go to really good schools on the continent. It would certainly be better for them than the ghastly public school system in Stoddard. It could be arranged so they'd spend their vacations here with you. Clemmie is really awfully good with children."

They seemed so very confident. "You people have it all arranged, don't you?"

"My dear Craig, sometimes perfect strangers have to step in and straighten things out. Don't go all rigid and stuffy about this. George and I are really very simple and uncomplicated people. We want Clemmie to have a happy life, with stability and love. We think you could give that to her. And she should have children of her own. George would make such a reekingly fatuous grandfather."

"I probably will. Craig, why don't I have Harvey draw up a tentative contract. That's Harvey Tolle of Tolle, Rufus, Kell and Burney."

"I'll have to think it over."

"We *know* that, my boy. We are aware of that."

"But," Mimi said, "the very least you can do is make your peace with Clemmie while you're thinking it over. The child is miserable. She thinks you don't want her because of her past misadventures. And if you do have that idea in your mind, please be tolerant. Try not to think of the things she's done to herself. With Clemmie it has always been like a sickness. She was hitting back at the world. Just think of what she *is*. A healthy and lovely girl with a quick mind and lots of talent. And think of the life you will lead together. I don't want to sound smug, but nothing can go frightfully wrong when there's enough money. It's so easy then to escape the sordid. You can live with a certain flair, and style and—precision. It makes a wall you can live behind, safe from the more unpleasant kinds of intrusion. I'll confess something, Craig. I was going to help George and help Clemmie just for their sakes. But you really are quite awfully nice in your own right, and I'm—I'm just terribly, terribly pleased."

"But . . ."

"I know. I have a dreadful talent for rushing things. But you will go talk to Clemmie, at least?"

"I—yes. I'll see her."

George called to the bar man and ordered fresh drinks and then said, "And, Jeff, go in and ask Mary if she has any of that cheese left, the cheese Mr. Cleef sent me from Denmark. We'd like that with some crackers."

They sat and talked easily about other people. They drank the drinks and ate the cheese and crackers. Some neighbors named Knight came over. Mimi's brother woke up, was introduced, and began to drink Martinis with remote efficiency. Another couple joined them, an asthmatic old man and a woman who looked like a chow dog, jangled with jewelry, talked in a little voice and used words that would jolt a sand hog.

When Craig left, George walked him to his car.

"Shall I let Harvey know you're going to stop in?"

The casual question brought the whole offer to the first point of decision. Forty thousand. And expenses.

After one bad scene with Maura. And then maybe it
wouldn't be too hard to get into the habit of not thinking
about her. Not remembering. No painful job interviews,
like the one with Maleska. No look of contempt in the
eyes of an Ober.

A life of pleasant sunshine and blue pools and a man
to make the drinks.

"You can tell him I'll be in to see him."

George shook his hand hard. "And you'll see Clemmie?"

"Yes."

George looked off toward the hills, a damp glistening
in his eyes. "I want to see Clemmie happy. I want to see
her happy at last."

Craig drove slowly back to Stoddard. The gates to
Christmas Ridge were gates to another world. Candyland.
Reach out and pluck from the money bush. It was too
simple to merely envy them. The emotion was more complex. Envy, incredulity and an inverted respect.

He knew that George would be pleased if Craig worked
no more than sixty days a year.

Forty thousand. Three times as much as he had ever
made. Security for Maura and the girls.

Maybe they were right, the people like Mimi and
George. Divorce was not truly an earth-shaking event. It
happened a hundred times a day. One bad scene and
it would be over. All over except for the legal part.
Maura wouldn't beg. She wasn't that sort of person. She
would go cold, hiding the hurt. The honest thing to do
would be fly over and get it over with. She might want
to stay there. He could ship the things she wanted. A
jobless man with children didn't have much choice. And
even if she came back, it would never be the same. Not
after having Clemmie in the house, in their bed. Marriage
couldn't be the same. And he had alienated all their
friends. He could make the vacations for Penny and Puss
very special affairs. Buy them wonderful things. Maura
could live very well in England on a thousand a month,
probably as well as with two thousand here. She was a
handsome woman. She could easily make a new marriage.
And marry one of her own people. Clemmie loves me and
needs me. Money is a lovely cushion against pain. Any

man in the world would give an eye for this kind of a chance. And he could carefully spit in the eye of Ober, and Upson, and Rowdy and Commerford.

And he knew what the first step had to be. The very first step. He drove to the Jardines. Irene let him in. She was very cool. She and Al, who had just come home, were having a drink on the back terrace. Al made him a drink while he apologized to Irene for the way he had acted. Irene unbent slightly.

Al brought him his drink. He said, "I talked to Johnny Maleska. He thinks you need a rest."

"I'm going to get one, Al. Paul Ober let me resign. They had my personal things all packed and ready."

"That's not a surprise. But it's a damn shame."

Craig glanced at Irene. "Did Al tell you my sordid story?"

"Yes. And I don't think you ought to be flip about it. You ought to be terribly ashamed. Can you get another job before she gets back?"

"I have an offer."

"Any good?" Al asked, interested.

"It pays three times what I've been getting."

Al stared at him. "You serious?"

"Very serious."

"That's great!" Al said too heartily.

"There's a string attached to it. I'm going to fly over and ask Maura for a divorce. She may want to stay over there."

Irene gasped and said, "You *can't* do that!"

He looked at her. "I'm going to do that. And I'm going to marry the Bennet girl. And I'm going to work for her father."

Irene quite suddenly looked much older. "You complete fool!"

"I don't think so."

"What's the matter with you?" she demanded. "You act as if you were talking about going down the block for cigarettes. My God, Craig! You're in trouble. All right. But this isn't any way out of it. Maura will help. She'd want to help. You have to let her help."

"Shut up, Irene. Please," Al said in a tired voice.

Craig stood up. "Thanks for the drink. This is what I

want to do. It's going to be very pleasant. Somebody left a gate open and I got into the clover. I thought you should be the first to know."

Irene got up abruptly and left without a word.

He looked down at Al. "Do you wish me luck?"

"You're a shallow, selfish, opportunistic son of a bitch."

"Do you wish me luck?"

"You're having a change of life and you can't handle it."

"Do you wish me luck, Al?"

"I won't wish you luck. I'll give you advice. Don't install any mirrors in that clover patch. Your digestion will be better."

"Good-by, Al."

"I'll send you a bill."

"Make it big enough. I can afford it."

"You've said good-by."

He went out and got in the car. He felt curiously like a man made of wood. A good tough wood, like maple, or apple. The joints were cleverly carved and they worked smoothly. Two glass eyes were set neatly in the wooden face. Wood was durable. It would last very well. The wooden man could go and tell the flesh and blood wife that the marriage was over, and he wouldn't have to feel a thing, because from chest to shoulder blades, all the way through, the wood was firm, without knot or wormhole.

CHAPTER SEVENTEEN

MONDAY, the nineteenth of August, was a day of violent thunderstorms. They came down the shallow valley, one after another. The sky was so dark that from the big window of Clemmie's apartment he could see lights on in the office buildings in the heart of town.

The airconditioning had been installed the previous week. Clemmie felt headachy and out of sorts. She described it as 'grismal.' She lay on the couch by the windows in sheer nightgown and bed jacket, propped on pillows. In mid-morning he had gone out into the rain and found her the sort of novel she had requested. "Something full of bosoms and sword play and naval broadsides, honey."

She would read for a time, and then watch the storms. He stood by the couch and looked out the window. She was watching a storm. He looked down at her. Her face was turned away. He could see the curve of her cheek, the long dark lashes, a tiny edge of the blue pigmentation of one eye. Ever since Friday evening when he had returned to her, ever since those first hours of reunion, she had seemed curiously remote and restless. She had been triumphantly happy when he had come back to her. And she had made him repeat, over and over, that he was going to divorce Maura.

She turned and looked up at him. "I would like more tea."

"Coming up."

"And see if you can keep it out of the saucer this time, dear."

"Want an aspirin with it?"

"Not this time."

She was reading again when he took the tea to her. She didn't look up and he put it on the small table he had moved over near the couch.

"Book any good?"

"What? It's all right. The heroine is a nympho and the hero obviously has satyriasis, so they're beautifully matched."

She moved her legs with obvious reluctance when he sat on the corner of the couch. He watched her read, watched the movements of the pupils of her eyes. They took three jumps across each line. She nibbled at the skin at the corners of her nails.

After ten minutes she slapped the book shut, dropped it onto the floor and looked at him with irritable impatience. "Are you just going to sit and stare? Can't you think of anything to do?"

"I didn't know I was bothering you."

"The way you keep mousing around bothers me. When are you going to take your trip?"

"You've asked me that forty times."

"Then that would make this the forty-first time, wouldn't it?"

"The flight leaves New York on the twenty-sixth. That's a week from today. I get back to New York on Saturday. And your father bought the ticket."

"You didn't have to say that."

"I wanted to make sure you had all the information."

She gnawed her thumb knuckle for a few moments while she watched him. The cool intensity of her stare made him uncomfortable. There was no friendliness in it.

"I've decided you shouldn't go without warning, Craig."

"What do you mean?"

"Your tactics are wrong. We'll do it my way. You are going to cable her and tell her when you are going to arrive in London and tell her you want to speak to her on a matter of importance. Make it clear she isn't to bring the children. You're too soft-headed to handle this thing up there in that Long Melford place, with the children whimpering around and Maura beating her breast. You've got to meet her on neutral ground. I won't have it any other way."

He wanted to do it his way. But he thought ahead to the inevitable scene. It was easier to let her win the small victories.

"Whatever you say, dear."

"Whatever you say, dear," she said, mimicking him. "Then write the cable, will you?"

"Isn't it a little soon?"

"WRITE THE CABLE! There is paper in the table drawer over there. And let me see it. Write it and send it and let her stew for a week. She'll think too much. She'll be off balance, and a hell of a lot easier for you to handle."

He wrote the cable. She picked up her book again. She approved of the third draft, changing it in only one respect to make it read a 'matter of great importance.'

"Phone it in, dear."

"Now?"

"No, for God's sake. Wait until midnight."

"Why are you getting so upset?"

"I'm tired of waiting for this thing to be over."

As he phoned it in he was looking toward her. She

watched him with a curious intentness. When he hung up she picked up her book again. He roamed the room, got himself a glass of water, wandered back to the couch.

"Heat up the tea?"

Again the book slapped shut. "I cannot stand you dithering around this way. You are really getting on my nerves. Why don't you go to your house for a while?"

"You're certainly in an ugly mood, Clemmie."

"I feel lousy. You make me feel worse. Just get out."

He shrugged. He was at the door when she said, "Craig?"

"Yes."

"Come back here."

He went back to the couch. She held her arms up to him. "You have to kiss me before you go. No, not like that. There! I'm sorry I'm cross. But, darling, please don't let me get bored. Don't ever let me get bored. Promise."

"I won't."

"Come back tomorrow, dear. At noon. I'll be in a better mood then."

"All right, dear."

He went back the next day at noon. Her mood was worse. She was like something caged. She was obviously avid for a quarrel. He delayed it as long as he could. They made up after the first quarrel, and then she grew sullen and the second quarrel was worse. At its peak she walked out, slamming the door behind her. She didn't come back until ten at night. She was quite simply and helplessly drunk. Her lipstick was smeared and her blouse was torn, and he could get no coherent information out of her. He slept on the couch. She had a bad hangover on Wednesday morning, but she seemed contrite and more agreeable. She claimed to have blacked out the previous evening. She said she had no idea how she had torn her blouse or smeared her lipstick, but he was almost certain she was lying. And he did not care to press the point. It was easier to accept the lie than to precipitate the quarrel.

On Wednesday afternoon they went for a ride in the Austin-Healey. She drove. The further she drove the more erratic and reckless her driving became. He knew she was trying to make him object, and he swore that he wouldn't. But when she lost control on a curve at ninety, and barely regained it in time, he became angry.

"What the hell are you trying to prove? For God's sake, take it easy!"

And from then on she drove the little car at thirty-five miles an hour, refusing to speak to him.

On Thursday morning he went in to see Harvey Tolle. They discussed the draft of the contract Tolle had prepared. A few minor changes were made. Craig said he would come in and sign it on Friday. Tolle was precise and not friendly. He saw Chet Burney in the hall as he left. Burney looked startled, seemed about to speak and then turned away.

When he returned to the studio apartment at noon, Clemmie was out. She had not said anything about going out. He felt a dulled annoyance with her, not vital enough to be classified as anger. He made himself a sandwich, drank a bottle of beer, put on some records and tried to read. The rasp of the atonal music annoyed him, and he could not lose himself in what he was trying to read.

He wandered restlessly and aimlessly around the silent apartment. Everything was going to be fine after his trip, after the remarriage. He'd managed to land on his feet. Clemmie was being sulky and difficult because of the strain they were both under. When it was over she would be gay and loving again.

He went into her room and looked at her racked clothes and tried to remember what she had worn at this time and that. There was a fragrant pathos about her empty clothing, a small-girl arrogance and vulnerability.

It was after four in the afternoon when he heard her slow step on the steel stairs. He opened the door for her. She gave him a remote look which he could not understand, and said, "Are you still here?" as she brushed by him.

"Where did you think I'd go? You didn't say you were going out."

She went over and sat on the couch in front of the big window. "How do I know where you'd go? And I didn't say I was going out. Do I have to? Why don't you get some little slips made out? Then I can have them signed when I want to go out. And you can file them or something."

"Where did you go?"

She looked at him without special interest. She yawned, making no effort to cover her mouth. He saw the even teeth, the up-curl of pink tongue. "Out," she said. She kicked her shoes off.

He looked at her and wondered why he had not identified her expression and her manner more quickly. He had seen her look that way too many times to be mistaken. He had caused her to look that way too many times. It was her sated look, a heaviness that came over her after a prolonged act of love. When he recognized it, unmistakably, he felt his heart twist in a cruel and sudden way.

"Don't I deserve more than that?"

"Just what do you deserve, dear Craig? Maybe you could stop looking like a male Joan of Arc. If you tried hard. Somebody called up. I went out. I went out to lunch. I came back."

"Who were you with?"

She yawned again, and it squeezed her eyes shut and made her shudder. "Oh, for Christ's sake, Craig! Will you please drop it?"

"I don't like this. I don't like what's happening."

She looked at him in mock surprise, arch and ironic. "You don't like what's happening! Gracious!" Her eyes hardened. "Maybe you need a guide book. Maybe you can memorize the instructions in the back. You don't own me and you never will own me. And I refuse, at any time, to permit you to bore me. So stop being so incredibly middle-class, and possessive."

"Who were you with?"

"An old friend. Go to hell, Fitz. Kindly go to hell."

"What are you trying to do to us, Clemmie?"

"I'm getting very bored with that question. My God, it will be a relief to have you gone for a few days. Why don't you go today instead of Monday. Daddy can fix the reservations. He's very matey with some kind of wheel at BOAC."

"Why have you changed?"

"I haven't changed. I haven't changed a bit. This is Clemmie, remember? Clemmie never changes. Damn it, stop picking at me. You've fallen into a feather bed, haven't you? You've been suitably and quite extravagantly purchased, darling, because it has been decided that Clemmie needs a husband. I'm going along with the gag.

But I will *not* be nagged and questioned and chained to the bed post."

He looked at her for a long time. "Clemmie never changes," he said. "I should have understood that."

"Are you getting a little brighter, possibly?"

"Possibly. I was something you couldn't have. So that was your motivation. Not love. A sort of emotional voracity. I had to be devoured. You despise men. You've been faking all along, faking all of it. You had to win. You had to turn me into something entirely gutless, and as soon as you'd won on every last count, then you lost interest."

She stretched and leaned back and smiled at him. "Parlor psychiatry is such a pretentious game, honey. You see, I've heard this song before. Always with the same kind of indignation. But usually they bring up the analogy of the spider that eats her mate. You didn't happen to think of that, did you?"

"I would have."

"Of course, because your thinking is trite. But you make it all so dramatic. It isn't that earth-shaking. It's time I was married. And you'll do nicely. You can have a lovely time being Clemmie's husband. But you won't own me. If I want to go out, I'll go out. And if I want to go on a trip, I'll go on a trip alone. You'll have no complaint coming, and no complaint to make. And you're going to try in every way you can to keep me from being bored, because you are going to learn that when I'm bored, I'm not pleasant to you. That will be a very simple conditioned reflex for you to acquire. And we will live precisely the way *I* want us to live, and there will never be any complaints because you never had it so good. And if, from time to time, you happen to feel any cute little horns sprouting, it's because you've been boring and stuffy and tiresome. As you have the last few days."

"Are you trying to admit what you did this afternoon?"

She got up quickly and walked over to him and stood with her hands on her hips, her face tilted up. "Now, you see, you've made me angry, dear, and that's another thing. That's a thing to be especially avoided. You'll have to learn that. Now I want you to think very very carefully. Think of all the aspects of it before you answer. Decide if you want to ask me any more questions about this afternoon. Because, if you do, I will give you the most God-damned detailed report you ever heard. And, if you don't ask me, I will tell you nothing, and you will feel a lot better about the whole thing, I guarantee. Well?"

He looked down at her, into pale eyes. Looked at a cold and ruthless strength. He moistened his lips and looked away and said, "No more questions."

She patted his cheek lightly and went back to the couch. "That's a good sensible man, darling. You learn very quickly, don't you?"

"I guess so," he said dully. He felt as though he had been beaten with clubs.

She took her nylon stockings off, peeling them down her slim muscular legs. "Come here, dear," she said.

He went over to the couch. He thought she was looking at him most oddly. She handed him the stockings and he took them and looked at her, confused.

"Be a dear and rinse them out, will you?"

"What?"

"Rinse them out. It's very easy. There's a bottle of liquid detergent on the second shelf in the bathroom closet. Use a couple of drops in warm water. Squeeze them gently. Then rinse in clear warm water and hang them over the edge of the shower stall. Then you can make us a lovely drink."

He looked into the implacable eyes, and turned and went into the bathroom. He washed the nylons. He ran more water into the sink and started to rinse them.

And quite suddenly, and without warning, he saw himself. He looked down upon himself from a great height, and saw a worn and baffled man doing the work of a personal maid for a dark and handsome and vicious girl. He saw his bowed and obedient back. Captive creature. All the routes of escape had been so carefully nailed shut.

All routes but one.

He straightened slowly until he stood tall, his shoulders square. Tears of anger filled his eyes, rolled down his cheeks. He went out into the big room, the soaked ball of stockings in his hand. As she turned toward him, he hurled them at her with all his strength. It was a silly and petty gesture, but the stockings, heavy with water, struck her face with an oddly satisfying whacking sound and clung there for a moment and fell into her lap, and he wanted to laugh at how wide her eyes were, how wide and how shocked.

"Craig!" she said.

He walked to the door on legs gone wooden and stilt-like, moving slowly but with an immense determination. As he got the door open she caught his wrist and yanked him back with a frantic strength.

"What are you doing?"

"The animal escapes," he said. "The animal gets out for good."

"You're out of your mind!"

He turned back toward the door and once again she spun him around. He pushed her away so violently that she fell, and gave a small cry of pain and scrambled up and stood looking at him.

"Don't try to grab me again," he said heavily. "I don't think it's a good thing for you to try to do that again. I don't think that right now I'm entirely rational, because I can look at you and I can think how it would be to see you with one of those stockings knotted around your neck, and I can see you dead, with your face black. So don't come near me, because I don't know how close I am to doing that."

He went down the steel stairs, planting his feet carefully because he knew he could easily fall. He heard her behind him. "Craig, my darling! I was just being bitchy. My dearest, it didn't mean anything. Honestly. Please come back. Please! Darling, I was just upset."

Upset by whom, he thought. She followed him out to the car. She stood in front of his car, trying to smile at him, and he heard her say, "You'll have to run over me, darling. I can't let you go like this."

He put it in gear and stepped on the throttle. She jumped wildly to one side, and he caught a flash of frightened eyes. When he stopped at the alley mouth he looked in the rear vision mirror and saw her picking herself up.

He drove back to his house and put the car away and went in, and it was a place where some people he had once known had lived. He hadn't known them very well. He felt like an intruder, as though they might come back at any moment, Mr. and Mrs. Fitz and their daughters, and find him here and wonder who he was.

Clemmie arrived forty minutes later. He would not let her in. He locked the doors. She circled the house and saw him through the windows and called out to him in an anguished voice, but he would not let himself hear what she was trying to say.

He did not know when she went away. The phone began ringing. He counted the rings the first few times she phoned. Then he was able to close his mind to that, too. It was a meaningless sound that happened at random intervals.

He did not know what time it was. He knew that it was dark, and that he sat in his chair in the living room with bowl of ice, bottle of bourbon, glass and pitcher of water. He made the drinks in the reflected yellow glow of the sodium vapor lights, and drank them down, but they had no effect.

"Craig, darling!" she said, and her voice was startlingly close. He turned his head slowly and saw her head framed in the window, face close to the screen, so that the yellow light was behind her and the moving car lights touched her cheeks. He wondered what she was standing on. Perhaps she had driven her car into the shallow front yard as before.

"Craig, let me in, beloved."

"No."

"Darling, this is all a mistake. I'm sorry I hurt you. I won't do it again, ever. I promise with all my heart. I know I was being a dreadful bitch. I apologize."

After a few moments he got up and went over to the window and knelt on the floor so that their faces were at the same level and a foot apart, separated by the screen.

"Kiss me through the screen," she whispered. "It might be very gay."

"You don't understand yet."

"I just understand I hurt you and I want to make it up to you."

"No, you don't. You found one more little area of rebellion, you think. And you want to eliminate it."

"I'm not that horrid."

"It isn't a little area of rebellion. I'm drunk I think. The words come slow. It isn't rebellion, Clemmie. It's revulsion. All of a sudden I'm cured of you. All the way.

I don't know what did it, exactly. Maybe a little pocket of character you overlooked."

"Please let me in, darling. In a little while everything will be all right."

He thought it over. His mind seemed to move very slowly. She was whispering provocative things to him, trying to stir him in a sensual way, but he paid no attention to her devices.

"Listen," he said, and she stopped talking. "Like you said to me, today. Think this over very carefully before you answer. Think of all the aspects of it. A couple of minutes ago you said you can't live without me. Think very carefully. If you ask me again, I will let you in. I'll unlock the front door and you can come in. And when you come in, I'll kill you. I'll try to do it in a way that won't hurt you too much, and I'll try to make it quick. And when I do it, I won't feel a thing. I'll feel absolutely nothing toward you."

After a silence she said, "Don't try to bluff me, dearest."

"Think it over. I never meant anything more in my whole life. It's your choice. I'll kill you as efficiently as I can, and in a sense I would merely be returning a favor. I will knock you unconscious and carry you up and drown you in the tub. Once I had to drown kittens. I didn't like doing it, but did it. Do you want to come in?"

She slid down into the seat of the little car and drove away. He knelt by the window a long time, his body cold. He got up stiffly and went back to his chair and there was just enough ice left to make another drink.

George Bennet arrived at ten in the morning. Craig recognized him and opened the door and let him into the front hall, and blocked the way when George tried to move on into the living room.

"You look like hell, Craig. Are you sick?"

"In a sense. Stay right there a minute, George." He went and got the airline tickets and brought them back and handed them to him. "You can get a refund on these."

"Now let's talk this over, Craig. Let's not be too damn hasty. Harvey has the contract ready."

"That's nice. But I'm not for sale. Not any more."

"I told you I'd expect diligence. You remember that.

My God, man, I wouldn't be buying you for Clemmie. Don't be so melodramatic."

"I'll take the job."

"That's better."

"I'll take the job under one condition. That I never have to see or speak to your daughter again. Is it still open?"

"You're being foolish, Craig. I understand these little spats, these lovers' quarrels. My God, Clemmie's mother was a very highstrung and temperamental woman. It was hell trying to live with her. I'm an expert in quarrels. But this must have been more serious than most. I hope it may concern you to know that Clemmie is under a doctor's care. She was hysterical when she arrived last night at midnight. Why she didn't kill herself in that little car, I'll never know. Here, take the tickets back, Craig. You don't want to do this to Clemmie."

Craig felt so weak he leaned against the wall. "The tickets won't do any good. I cabled my wife to ignore the other cable. It was a very short cable. It said, 'Ignore previous cable. I love you.' That's all it said. Love is a hell of a curious word, George."

"We had this all straightened out."

"It nearly got straightened out last night, George. She was here, murmuring her little obscenities through the screen, and I was perfectly willing she should come in. I told her she could come in and I would kill her, but that didn't seem to be what she wanted."

"Kill Clemmie!"

"Why not? She isn't any use to herself or anybody else. I can understand her, after a fashion."

Bennet stared at him. "Are you out of your mind?"

"Not entirely. There is a cute and bright and provocative little girl. Give her the slightest hold on you, and she has to grind you into the ground."

"This is just a spat."

"I'm tired, George. I'm tired of you and your moneyed confidence and your big house and your sick friends and your slut daughter. You people have worn me out. Your daughter isn't a person, she's a disease. She ought to be put away. Her heart is rotten. Honestly, George, I'd as soon marry a leprous cretin as get mixed up with you Bennets."

George was thick and quick and his brown hands were astonishingly hard. Craig felt a remote satisfaction as he bounced off the wall and was thrust back and hammered against the wall again. He lay on the floor for a long time, his cheek on the polished hardwood. Finally he sighed and pushed himself up onto his hands and knees and spat blood and a fragment of tooth, and got up by holding onto the wall. He wavered into the kitchen and held his head under cold water.

Craig was mowing the back yard on Sunday afternoon when he looked up and saw Al Jardine standing at the edge of the driveway. Al did not smile. Craig walked over to him. "Something you want?"

Al shrugged. "A cold beer, if you've got one."

Craig hesitated, then went in and got two cans, opened them and took them out. They sat on the back steps.

"What else do you want?"

"Who worked you over?"

"George Bennet. Friday morning. It doesn't look as bad as it did."

Al nodded. "Ran into Chet yesterday and he told me that Harvey Tolle told him that your fancy job with Bennet went down the drain."

"I ran it down the drain."

"Nice pay."

"The hours were too long."

Al glanced at him. "I think I see what you mean. One reason I came over, I was off base when you stopped by. Jesus, the least I can do is be tolerant. That's one thing I should have learned from the business I'm in. There shouldn't be a complete collapse of friendship just because I disapprove of your actions."

"Irene know you were coming here?"

"She knows I've been upset ever since. She sort of suggested it."

"Thanks to Irene. I'm sorry for the way I acted."

"I thought about it. It isn't you. It's a disease of our times. And, I suppose, of our income group. And age group. The tensions pile up. Then, when you go off the

eep end over a chippie, it's just a sublimated form of
uicide. Or as childish as the kid breaking all his toys in
n attempt to punish God and his parents."

"Pretty it up as much as you can, but basically there's
o decent excuse for it, Al. Ever."

"Cured this time?"

Craig spat into the grass. "Completely."

"What are you going to do?"

"It's quite a problem."

"When do Maura and the girls get back?"

"On the sixth. On the Queen Elizabeth."

"Meeting them?"

"I guess so. I don't know for sure. I haven't been very
ecisive about anything. I tried to be decisive. I felt so
ckened by myself that—you don't want to hear all this."

"I came over to hear all this."

"All right. I wrote a suicide note. Six pages. Longest
ote in history. Anita's method seemed fine. I guess I
ould have made the cut. The blade was sharp enough.
ut I felt like such a damn fool, sitting there in a hot
ub. Gulping big sobs. Feeling so damn sorry for myself.
ears running down my face. Then I understood I just
anted to get out, go out the quickest door so I wouldn't
ave to try to look Maura in the eye, and I wouldn't have
look at my kids."

"Jesus!" Al said softly. "So now what?"

"I'm taking little steps. One at a time. No big plan. I'll
ork around here until it's time to go meet them. I'll de-
ide whether I'm going when the time comes .The more
ork I do around here, the better price we can get for
he house. I understand a few things. We're through in
his house. I'm through in Stoddard."

"I know that."

"So you don't let yourself think too far ahead. You take
ittle steps, one at a time. Convalescent steps. Whether
meet her or not, sooner or later I've got to sit down
nd look at her and tell her the whole thing."

"How about a job?"

"There's enough money to last a while. I'll think about
hat afterward."

Al finished his beer, set the can on the porch, took an
nvelope out of his pocket. "This is maybe to ease my con-

science. I phoned a friend this morning. I said you ma
stop and see him. I said I didn't know when. Joe Casswell
Casswell Products, Eldon, Pennsylvania. Up in the north
east corner of the state. Employs about three hundred
making wood products, sectional furniture, that sort o
thing. Big mail order business. He's in the market for
production manager. He wrote me six months ago to kee
my eyes open. I recommended you. Ask for ten. You ma
get nine." He handed Craig the envelope.

Craig said, "Al, I . . ."

"Whatever it is, don't say it." Al stood up and Craig
stood up. Al took his hand, gave it a quick hard pressur
and said, "Luck, boy." He went across the yard an
around the corner of the house and was gone.

Craig sat again and opened the addressed envelope. A
had scrawled on a sheet of letterhead, "Joe, this will in
troduce Craig Fitz, the man I told you about over th
phone. Best regards, Al."

Craig sat in the sun. He put the envelope aside, care
fully. The sun was hot on his arms, and he could smel
the warm scent of freshly cut grass. He thought of Clem
mie and it seemed to him that, in this moment, he had
taken another short step further from nightmare.

He thought, This makes the next step a little easier
Now I know I can meet them. And somehow I know
can make myself tell her. I could leave earlier. I coul
drive to Eldon, talk to Casswell and go on to New York

He went out into the back yard and began to push th
lawn mower again, cutting the high grass.

Then it will be her choice.

And he reached the end of the lawn and stood ther
and closed his eyes tightly and clenched his hands aroun
the handlebar of the lawn mower.

But, he thought, it won't be entirely her choice. I won'
let it be all her choice. I'll go down on my damn knees t
her. I'll beg her mercy and forgiveness. And may Go
help me.